CW01085364

THE BLACK ROCK KILLINGS

WES MARKIN

Boldwood

First published in Great Britain in 2025 by Boldwood Books Ltd.

Copyright © Wes Markin, 2025

Cover Design by Head Design Ltd.

Cover Images: Alamy

Every effort has been made to obtain the necessary permissions with reference to copyright material, both illustrative and quoted. We apologise for any omissions in this respect and will be pleased to make the appropriate acknowledgements in any future edition.

A CIP catalogue record for this book is available from the British Library.

Paperback ISBN 978-1-80483-799-3

Large Print ISBN 978-1-80483-798-6

Hardback ISBN 978-1-80483-800-6

Ebook ISBN 978-1-80483-797-9

Kindle ISBN 978-1-80483-796-2

Audio CD ISBN 978-1-80483-805-1

MP3 CD ISBN 978-1-80483-804-4

Digital audio download ISBN 978-1-80483-803-7

This book is printed on certified sustainable paper. Boldwood Books is dedicated to putting sustainability at the heart of our business. For more information please visit https://www.boldwoodbooks.com/about-us/sustainability/

Boldwood Books Ltd, 23 Bowerdean Street, London, SW6 3TN

www.boldwoodbooks.com

To Eunan, nephew and godson

PROLOGUE
2021

With the back of his hand, he widened the gap he'd already made in the condensation on the bathroom mirror.

Twenty-eight years old and the fine lines were etching out from the edges of his eyes. Time was relentless. Opportunities slipped away in the blink of an eye.

His damaged left ear tingled. He turned his head slightly to look at the scar tissue. Then he reached up to stroke the nub where his lobe should've been.

He thought of his parents' incompetence. Their inability to care. Their failure to protect him.

His ruined ear had been tingling for days now.

It was just no good.

He left the bathroom and stood behind the leather Chesterfield. Sarah was watching the evening news while she sipped from the glass of champagne that he'd given her.

He'd always admired her drive, her intelligence, her unwavering focus. After all, he possessed the same attributes.

But their paths had diverged. They were marching in opposite directions.

The tingling intensified.

He reached up to the scar tissue, rubbing it, trying to put some warmth back into the damaged nerves, to settle them, yet knowing, deep down that there was only one way of doing that.

Today, Sarah had achieved her ambition. She'd become a headteacher.

The champagne was well deserved.

He rubbed his ear.

When the champagne glass slipped from Sarah's hand and shattered on the parquet floor, he abandoned his ear and stepped up behind her. He laid a hand on her shoulder.

Sarah groaned, her head suddenly snapping backwards.

He reached down and touched the damp skin of her contorted pale face.

'I feel awful...' she said.

He nodded and stared over at the mantelpiece. A collection of framed photos. Their wedding day, their trip to the Great Wall of China, pictures of her family – not his, of course. *Never his.*

The hand on her shoulder was suddenly empty.

He looked down.

She was on the floor now, clutching her chest.

'I'm proud of you...' he said. And he was. He really was.

But that wasn't the point, was it?

There was nothing left to say. He sighed. With a reset, simply came acceptance and resignation.

He stood there for almost seventeen minutes as she died, listening to her pleas.

When she was past the point of no return, he circled the Chesterfield and lowered himself to her side. He brushed a strand of hair from her twitching, damp forehead.

She stared up at him, her eyes wide. Her lips moved, trying to form words, but only managing a series of strangled whimpers.

Her body convulsed, her back arching as she fought for breath. He held her gently but firmly, waiting for the rolling eyes, the bluish tinge, sporadic twitches, and then stillness.

He remained there, cradling her body, for several long moments. The room was silent save for the continued drone of the television.

He bent down, pressing a soft kiss to her forehead.

Then, when he was certain that the tingling in his scar tissue had stopped, he retrieved his mobile and phoned the emergency services.

* * *

North Yorkshire Moors

Paul and Colin Riddick watched the shimmering light dance on the surface of the Gouthwaite Reservoir.

Behind them, their tent flapped in a chilly breeze.

Shivering, Paul huddled closer to his dad for warmth. He was only eight, and this was his first time camping. Colin, weathered by age and shaped by his own childhood experiences of visiting the wild with his father, understood, and draped a large arm over his son's shoulder. Then, he pointed upwards into the sky. 'See them stars there, son? That there's Cepheus... he was a king.'

Paul struggled to make anything out in the mass of stars. He squinted, pointing up. 'Where, Dad?'

Colin took Paul's small hand in his own and tried to aim his finger towards Cepheus. 'There... see? A house with a pointy roof. Got it now?'

'Yeah.'

'Them ancient Greeks reckoned Cepheus were a king who'd do owt for his family.'

Paul's eyes widened. Colin moved his hand, taking Paul's pointed finger along on the journey. 'See the harp?'

'Yes.'

'A special one, that is. Lyra. It's said to represent the love between parents and their bairns.'

Paul was warmer, but not entirely comfortable. He leaned further into his father's sturdy frame. 'Do you think there are astronauts up there, Dad?'

'Aye. Without a doubt.'

'Cool.'

His father laughed. 'Would you like to be an astronaut, son?'

Paul wasn't sure. He'd seen documentaries, and some of those astronauts had to spend ages away from their families. 'Would you come with me?'

His father laughed again. 'Bit long in the tooth for that, son. Not sure NASA would risk any nice Apollo spacecraft on someone like me. Besides, when you're old enough to get up there, you won't want me tagging along!'

'I would,' Paul said. He loved spending time with his father.

A comfortable silence settled between them while Paul gazed at the stars in wonder and thought of astronauts and all of their wonderful adventures. He felt warm now. Safe in his father's embrace. Nestled and at ease among the rolling hills of North Yorkshire.

'Y'know, Paul,' his father said. 'I were just like you once. Full o' life, full o' dreams... and my father, God rest his soul, was always there, listening. He were a scout leader. A scout leader! You know? Have I ever told yer that?'

Paul nodded. 'Yes.'

'He took me everywhere, did your grandad... taught me everything a whippersnapper should know. How to tie knots that'd hold fast in any storm, how to track animals by their prints, how to find food in the wild, and navigate by the stars. He even taught me how to whittle... I were never much good at whittling. Bloody hell, excuse my language, son, but whittling... I'll teach you, too.'

'I'd like that, Dad.'

Silence enveloped them again. This time, the world around him seemed to shimmer oddly, and the stars above pulsed with an otherworldly light. It was a strange sensation, but not one that unnerved him.

Then his father sighed. 'I'm sorry, son. I really am.'

'What for?'

'Not being there for you... enough.'

'It's okay. We're here now.' He looked up at his father.

Colin nodded, but his eyes were sad. 'Aye... I should've done this more often, though. Should've been there for you like my dad were for me. Always there.' He nodded up at the constellations again. 'Like *those* stars, see... not some shooting star passing through. My father taught me something special, Paul, and I didn't harness it. I were too busy chasing the next quid. Chasing things that don't really exist. That don't make a true difference. Chasing ghosts.'

Paul nodded. His father's words were heavy, but he knew them to be true.

An icy wind caused the tent to flutter behind them, and the glassy surface of the lake to ripple.

There was a whisper riding the wind.

I'm here, Paul.

He looked back up at his father, eyes wide. 'Dad, did you hear that?'

Colin shook his head.

Right here.

Colin cocked his head, listening intently. After a moment, he nodded slowly. 'Aye, there's definitely something out there, lad.'

'Are they the ghosts you mean?'

'No. I think those whispers are very real. But it's up to you to tell the difference now, lad. Between that which can help you and guide you, and the nothingness, the ghosts of what once was, which pull you further and further away.'

* * *

2023

He watched the steam rising from the cup of *cafezinho* on the coffee table.

He shifted his gaze upwards towards the muffled thuds and shuffling. Camilla, his wife, was assisting her weakening mother.

The fifth mission to the toilet that evening.

His damaged ear itched.

In the shadows at the corner of the room, he saw movement.

Clive the Rottweiler.

He knew Clive wasn't really there. Not really. And yet, his ear, and the presence of that infernal dog... it was a lot to take in.

After Camilla had settled her mother, she joined him on the sofa. He smiled at her. She picked up her cup of *cafezinho* with trembling hands.

'If I pick up more *turnos*, we can *pagar* to hire nurse.' Her native language crept into her words, as it often did when she was worn out. '*Só* for *algumas* hours *cada* week.'

He nodded, but inside he wasn't convinced. She already worked every hour God sent! He attempted to reply completely in Portuguese. '*Mais turnos? Você já trabalha demais.*'

Camilla insisted it would free up more time for them. '*Mas isso poderia liberar mais tempo para nós.*'

He nodded. Right now, her voice sounded muffled and distorted to him, as if filtering through water.

Thirty years old.

His life, like sand, through an hourglass.

The movement in the room's corner caught his attention again.

Clive the Rottweiler stepped out of the shadows, working his teeth methodically on a small knot of flesh.

He rubbed his itching scar tissue, willing the beast away. But Clive snarled, continuing to chew. Dark, soulless eyes bored into him.

He felt a tight grip on his left arm, and somewhere, he could hear Camilla's moans.

His eyes locked with the animal's as he struggled to respond to Camilla, even as he heard the crashes and cries of pain.

The itching had become more like burning now, and he wondered if he was making it worse with his incessant rubbing, or whether it was deteriorating of its own accord...

He turned his head to see Camilla. One hand clutched at her chest, fingers clawing desperately at the fabric of her shirt. The other reached out towards him, trembling, beseeching. Her eyes, wide with panic and incomprehension, locked onto his.

He looked at Clive again and closed his eyes. He didn't know for how long.

When the itching had finally stopped, he opened them to find that the dog was gone.

A crackle burst from the baby monitor on the side table. Camilla's mother's voice, thin and reedy, called out in Portuguese, asking for help.

He picked up the monitor, pressing the button to respond.

'*Sinto muito.*' His voice was calm as he apologised. '*Acho que Camilla acabou de ter um ataque cardíaco. Descanse enquanto eu chamo alguém,*' he said.

I think Camilla just had a heart attack. Rest while I call someone.

* * *

2025

His body, slick with blood, cradled in her arms.

It was an image that was now forever with DCI Emma Gardner.

And it came to her often when she closed her eyes.

It didn't matter that he hadn't died of that knife injury because the shock of finding him that way, on the edge of death, had wounded her in ways that would be difficult to heal.

She swallowed, opened her eyes, and stared down at the still form of her colleague and close friend, DI Paul Riddick, who'd been wheeled out of surgery just hours ago.

While the knife wound hadn't killed Riddick, it had created a problem that eventually would. A bacterial infection, coupled with years of alcohol abuse and the emotional toll of losing his wife and children to tragedy, had left his heart beyond repair.

Today, however, had ended in hope.

After a six-hour operation, someone else's healthy heart now beat in his chest.

She sat with him in the ICU, as the ventilator hissed and his chest rose and fell rhythmically. Recalling images she'd seen online, she gazed at the layer of bandages, imagining the fresh surgical scar beneath. Her eyes then traced the maze of IV lines delivering a cocktail of immunosuppressants, antibiotics and pain relievers directly into his bloodstream.

The myocarditis had ravaged his heart, causing extensive damage that even the best medical care couldn't reverse. Now, his face seemed younger somehow, free from the lines of pain and worry that had become as much a part of his personality as his appearance.

She wondered where Riddick's mind was now. He'd recently endured hell to rescue four children who had been trafficked. She hoped he was somewhere calm, getting the rest he so desperately needed and deserved.

She reached out, her fingers hovering over his hand before gently clasping it. His skin felt cool beneath her touch.

'I'm here, Paul,' she whispered, her voice thick with emotion. 'Right here.'

She remained by his side a while longer. The hospital staff had been kind to her in allowing her this much time. They'd recognised her dedication to him over the past weeks.

Eventually, she straightened up, reluctantly releasing his hand. As she turned to leave, she cast one last look over her shoulder. The steady rise and fall of Riddick's chest, the quiet beep of the heart monitor, the gentle hiss of the ventilator – all formed a symphony of life, of second chances.

And then she was gone, stepping momentarily from his world and back into her own.

1

After walking around Knaresborough Castle, Imogen Ashworth took the footpath across the moat to Bebra Gardens. It was among these steeply sloping shrub beds and limestone rockeries that Alistair had first proposed to her.

Smiling, she regarded the strawberry tree, beside which he'd got down on one knee. Then she turned her admiration to the majestic cedars.

However, the next thing she saw, sent a chill through her.

The children's pool.

It was winter, so the pool was not in use, but her knowledge of how kids splashed and played in it over summer was a heavy blow.

Children.

Not for you, Imogen... No, never for you.

The finality of that thought pierced her like an icy blade.

She took her place on one of the weathered wooden benches, some way out of sight from the pool. It was a frosty night and overcast, so it was quiet, and at the moment, she was alone.

With a tissue, she dabbed at her eyes, and watched the sun descend. Muted oranges and purples, the bare branches of the trees, the fading light, everything reminded her of death. And even though no one had died, the prospect of her being unable to give life felt exactly the same. She was barren. She couldn't nurture, nourish, grow... did that not make this mournful atmosphere a fitting backdrop to her despair?

It had been two months since the miscarriage, but life wasn't getting any easier.

Time was not healing.

The doctor's words echoed in her mind. That the miscarriage had caused too much damage, and that she wouldn't ever be able to conceive. Scar tissue. Adhesions that would prevent any future pregnancies from taking hold. Even with the advances of modern medicine and the possibilities of IVF, her chances of carrying a child to term were now virtually non-existent. It had shattered her.

Imogen's hand moved to her stomach, where before Christmas she'd protected something that was now lost to her forever.

Today, Imogen had gone to speak to someone about the adoption process. Alistair wasn't keen, but she was determined to find out all she could about it. That he'd refused to come, and hadn't taken the time off work wasn't a glorious moment in their struggling relationship, but she hoped he would come round. He'd always dreamed of being a father, holding his own child, and she'd caught him lying awake, in the early hours of the morning, these last weeks. He'd denied he was in pain, but she knew he was.

This evening, they'd planned to meet here after he finished work.

Who knew? Maybe the place in which he'd proposed would rekindle something in their flagging relationship?

Maybe this could be the moment when he'd be receptive to her suggestion of adoption, listen to the logistics of the process and unburden himself of sleepless nights.

As the last rays of sunlight dipped below the horizon, illuminating the limestone cliffs that bordered the park, Imogen saw him. Alistair, her husband of under a year, father of the child she'd lost, walked towards her with measured steps.

Emotions swirled within her, and she wasn't sure what she was feeling as he approached.

This had been the way of their lives for two months now.

Was it love, still?

Yes... certainly... no question.

But there was definitely something negative. Resentment? Likely.

Guilt? Even more likely.

He rarely spoke about his feelings. In fact, the only time he'd truly opened up to her was when she'd fallen pregnant, and he'd confessed how desperately he'd always wanted to be a parent.

But she knew he was in pain.

And not just because of the wide-eyed staring in the early hours, although that was a significant clue. But because she could feel it radiating from him now. Seeping from every pore. Much like her own pain did.

In his hands, Alistair carried two cups of coffee, the steam rising in delicate wisps in the cooling air.

Alistair sat down beside her, offering one cup. Their fingers brushed as she accepted it, a slight gesture of intimacy that was so welcome right now that it nearly broke her composure. They shared a brief kiss, but she feared it came more from comfort than passion.

They discussed how beautiful the gardens were before settling into a companionable silence.

This was what had first attracted Imogen to Alistair less than two years ago – his quiet, reflective nature. In a world that often seemed chaotic and overwhelming, he was her calm centre. He met situations that would have others shouting and gesticulating wildly with his steady gaze and thoughtful words. It was a quality she relied on, especially now.

As they sat together, sipping their coffee and watching the last vestiges of daylight fade from the sky, Imogen studied Alistair's profile.

She noticed him playing with his damaged left ear. Rubbing it between his thumb and forefinger.

It seemed a relatively new tic. She hadn't noticed it at all in the first year of their relationship. In fact, it had only emerged during those traumatic days of miscarriage, and the doctor's bleak prognosis.

'Is your ear okay?' she asked and then took a mouthful of coffee.

He nodded. 'Sometimes... in the cold. It itches.'

She recalled his story of what had happened. How when he was a toddler, another child at the nursery had bitten it. Infection had set in, and eventually, a fair chunk of his lobe had to be cut away.

Imogen leaned over and gently kissed his damaged ear. 'I'm sorry,' she whispered.

'What for?'

'My body.' Her voice trembled. 'It's ruined everything.'

Alistair looked at her. She tried to read his facial expression but couldn't. Her father, Roy, had pointed this out to her more than once, claiming to not be able to read him. She'd dismissed it then, but recently, her father's words often came back and echoed in her mind.

'Don't... it isn't your fault.' Alistair drank more coffee and then set it down by his feet and turned to face her again.

She desperately sought the love and sympathy in his eyes, but she felt intensely paranoid that she was merely imagining it.

Were they ending?

Had she, and her bloody body, blown it?

'Shush,' he said, pressing a kiss to her forehead. 'It's me that's sorry... sorry that I can't make it right.'

It seemed genuine.

Imogen finished the coffee. She, too, placed her empty cup on the ground. She felt fresh tears welling up. 'Do you want to hear about how the adoption process works?' she asked, the question hanging heavy in the air between them.

Alistair was quiet for a moment, staring ahead, his gaze distant, as if looking into a future only he could see. When he finally spoke, his voice was low and determined. 'Yes... Not now... but yes. I'm ready to start again.'

There was something in the way he said it, a certain weight to his words that Imogen couldn't quite decipher but seemed off. However, in that moment, wrapped in the cocoon of his presence and the love she felt for him, and the positivity of him saying he would listen, she nodded and took it as a good sign.

'Start again,' she repeated, leaning into his embrace as the first stars appeared in the darkening sky above Bebra Gardens.

'Cepheus,' Alistair said. 'The one that looks like a house. See it?'

'Yes,' she said. She sat up and peeled off her jacket. 'I'm suddenly feeling hot.'

She leaned back into him and gazed up at Cepheus again. 'I love you.'

And she did. She really did.

She rubbed her stomach again. Not from loss this time, but from indigestion.

Coffee this late really didn't agree with her.

2

Gardner stared up at the ceiling. Sometimes the patterns drawn by the streetlights helped her sleep. But not tonight.

She felt Lucy O'Brien's soft breath on her cheek, her arm draped loosely over her stomach, and let out a quiet sigh.

The detective was both her lover and her colleague.

Junior colleague. By sixteen years!

Gardner's fingers absently traced the contours of O'Brien's hand. She couldn't deny her potent feelings, but a nagging voice in her head questioned whether this relationship was not only inappropriate but also a convenient distraction from the chaos unfolding in her life.

The past six weeks had been a whirlwind. Gardner had been a woman possessed, dividing her time between her critically ill friend, two children, a high-pressure job, and this new, burgeoning relationship.

She turned her head slightly so she could see O'Brien's sleeping face.

You've been a rock, Lucy. A rock.

Tonight was a perfect example. O'Brien had been waiting

with a bottle of wine, a takeaway, and two children settled and tucked up in bed. With the au pair away visiting family, O'Brien had stepped in without hesitation.

But if I'm taking advantage, tell me. Stop me.

Gardner looked back up at the ceiling. Her feelings for O'Brien were genuine, but so were her feelings for Riddick. Albeit different. Very different.

She'd been careful to steer conversations with O'Brien away from Riddick. How could she explain the way her heart clenched every time she saw Riddick pale and vulnerable in that hospital bed?

The rational part of Gardner's mind kept reminding her that a life with Riddick was a near impossibility. His alcoholism, violent tendencies, the ghosts that plagued him – could he ever truly heal enough for a successful relationship?

In contrast, despite the potential for workplace gossip, a future with O'Brien seemed more realistic, more attainable.

Yet, the prospect of losing Riddick – first from the stabbing, then from his infected heart – had brought Gardner to the edge of a dark chasm. And Gardner feared this trauma had driven her into O'Brien's arms, which felt immoral.

She shifted slightly, careful not to wake O'Brien, as her mind continued its relentless cycle of thoughts.

Gardner recalled the young detective leaving cereal bars on her desk when she'd been overworked, a small gesture that had touched Gardner more than she cared to admit. She thought back to the time when O'Brien had been first on the scene during the turbulence with Neville Fairweather. The tall, mysterious entrepreneur who circled her like a shark. His intentions always ambiguous and dangerous. O'Brien had been a lifeline during that shadowy time, offering safety to her and her children.

Then the memory of shots fired behind an old farmhouse flashed through Gardner's mind – and those agonising minutes when she'd thought O'Brien had been killed.

Gardner looked over at the young detective's face. Her smooth skin glowed in the streetlight, a stark contrast to the worry lines that had etched themselves on Gardner's face over the last decade.

It was yet another reminder of the gulf between them.

But O'Brien made her smile more than anyone and made her feel alive in a way she hadn't in years. The weight of her responsibilities seemed lighter with her around. The young detective's smile could illuminate a room. Her laugh was infectious.

When they were together, Gardner felt like she could breathe again. Had she ever really felt that way with Riddick?

O'Brien had put in a transfer request this week, ostensibly for career development. The real reason: Gardner and O'Brien shouldn't be working together, not with their personal relationship complicating things. Gardner's stomach twisted at the thought of losing O'Brien at work, even as she knew it was the right decision.

Gardner turned on her side, away from her sleeping colleague, and closed her eyes.

Behind her, she heard O'Brien's sleep-softened voice murmur, 'I love you.'

The words hung in the air, heavy with expectation. Gardner's throat tightened, her inability to respond feeling like a betrayal.

She wanted to say it back, knew that part of her meant it. But the words caught in her throat, tangled with thoughts of Riddick and the uncertainty that clouded her future.

In the darkness and silence, she carried the weight of her painful choices into an uneasy sleep; her dreams a tangle of desire, duty and doubt.

3

Gardner jolted awake.

Her mobile phone was glowing. She reached for it, her hand trembling slightly as she recognised the name on the screen.

Neville Fairweather.

She read the message, her stomach churning. The clock on her nightstand showed 3.17 a.m. She sighed, knowing sleep would now be elusive. She thought of the kitchen cupboard downstairs and what it contained.

It seemed a good option.

Downstairs, while she took a long sip of Merlot, she read the message again.

> They've brought forward Jack's release. He comes home tomorrow. Further details to follow.

She shook her head. Jack Moss, her brother, who'd been serving time for assault, was coming home. Or, more precisely, to *her* home, because he didn't have one.

What a bloody nightmare.

She took an even longer sip of Merlot than before.

Of course, she'd known this day was coming, but this week, and certainly not tomorrow, hadn't factored into her planning.

She had, at least, hoped that Riddick would have been out of the woods first.

However, she should've been prepared for this. When Neville was involved, anything was possible.

Gardner set down her glass, taking a deep breath as memories washed over her. She was ten years old again wandering around Malcolm's Maze of Mirrors at the fairground, terrified because it was late, and no one else had been in there.

At least, until Jack, her eight-year-old brother, had crept in, holding a large stone in his left hand.

She recalled his empty eyes and her own confusion.

Then she remembered him swinging that stone and everything turning white.

Gardner's hand unconsciously moved to the faint scar hidden beneath her hairline, and she exhaled.

Time had fixed her fractured skull, but it'd never fixed her little brother.

Their parents, and herself for a time, had tried to manage it, but failed.

The emptiness and the capabilities that existed within Jack couldn't be fixed.

Gardner finished her glass and poured herself another before making her way back upstairs. She paused outside Rose's room and pushed the door open. The night light spilled across the sleeping form of the nine-year-old girl. Her adopted daughter.

Jack's biological daughter.

Rose stirred slightly in her sleep, her face peaceful and untroubled. Gardner felt a lump form in her throat. To think that this beautiful girl was only a year older than Jack had been when he'd swung that stone and almost killed her.

What have I done?

She thought of the promises she'd made to Neville Fair-weather, and Jack, and this innocent child lying asleep. Not forgetting the other eight-year-old child in the adjacent room. Anabelle.

Jack, her unpredictable and dangerous brother, was coming here and she'd agreed to it. If she hadn't allowed it, then Jack would have had to stay in prison, and he'd have been dead by next month.

What choice had that given her? Condemn her brother, Rose's father, to death? Or do what she could to help him?

Gardner's fingers tightened around the stem of her wine glass. She wasn't built like Jack – she couldn't allow him to die.

Still, she'd been clear as day to both Neville and Jack.

One chance.

At the first sign of trouble, those gunning for him inside would be the least of his problems.

She'd kill him herself.

4

———

Gasping for breath, Roy Linders made it to the private waiting room without collapsing. Considering his age, and that he'd not run like that in over ten years, this was no mean feat.

He opened the door and saw the single occupant, Alistair, Imogen's husband, in a chair. He had his elbows on his knees, his head in hands, and he was leaning forward.

Roy stepped in and the door closed behind him. 'Where is... she?' He forced his words out between rapid breaths.

Alistair raised his head and regarded him, his eyes red-rimmed.

Roy leaned against the closed door, afraid he might fall over. 'Well?'

'I'm sorry, Roy...'

'Where the... hell... is Immy?'

Alistair had a vacant expression on his face. 'She's gone.'

'What?' The way his insides suddenly seemed to churn made him stagger to one side. 'Eh?'

'Gone...'

'No,' Roy said, shaking his head. 'No...' He took a deep breath and stood up straight, regarding the shell-shocked man as he buried his head in his hands again.

'Alistair!' Roy bellowed, his voice echoing in the small room. 'Bloody snap out of it... Immy.'

Alistair lifted his face. 'Gone.'

'No. What happened?' Roy pressed.

Alistair didn't respond this time. Just stared off into space.

Roy couldn't handle the silence. He started forward, confused. Angry. *This bloody kid!* He made no sense. Never had done. He'd always been wrong for Imogen.

I said it from day bloody one!

'Alistair? What happened? Tell me lad, before I drag you to your sodding—'

'She collapsed... just collapsed.' He made eye contact with Roy. 'A heart attack.'

Heart attack?

His insides churned again and he staggered all the way back now, until the back of his legs caught a chair and he went down into it. 'No... no... not again...'

Roy's mind reeled, memories of another hospital, another loss, flooding back. A doctor telling him that Elaine was gone. *Heart attack.* It made no sense. *She had the heart of an ox!* He'd told the doctor that. Didn't matter. It didn't alter the outcome.

'It can't be.' Roy shook his head. 'You're wrong... you have to be.' His voice was a hoarse whisper. He glared at Alistair again. 'She's not even thirty!'

'I don't know,' Alistair said, shaking his head.

'Why not? Who have you spoken to?'

Alistair lowered his head again.

Shit. The man was a bloody lemon.

And he was cursed.

Their family was cursed.

He narrowed his eyes, studying the grief-stricken husband. 'Were you with her?'

Alistair said something, but he couldn't understand him through his hands.

'Speak clearly, man!' Roy raised his voice.

Alistair looked up. 'They tried to bring her back.'

Roy raked his hands through the short tufts of hair he still had on the side of his head.

He just didn't get it.

He glared at Alistair. *I was always right about you. You make no sense. Never have done. Never will.*

This despair didn't feel real.

Alistair looked too calm, too placid. It was unsettling.

If he'd been Alistair, he'd have been tearing up trees, demanding answers.

Roy was an emotional man, had always worn his heart on his sleeve – that was how he preferred his folk. Not this lot, with their cold, calculating eyes.

Roy steeled himself. Well, if you're too weak. He lurched to his feet. 'I'm going to find the doctor.'

As Roy stomped towards the door, he cast one last glance at Alistair. The younger man's shoulders had begun to shake, silent sobs wracking his body. For a moment, Roy hesitated, torn between his need for answers and a flicker of sympathy. Then, with a shake of his head, he yanked open the door and strode into the hallway, determined to find out the truth about his daughter's fate.

5

Gardner sat beside Riddick's bed. She held his hand while keeping her eyes fixed on his face. The ventilator was out now, and there seemed to be a little more colour in his cheeks. Apparently, he'd been awake only an hour before she arrived. She was disappointed to have missed him, but that didn't temper her happiness that things were progressing smoothly.

She'd hoped his eyes would open during this twenty-minute visit, but it wasn't to be.

Instead, she found herself studying the steady rise and fall of his chest, marvelling at the fact that he had someone's heart beating within his chest. It really was a miracle.

As her visit drew to a close, she kissed him on the crown of his head and told him to keep fighting. She bumped into Dr Euan Gresham, the surgeon who'd performed Riddick's heart transplant, outside the room. He was a tall man in his fifties with long, thin fingers and Gardner couldn't help but imagine their spidery movements as they worked on the most important of organs in the body.

'Morning Emma,' Euan said. 'Paul was having a good old look around this morning, I believe.'

'So I hear,' Gardner said, a hint of regret in her voice.

'Looking for his guardian angel, no doubt.'

'Give over. There's only one guardian angel around here, and that'll be you. Six hours you were with him. That must take some focus.'

'Don't underestimate your role in it, Emma. He was calm.' He winked. 'I suspect he's a good reason to live?'

Gardner narrowed her eyes, suspicion creeping in. 'What's he said to you?'

He smirked. 'Who? Him? Nothing, of course. He was asleep the whole time, remember?'

'Hmm.'

'Anyway, he should become a lot more alert over the next day or so.'

'I've taken a couple of days off work,' she told the surgeon. 'I'll be available at a moment's notice if anything changes.'

Euan smiled and nodded. 'And I'll be in touch if anything does.'

As Gardner turned to leave, she paused and turned back. 'Dr Gresham... thank you. For everything.'

The surgeon nodded again, his eyes warm with understanding. 'Just doing my job, Emma. Now, go take care of yourself too.'

The Gouthwaite reservoir was still.

Colin rested the last of the logs alongside the others. 'Right then, son... that'll be enough...'

Paul knelt and ran his fingers over the wood. 'Have I chosen well, Dad? This wood is going to really float!'

'Aye,' Colin said. 'It's a decent enough foundation, and nothing is worth building in life without a foundation.'

Paul nodded, feeling a swell of pride over his father's approval.

'Still... a good foundation isn't the only part. In fact, the most important part is the ropes. Without the knots, it could still fall apart.'

Paul watched intently as his father's weathered hands moved with practised ease.

'This here's a sheet bend, also known as a weaver's knot,' Colin explained. 'Good for joining two ropes of unequal thickness. You try it...'

Paul attempted the knot, his brow furrowed in concentration.

His first try was clumsy, but Colin's patient guidance helped him improve with each attempt.

'It's a weird knot,' Paul said.

His father laughed. 'Aye, it is. The strangest ones are often the strongest. Let's try a bowline. This one's known as the "king of knots" – it won't slip or jam, no matter how much strain you put on it.'

Paul struggled with this one. After several failed attempts, he sighed. 'I don't think I can.'

'Well, if you don't' – he nodded down at the half-finished raft – 'then you'd be stranded. And what's the use of all that?'

Determination set in Paul's jaw as he tried again and again, his small fingers working the rope until finally he managed it. He cheered.

'Now, the square knot,' Colin said, demonstrating another technique. 'Simple, but effective. It brings proper balance.'

Soon, the scattered pile of logs was a sturdy craft, bound by an intricate web of knots.

Paul ran his hand along the raft's surface, feeling the solid construction beneath his palm. 'It's stronger than I expected.'

'Aye, that it is,' Colin agreed. 'Now, what do you say we give it a proper test?'

With a grunt of effort, they pushed the raft into the water. It bobbed for a moment before settling.

'Go on then,' Colin encouraged. 'Climb aboard.'

Paul hesitated, a flicker of fear crossing his face. 'What if it sinks?'

Colin laughed. 'What's the worst that can happen? You get wet! But have a little faith, lad. There's a firm foundation, and we've strong knots.'

Taking a deep breath, Paul stepped onto the raft. He tensed, expecting to feel it give way beneath him, but it held firm. Slowly, he lowered himself to sit cross-legged at its centre.

'There you go,' Colin said, pride clear in his voice. 'Steady as she goes.'

With a firm push, Colin sent the raft gliding out onto the lake. Paul gripped the logs tightly at first, but as the raft continued to float steadily, he relaxed.

The shore receded, and Paul found himself surrounded by the tranquil expanse of the lake. A burst of joy welled up inside him, and before he knew it, he was whooping with delight.

'It's working, Dad!' he called out, his voice echoing across the water. 'It's really working!' He closed his eyes, basking in the sun's warmth on his face and the gentle rocking of the raft.

'Like I said, a firm foundation and strong knots,' his father called out.

But hearing those words again caused Paul's joy to suddenly recede, because no matter the foundation and the knots, nothing was forever.

One day, this raft would sink.

Gardner was planning to return home for some breakfast before coming back late morning to visit Riddick.

As she left the hospital, the weight of her impending responsibilities pressed down on her. The looming spectre of her brother, who she'd be welcoming back into her life this afternoon, felt like a dark cloud on the horizon.

Shit.

What a time to deal with this!

She'd been absolutely desperate to keep this week undisturbed. Completely. To be there totally for Paul for every second that they'd allow her.

Now, things had just got very complicated.

Neville Fairweather had moved far more quickly than she'd expected.

As she crossed the road to the car park, she caught sight of the puppeteer himself and swore out loud.

He was leaning against a sleek black Tesla parked alongside hers.

Receiving a text in the middle of the night had been disconcerting enough, but having the smug bastard track her down to a hospital car park was completely bloody infuriating.

But that was Neville all over. He moved in the shadows, and he'd been scaring the shit out of her since he'd first announced his presence a year back.

As she neared him, he gave her a swift nod and climbed into his car. His intentions were obvious. He wanted her in the vehicle too, sitting alongside him.

Gardner hesitated, holding the handle of the passenger door for a moment. With a resigned sigh, she changed course and climbed in. 'New car?'

'We've a pool of them. I checked it out before one of my bodyguards could stop me. Thought it best I came alone... Feels less intimidating for you.'

Gardner observed him, noting his long white hair pulled back into a neat ponytail and his neatly trimmed beard framing a face that appeared to be constantly torn between a smile and a smirk.

'Tracking me down to the hospital. Ensuring my brother's early release. It all still feels intimidating, I'm afraid.'

His phone buzzed in his pocket. He hoisted it out, looked at it and grinned. 'Doesn't take much to piss my guard dogs off. They think I'm a liability! You think this setup is intimidating, Emma... try to live in a world where you've no freedom whatsoever.'

'Difference is: you chose it. I didn't choose this.'

He nodded. 'Yes, I chose it, all right. I believe in what I do.'

'Which is?'

Neville raised his eyebrows and gave her an expression that suggested she should know better than to ask that question.

Gardner's mind raced, piecing together the fragments of information she'd gathered about Neville over the past year. She recalled their first meeting when he'd appeared out of nowhere, claiming to be from Wiltshire, her own place of origin. He said he'd been house hunting and was eyeing up Gardner's estate, when he'd stopped Rose from running out onto the road.

But it'd all been a ruse. Neville had known who Gardner was. Just as it transpired he now knew her brother... But how did he even know Jack?

It was anybody's guess.

There was also another intriguing connection. Fairweather was the biological father of Collette Willows, a colleague Gardner had lost in the line of duty before she was seconded to North Yorkshire. At first, Gardner had been paranoid that he was holding her to account for Collette's death, but this, it now seemed, wasn't the case.

Jack, her sociopathic brother, was the sole reason Gardner had Neville's attention.

'Emma, believe it or not, I'm here to express my gratitude,' Neville said.

'I don't believe it.'

He nodded. 'I don't suppose you do, but it's true. Without you, I couldn't have arranged Jack's early release. That he'll be staying with his reputable DCI sister carries considerable weight. You're the reason he's out of significant danger.'

'And what if he brings that danger with him? He's a criminal. There're children in the home.'

'One of which is his daughter, whom he adores. He wouldn't put her at risk.'

'Jack isn't like everyone else, as well you know.'

'Maybe not, but that sense of loyalty to his daughter... and to you... will keep you all safe.'

'To me?' Gardner laughed out loud. 'He almost killed me when I was ten. He brained me with a stone.'

'Almost. Did he not have ample opportunity to finish the job?'

'He was eight. He probably thought he had done.'

Neville shrugged. 'Look. I can only report on the man I know now. You and your children are in no danger. In fact, arguably, you're safer for his presence. He'd sacrifice himself before letting any harm come to you all.'

She wouldn't bet on this. She knew her brother well, and although he'd definitely fight for Rose, she'd doubts about whether he'd fight for her. 'So we're safe from those who want my brother dead?'

'Absolutely. Outside of prison, we can keep tabs on these individuals. Besides, none of these people would go near a DCI's home and risk a shit storm. These are people who like to stay invisible – although, they're failing miserably where I'm concerned.'

'So, you're 100 per cent?'

'Yes, just because you're still here. If they were ever going to move against you, do you not think they'd have done it by now? You're high risk for them. You carry headlines, Emma, and that's exactly why we need you to look after him until it's over, because they won't come anywhere near your home.'

'Until what's over?'

Neville looked away.

'Really? Ridiculous!' She snorted. 'You're genuinely not going to tell me, are you?'

'There's nothing you need to know or probably want to know.'

'I'm putting my career on the line with your shady business.'

He laughed. 'No... you're really not.'

'Oh, and how do you work that out?' she asked, frustrated at being kept completely in the dark.

'Because what we're involved in is morally sound.'

Now that was intriguing, and implausible. 'Eh? With Jack involved? Morally sound?'

He nodded. 'Yes. You've my word.'

'I feel like I've walked into another bloody dimension. You were mixed up with KYLO Ltd... how could I even believe you're morally sound?'

Neville had been a major shareholder with KYLO Ltd. In Gardner's recent investigation, KYLO had been connected with babies being stolen from homeless women.

'Not fair, Emma. You knew I'd sold my shares long before that. Also, who was it that led you to the truth in that investigation?'

'Only so I'd be indebted to you.'

He shook his head. 'You think telling you that was really necessary to get what I want? We're here now, irrespective of the KYLO situation. I told you the truth because it was the right thing to do. I also do things for the people in my circle. I consider you part of that. That was the real reason I helped. It is also why I ensured the survival of your friend Paul Riddick.'

Her eyes widened. She turned and stared at him, taking a sudden sharp breath. 'What?'

He smiled. 'How is Euan by the way?'

She was lost for words.

'Oh, come on, Emma, you didn't really think you'd ended up with the best heart surgeon in the country by chance?'

She flinched and looked away.

'Didn't you notice how quickly they found a matching heart donor? How smoothly it's all gone?'

She took a sharp breath.

'Yes, I tried my best to ensure he survived...'

She exhaled. 'By jumping the queue?'

'Would you rather I hadn't have done?'

She glared at him. He was reading her like a book. Would she have risked losing Paul based on doing the right thing? Of course not, but she didn't want to admit that to this patronising idiot. 'Hardly moral, is it?'

Neville smirked. 'Answer my question – would you rather I hadn't have done?'

'He would have said no.'

'Who, Paul?' Neville said. 'Good job we didn't ask him then.'

She closed her eyes and sighed.

'Look, Emma... everything we do, *I do*, it comes back to loyalty. You've been loyal, are being loyal. And your life is a week, maybe less, away from normality. Jack will leave, resettle. Rose will be raised by you. And with that loyalty, know this: the duty you're performing will follow you around positively for the rest of your days. Now, my phone is buzzing, which means my entourage is getting even more pissed off. I need to return to them. I'd wish you luck, but you don't need any. This will be smooth.' He started the engine.

'Is that it, then? Goodbye? No more unexpected visits?'

Neville nodded.

'Good.' She exited the car and as she slammed the door, she muttered, 'Now, piss off.'

Despite starting his engine, he waited. When it was obvious he would not leave first, she got into her car and drove away, catching sight of Fairweather in her rear-view mirror. He sat there, unmoving, watching her leave.

8

It had been a challenging twenty-four hours for Alistair.

Between the tragedy that took Imogen from his life last night, and the confrontation with her suspicious father this morning, he'd operated in a chaotic whirlwind.

And throughout everything, Clive's canine eyes remained on him. That nub of flesh pinned between incisors.

But now, as he folded and placed each piece of ironed clothing into his suitcase, he felt some reprieve. Clive was gone again, for now. It was time for a reset.

He never rushed the packing. It almost felt like a ritual. A firm sense of order.

Each folded garment was a sign of renewal. Hope.

Before closing the case, he checked the minimal contents. Three pressed shirts, two changes of underwear, two pairs of trousers.

Alistair didn't want to appear as if he'd prepared himself and fled. A question mark was always better. Create the suspicion that he'd chosen another, more final, exit from existence.

Let them look for a time, and then let them believe he was at the bottom of a river somewhere.

Afterwards, he went to the bathroom and drank a glass of water. He examined his face.

Thirty-two.

Still time.

Too busy focusing on his face, he put the glass down too close to the edge. It slipped and smashed on the floor at his feet.

He lowered himself, pulled the small plastic toilet bin towards him, and began placing the broken shards in it.

Reminded of something from another time, another life, so long ago, his heart raced...

His trembling, small hands moved fast. Each shard went into the plastic bag. He needed to be quick. Before she saw... but he needed every piece...

On one shard of the broken cup he saw his mother's name.

On another shard, his father's.

Originally, the glass had depicted both their names with a love heart between them.

He saw his mother watching from the door. She was swaying. Her mascara smeared beneath bloodshot eyes.

'I'm sorry,' he said, moving faster. 'I'm sorry...'

She laughed. She mustn't have realised it was her favourite cup. 'Pick up every piece, no mess.'

He saw her moving towards him. He scooped up the shards, and only stopped when he felt her presence directly behind him.

'How?' she asked.

'It was an accident,' he said.

Silence.

He sensed she knew now.

Her special cup.

'You stupid boy.' She pushed the back of his head. 'Idiot. Go to your room.'

'Let me help—'

She smacked the back of his head this time. Everything flashed. He felt a piece of glass bite into his fingers.

'How dare you answer me back,' she said.

He ran, crying, but stayed at the top of the stairs. Sitting, watching. Blood dripped from his cut finger onto his trousers.

First, his mother cleaned his mess, and then she washed down pills with wine.

The memory faded, and the bathroom came back into focus. Alistair clenched his right hand. When he opened it, he regarded a long cut across his palm, blood beading along its length.

'I'm ready to start again,' he said, repeating what he'd whispered into Imogen's ear. 'Start again.'

He wrapped a tissue around his hand to soak up the blood and then finished cleaning up the glass.

After he zipped the suitcase closed, he lay down, his body sinking into the mattress. The cut on his palm stung. The ceiling above him seemed to spin. He was tired.

He thought of the moment he'd pointed out Cepheus to Imogen... the pointed house in the night sky. Another memory intruded...

The bedroom door creaked open.

He trembled beneath the blanket.

'Are you awake, sweetheart?' His mother's voice was no longer full of anger.

He felt the mattress dip as she sat beside him. He felt her hand, cool and slightly damp, slip beneath the blanket and brush his hair from his forehead.

'Show your mother those beautiful eyes,' she said, pulling the corner of the blanket back.

He looked up at his mother's face. In the dim light, with her make-up washed away and her hair softly framing her face, she looked like an angel. She lifted his injured hand, pressing a gentle kiss to the small plaster over the cut on his finger. 'Does it still hurt, my little star?'

He wanted so badly to believe her, to sink into the warmth of her affection, but he couldn't.

She lay down beside him, looping her arms around him, pulling him close. She stank of alcohol.

'You're the star at the centre of my constellation. You know that?'

'Yes,' he said. It was the answer she expected.

'Everything revolves around you,' she murmured, her breath warm against his ear. 'Everything.'

He allowed himself to get closer. He wanted to forget the screaming, the broken glass, the stinging slap of her hand on the back of his head.

He was ready to start again.

'That's my good boy.' His mother sighed, her voice growing heavy with sleep. 'My perfect little star.'

Alistair opened his eyes and sat up.

He looked at the packed suitcase. Everything was ready. Everything was in order.

He took off the tissue. The cut had stopped bleeding, leaving a thin, red line across his palm.

And then thought of the last thing he'd ever said to his mother. He said it out loud. 'Stars burn out... and then everything starts again.'

9

Gardner felt unsettled by the silence at home.

The children were at school, and her Polish au pair, Monika, was away.

As she nursed a cup of tea in the kitchen, Gardner's mind wandered to the impending arrival of her brother. The thought of him sitting opposite her at the table by day's end made her stomach somersault.

From an early age, even before he'd fractured her skull in the hall of mirrors, it had been clear that something wasn't right with her younger brother.

Behind those empty eyes, something sinister simmered.

Their parents, however, had been blind to Jack's true nature. They doted on him, leaving Gardner to fend for herself.

Eventually, it had cost them. His behaviour, erratic and dangerous, was challenging and she watched as Jack ground them down.

Gardner, meanwhile, had quickly learned to be very self-sufficient. No doubt, the experience had caused her trauma, but she was grateful for the independence and resilience that she'd developed within herself.

By his early twenties, Jack had become lost in the shadows. His activities until his thirties remained, until this day, shrouded in mystery.

To think now that Neville Fairweather was involved with that felt surreal.

She wondered, now, if she would ever find out what really happened. Neville didn't seem willing to fill in any blanks for her. In 2013, Jack was convicted of manslaughter after accidentally hitting someone with his car. It had turned out that the unfortunate victim was part of a gang. For many, that was not coincidental and had all the markings of some kind of gang hit. But his affiliations with the rival gang were impossible to define, and the case was downgraded. He stuck fast and robotically to his story. The fog lights of an oncoming vehicle had dazzled him. The driver of the other vehicle was never located.

Because he didn't exist, Gardner thought.

Still, there'd been enough doubt to keep Jack's prison sentence short.

Before his incarceration, he'd had a brief relationship with a heroin addict, which had resulted in Rose. Upon his release, he tried to integrate himself into Rose's life.

In 2023, Jack had shown up on Gardner's doorstep in Knaresborough with Rose, claiming he'd changed and needed help. Against her better judgement, Gardner had let them in. She'd had no choice, really.

Gardner would not close the door on a seven-year-old girl.

At this point, Gardner had seen a different side to her younger brother. She'd *seen* a genuine warmth in his eyes that was unrecognisable to her.

What followed was a violent series of events that led to Jack's arrest, and then imprisonment, for assaulting a local traveller.

Ultimately, Jack had been manipulative, knowing full well that Gardner wouldn't allow Rose to go into the system. Hence, her adopting the little girl.

Still, during her visits, Jack had appeared grateful and contrite. She hoped that this endearment to her would prevent more bumps on the road ahead.

Gardner's phone buzzed, jolting her from her thoughts. Chief Constable Rebecca 'Harsh' Marsh's name flashed on the screen. With her short black hair, masculine appearance, and impressive upper body strength, she'd also earned the moniker 'Dr Frank-N-Furter'. A far less politically correct approach. Gardner didn't use either name, whereas Rice, her less-than-PC colleague, used them interchangeably on a daily basis.

Gardner liked Marsh, more than many, but it was an ominous name to see on her week off. She sighed and answered, 'Ma'am?'

'Emma... how's the week been?'

'Up and down. Better now...' *If you take Jack's arrival out of the equation.*

'Good news. I did hear Riddick's operation was a success.'

'He's not out of the woods just yet.' She felt it important to make it clear she was unavailable.

'Ha. He was never in the woods, Emma. Wasn't it you that once said he was like a cat? Nine lives?'

She had. However, she'd added, at the time, that she wasn't sure how many of these lives he'd already used.

'Yes... it's looking positive,' she said, wanting to push the phone call on. 'How's everything with you, ma'am?'

'Phil is walking around HQ like a lost puppy.'

She couldn't resist a laugh over this. Phil Rice, the middle-aged DI, was as belligerent and stubborn as they came. You'd never know if he was an emotional wreck inside, because he was so bloody old school. Expressing weakness in front of anyone was a no-go. Much easier to mask it all with sarcasm, aggression and controversial viewpoints.

Still, when all was said and done, he had, under Gardner's guidance, shown flashes of being a decent copper, when she'd steered him away from antagonising colleagues and witnesses.

'What can I say? I'm the only one who can tolerate him.' *Now what the bloody hell do you want?*

'Emma, look... I know this is your week off, but I need a favour. A big one... or I wouldn't ask. Are you able to spare me a few hours?'

Bloody hell. 'That's a long favour. Sounds more like work, ma'am.'

'When did we call it work, Emma? This is a vocation. We do this because we love it.'

Gardner snorted over her use of sarcasm, and then followed it up with the most obvious of loud sighs.

'Like I said, Emma. I wouldn't ask if I had someone else with your capabilities...'

'You've Phil. He's mellowing.'

'Can't risk him – at least, not on his own. This is sensitive. I'm going to be insistent with this one. I do need this favour.'

Riddick in ICU, her brother about to descend on her life, a relationship that surely couldn't last with someone sixteen years younger...

...and now Marsh was calling in a favour.

And, if there was one person you never turned down, it was Marsh. Especially if you already owed her that favour, and Gardner owed her several. The chief constable had been supportive during Gardner's tumultuous start in Yorkshire, backing her decisions and shielding her from political fallout.

She'd also arranged support for Gardner when Neville had reared his intimidating head.

Still, Gardner had to try and wriggle. 'My life is upside down at the moment. The week off was the only way I could make sense of it.' And I explained that to you in your sodding office when I took the time off!

'This is a very personal favour, Emma. You're the only one I trust to bring in on it.'

And there it was.

A polite insistence that it was happening.

Why did everyone always make her feel like she owed them?

Marsh and Neville would get on like a house on fire.

'I remember you telling me about Michael Yorke, your mentor...' Marsh said.

Gardner shook her head. Emotional blackmail, too?

'You said that without him, you wouldn't be half the detective,' Marsh persisted. 'You wouldn't have been able to help half the people you have... Well... the same applies here. This is about my mentor.'

Gardner's interest was suddenly piqued. Who was that?

'Retired Chief Constable Roy Linders.'

'I've heard his name mentioned a few times. He was well respected.'

'And then some,' Marsh said. 'Many owe their careers to him... including me. Anyway, his daughter, Imogen, died of a heart attack yesterday evening.'

'I'm sorry to hear that.' Gardner sighed.

'She was in her late twenties.'

'Awful.'

'Fit as a fiddle.'

'I can't imagine.' And she couldn't. Losing one of her daughters, at any age, to anything, didn't seem like something that could be endured.

'Well... yes... all signs point to natural causes, except...' Marsh paused. 'Roy's instincts have gone haywire over the son-in-law, Alistair Ashworth. He always had good instincts. The best.'

Except, he's in shock and grieving, Gardner thought. *Instincts would certainly be compromised.* Gardner held back from suggesting it. Marsh was a perceptive individual; it wouldn't have gone unconsidered.

'He's not jumping the gun and tearing down walls. He's simply asked that we speak to Alistair, weigh him up, see if this is his paranoia, or if his gut feeling has a right to be flaring.'

'Ma'am, okay, maybe not Phil, but I can think of several other officers more than capable—'

'He asked for you.'

'Really? He doesn't know me.'

'Well, he asked for the best, which is you.'

Gardner couldn't help but snort. Now, she was using flattery. Nourishment for the ego.

'I owe him that.'

'How about you, ma'am? Many would say you're the best.'

'Ha! Nice try, Emma. I respect that. Truth is, I would if I could. But personal favours are wholly inappropriate for someone in my position. Plus, a chief constable marching in on a suspect early doors... well... talk about a fanfare.'

'But this is all still a personal favour, isn't it? No one suspected foul play other than Roy?'

'Yes, in a fashion, but I feel it will be less noticeable coming from you, and I meant what I said... about being the best.'

'And if I take Phil with me?'

'Of course. Look, Phil is great when you're holding his leash.

Just hold it tight, okay?' Marsh said. 'I'll send over the details on Alistair. I'll get Rice to meet you there around noon?'

Emma glanced at the clock. It was just past 10 a.m. now. She'd want to meet Rice for coffee first to plan their approach. 'That should work,' she said, mentally rearranging her day. She had to pick Jack up at two, and then at five, she'd be collecting the kids from after-school club. She was gutted that she couldn't see Riddick during the day. And she couldn't see him tonight after Jack's return, either! She certainly didn't want to leave him alone with the children on his first night.

Following another series of compliments and an expression of gratitude, Marsh rang off.

'Bollocks,' Gardner said, feeling that Marsh had just done a right number on her.

Didn't she have enough on her plate?

Things were getting out of hand. She texted Rice to arrange a meeting point for coffee, and then opened her laptop to research Alistair Ashworth, sighing.

The documents from Marsh were already in her inbox.

She noticed that they'd arrived half a minute before the phone call.

She couldn't help but laugh.

'I never had a bloody choice, did I?'

10

Caffè Nero was bustling. It was always the case when winter was biting.

It took Gardner a moment to spot DI Phil Rice at a corner table. As she approached, she noticed two cups of steaming coffee. Rice greeted her with a self-satisfied smirk, gesturing to the cup closest to her. 'Morning, boss. Large cappuccino, extra shot, one sugar. Just how you like it.'

She couldn't help herself. 'I've kicked the sugar, Phil.'

The smirk fell. 'Ah, bollocks. When?'

'Since I wrestled with my jeans just this weekend and the jeans won.'

'Trust you to change things up on me,' Rice growled.

She sat opposite him. 'I'll drink it just this once.' Gardner lifted the cup to her lips. 'My body's not as forgiving as it used to be. Unlike some.' She nodded at him. 'Who seem to age in reverse.'

Rice preened. Smirk resumed, he nodded. 'I think it's the new suit that's doing it.'

'Tailored?'

'Aye.'

Gardner took another sip of coffee.

'And, boss, if you don't mind, I'd like to point out that you don't look to me like you've put on any weight.'

'Careful, Phil. Compliments from you always make me suspicious.'

'Can't a man appreciate his superior's youthful glow without ulterior motives?' Rice asked innocently.

'Not when that man is you, no,' Gardner retorted. 'It's nice to see you, but enough of this creepy chat.'

'Fair enough. How's Paul doing?'

Gardner gave him a knowing look. 'Improving... but let's not pretend you give a shit.'

'Look, I may not be Paul's biggest fan, but I wouldn't wish any harm on the man. Contrary to popular belief, I do have a heart. Even if it's not a shiny reconditioned model like he's got. You have me all wrong.'

'Or... I've got you exactly right. And I'm probably the only one who does. You should be grateful for that. I trust you, and you were my first choice on this little errand...'

'And you believe you chose me? Marsh told me hours ago I'd be hooking up with you.'

'Bloody hell.'

'She knows how to play us like a couple of cheap fiddles. Mind you, women like that always get what they want.'

'Women?' She raised an eyebrow.

He adjusted himself in his chair, his face reddening slightly. 'Not women, women. That kind of women. You know? You get it, yeah?'

'Phil,' she said, her eyebrow still raised. 'It's nothing to do with gender. Have you never met a manipulative man?'

Rice nodded. 'Sorry... what I meant to say was it has more to do with her being a power-hungry, manipulative egomaniac.'

Gardner widened her eyes. *A tad extreme, perhaps.* Still, she hadn't seen him in over a week, so one bollocking was enough, plus he did have a point...

'You know, she actually instructed me to play nice and stay on a leash!'

'Really?' Gardner laughed. 'She used more or less the same words when speaking to me. She was keen for me to keep the leash tight, too.'

Rice snorted. 'Asking for a favour and then emasculating me in one fell swoop. How efficient she is.'

'Behave. The only thing that emasculates you is that kimono of yours,' Gardner said. She couldn't help herself.

Rice clutched his chest. 'Low blow.'

Gardner allowed herself a small smile before pulling out a file. 'Right, let's focus on why we're really here.'

'Ha. Yeah. You thinking waste of time, too?' Rice asked.

'I haven't thought much, to be honest, but be open-minded, Phil... Alistair Ashworth.' She took out her notebook. 'You read through everything we were sent?'

'Most... Let's go through the basics again. Warm us up.'

'From Surrey, initially. Has a law degree from Oxford.'

'Social mobility in full flow,' Rice said.

'He works in retail now.'

'Yeah... rather odd, huh? Courtroom to shelf stacking.'

'Not unheard of... leaving behind the rat race.'

'Aye... suppose not... especially if you've Daddy's money to rely on. And his parents are minted, yes?'

'True, but according to Roy Linders, Alistair is estranged from his family. Has nothing to do with them. They didn't even come to the wedding. Is he cut off from the money?'

'Perhaps. Might still be in the will? We could ask?'

'We'll put that down as a maybe question,' Gardner said. 'Remember this is a light touch... at least, until I have doubts.'

'There's no I in we, boss.'

'I know. But you always have doubts, Phil. About everything.'

'True.'

'So, we rely on my doubts. Leash... remember?'

He rolled his eyes.

'Roy has Alistair pegged as a loner. No friends. Never left Imogen's side when he wasn't working. Roy has really emphasised his creepiness.' Gardner pointed at Rice and smirked. 'A different kind of creepy to you, mind.'

'Good to know.'

'We've no criminal records... nothing on his driver's licence. Passport checked out fine. There's an extended stay in Rio de Janeiro in Brazil from 2022, before he met Imogen in 2023. He told Roy and Imogen that he'd been working in a bar over there.'

'A bar? Bloody hell, he really didn't want any part of the courtroom. Dancing the samba in Brazil... then, stacking Pringles at Marks & Spencer.' Rice broke off, looking thoughtful. 'Never mind leaving the law profession, why leave Brazil? I've just earmarked it for retirement.'

'Maybe he didn't like dancing the samba,' Gardner said.

'Miserable bastard.'

'Neither would you.'

'True. And yes, I'm also a miserable bastard.'

'Okay, let's think about Imogen.' Gardner's expression softened. 'Tragic. She had a miscarriage recently, and then found out she couldn't conceive at all. She collapsed in Bebra Gardens from a heart attack.'

Rice lowered his head. 'Awful. Poor woman.'

'Yes,' Gardner said. 'So, we need to be extremely sensitive.'

'You don't need to tell me, boss. This is Roy's gig. He's paranoid. It'll all turn out to be nothing.'

'Okay, so no blazing in based on a retired copper's grief-ridden assessment?'

He saluted. 'Aye. This man is bereaved. I hope you keep it toned down too, boss.'

She laughed. 'To live inside your world.'

'You know, boss, it can be a charming, pleasant world.'

'I'll take your word for it. Wait a moment... is that a glint in your eye? Have you struck gold with that dating app?'

Rice tilted his head from side to side. 'Yes and no. I'll start with the no. It's costing me a fortune. In this day and age, I thought things had moved on... but I end up paying for all the meals.'

'Really? Do you offer?'

'Yes, of course I do.'

'Well, there you go then!' Gardner guffawed.

'Eh?'

'In this day and age, quite a lot of folk don't have a pot to piss in! Then there's you. Who's going to say no when you're brandishing an American Express? Good on them is what I say. Someone offers them a free meal... take the free meal. To be honest, I'm even considering dinner with you now.'

He looked bemused. 'Really?'

She narrowed her eyes. 'That was a witty aside. *Only*.'

He sighed. 'You make a good point. I need to be more progressive. And just not offer.'

'Might work. You might look tight then.'

He groaned. 'I can't win.'

'Ha. Still, progressive is good. This is 2025.'

'Yes. I've been learning to use a lot of apps. It's a minefield, but I'm getting somewhere.'

'Have you started to send emojis yet?'

'I draw the line at little yellow faces.'

'You can change the colour of the faces now.'

'Anyone sends me a picture of a colourful face, I'll send back a picture of a pair of bollocks.'

Gardner's face fell.

'Not my own! An emoji one, of course.'

Gardner shook her head. 'That's okay then.' She finished her coffee. 'Now, shall we go over those questions for Ashworth?'

For all his faults, and granted, there were many, Rice was misunderstood.

He was, actually, good company.

A welcome distraction.

That said, the leash remained absolutely necessary.

As they began to review their approach for interviewing Ashworth, Gardner felt a small sense of relief. For a brief moment, the weight of her personal troubles – Riddick's recovery, Jack's impending arrival, her complicated relationship with O'Brien – seemed to lift.

11

'Watch your step,' Gardner said.

Rice looked down on Ashworth's well-manicured lawn and then hopped back onto the path.

The house was a modern two-storey affair with large windows and a pristine exterior.

She knocked and the door opened, revealing Alistair Ashworth. He wore a crisp white shirt tucked into well-fitted dark jeans, topped with a navy blazer. He'd also used product to comb his hair neatly to one side.

Although he didn't dress like someone reeling from shock, there were dark circles under his eyes, and he looked pale and gaunt.

Gardner showed her identification and introduced them both. She then followed up with, 'We're very sorry for your loss, Mr Ashworth.'

Alistair's eyes flicked between them. She tried to read his expression but couldn't. 'Thank you. What's this about?'

'We're simply here to check on your wellbeing,' Gardner said softly. 'Are you alone, Mr Ashworth?'

'Yes... I'm busy though... organising this and that... the funeral.' His expression remained neutral. 'Could it wait?'

'In situations like this, when the tragedy is so sudden and unexpected, it's prudent for us to follow up with family members.' She looked at Rice.

'Yes,' Rice said. 'Just to reach out.'

'And it takes a DCI and a DI to reach out?' Alistair raised an eyebrow.

He was exactly right, of course.

'Some questions will have to be asked,' Gardner said. 'That is expected.'

'And the fact that Imogen's father was a high-ranking police officer. Has that influenced this visit?'

'Not that I'm aware of,' Gardner lied.

Alistair stepped back, waving them in. She noticed he'd wrapped one of his hands in a clean, white bandage.

Alistair led them through to an immaculately presented lounge. The space was almost clinical in its tidiness – not a cushion out of place, classic artwork adorning the walls. A large bookshelf dominated one wall, filled with an eclectic mix of law textbooks, classic literature and travel guides. Gardner wondered if, in his grief, Alistair had embarked on a cleaning spree.

'Can I offer you both a drink?'

'We'll be fine,' Gardner replied.

Alistair gestured for them to sit on a pristine leather sofa, while he took an armchair opposite. The seating arrangement felt oddly formal, more like a business meeting than a condolence visit.

Gardner glanced at pictures lining the mantelpiece. Alistair and his stunning wife, Imogen, on their wedding day. Snapshots of them by the Colosseum in Rome and the Eiffel Tower in France.

Gardner wanted to give the impression that she was merely here in a supportive role, but was aware of how quickly that could slip. She would have to keep herself very focused.

'Do you have any family nearby to support you, Mr Ashworth?' Knowing he was estranged from his parents, she calculated that this could be a way in.

'No.' Sharp and abrupt, but not aggressive. 'They're far away.'

'I see.'

'How about Roy, Imogen's father?' Gardner suggested.

'No,' Alistair said. 'He doesn't like me.' He nodded. 'But I guess you know that already, don't you?' Again, not aggressive; he sounded distant, almost nonchalant.

'Oh, why is that?' Rice asked.

'My demeanour. *Apparently.* According to Imogen, anyway.'

'Your demeanour?' Gardner pressed.

'He's always been wary of quiet people... suspicious of them. So Imogen told me.'

'So, he considers you a quiet person?' Gardner asked.

'Yes.'

'And how did that make you feel?' Rice asked.

'It's not something I gave much thought to.' He looked at his watch. 'I don't want to sound rude, but I've got so many calls to make.'

'I understand. It must be hard. It's a shame you've no one local,' Gardner said. 'Is it not possible for your parents to travel?'

Alistair regarded her for a moment and then dropped his gaze. 'I no longer speak to my mother and father.'

'I'm sorry. That won't help... now, of all times.'

'I made my peace with it, a long time ago. Still...' He broke off, perhaps realising he was revealing too much.

'Still?' Gardner pressed.

'Well, it emphasises my loss, I guess. I stumbled on something so perfect.' He looked up at the pictures. 'Lasting... rich... with Imogen. More than I ever had from my family... and now, it's gone.'

Gardner noted that while he appeared sad, his demeanour wasn't that of someone freshly devastated. It was more like someone who'd already processed their grief to some extent. But she had to be careful in reaching conclusions. The bottom line was that grief manifested differently in everyone.

He made a point of looking at his watch again.

'What's so pressing, Mr Ashworth?'

'Pressing? Funeral arrangements, of course,' he replied.

'I think it's acceptable to spend some time processing everything first,' Gardner said.

'Like this?' Alistair looked at her. For the first time, she detected a slight change of expression. A ghost of a smile, perhaps? 'Is this discussion pressing?'

'We just wanted to see whether we could support, maybe ensure that there's nothing else for us to be worried about,' Gardner said.

'Worried about?' Alistair said.

'Regarding Imogen. Her death was unexpected. And once again, we're sorry about that.'

He nodded. 'Yes. Have you spoken to the doctor?'

'Not personally, no.'

'You're aware it was natural?'

Gardner nodded.

'So?'

'It always pays to be thorough... for everyone.' She nodded at him again to show she was only trying to be supportive.

'We noticed that you've moved a reasonable amount over the years.'

Alistair nodded. 'Yes... why are you bringing that up now?'

'It just caught my interest.' Rice said. 'Especially as you lived in Brazil for a time. Always fancied it myself. It must have been exciting.'

Alistair shrugged. 'It was okay. It had its difficulties. I always struggled with the heat.'

'Must have been warm running around a bar,' Rice said.

Alistair sucked in his top lip, paused for a moment, and then released it. 'You seem to know a lot about me already, considering this is merely a check-in. Anyway, to go back to your point. Yes, I've moved a lot. So? Isn't it just as likely to show me as lost, rather than confident?' He looked at the pictures of Imogen again. 'I finally thought I'd found something. So, I guess, I'll have to prepare to be lost again.'

Gardner exchanged a glance with Rice while Alistair was occupied with the images. Rice shrugged, indicating that he didn't really know what to make of it all.

She looked back at him and saw that he was adjusting the bandage. 'What happened to your hand, Alistair?'

'Just a cut.'

'You've wrapped it up well. Was it deep?'

Alistair shrugged. 'It wouldn't stop bleeding.'

'Sorry for this,' Gardner said, 'but it is necessary to ask. Are you a danger to yourself?'

'Only when I drop a glass, it seems.' He smiled.

Gardner didn't return his smile. In fact, she found herself becoming increasingly unsettled by him. His responses seemed rehearsed, almost too composed for someone who'd just lost their wife. She dropped her eyes, careful not to let her suspicions show. She didn't want him to see it in her expression.

'I think it's fair for me to ask a question now.'

'Of course,' Gardner said.

'Am I being investigated because of Roy?'

'This isn't an investigation, Mr Ashworth,' Rice said. His tone was defensive. Gardner hoped he would stop there. 'However, in instances such as this, a decision will have to be made on whether to have one.'

Gardner looked up at him and he caught her eyes. He read the signal that this was enough.

'Do I need my solicitor?' Alistair asked.

'Of course, that's your choice, Mr Ashworth. If that's your wish. But I see all this as merely a...' She needed a word. 'A debrief at this stage.'

'A debrief on my wife's death. I was there.'

Gardner winced internally at her poor choice of words.

'I know, and I can't stress enough how hard this must be, and how sorry we really are... but Mr Ashworth, you were there, and so, this conversation has to be had at some point. I just want to get it out of the way, so you can move on. Of course, a solicitor is something we can wait for if you want.'

Alistair's posture stiffened.

'As I said before,' Rice said. 'I've always wanted to go to Brazil. See the carnivals and that. I'm not much of a dancer, like, but I'd give it a go. What made you choose Brazil, Mr Ashworth?'

It was obvious to Gardner that Rice's abrupt change of topic was intentional. He wanted to prevent Alistair from clamming up.

Still, Alistair looked uninterested. 'I was lost, attempting to comprehend myself and my upbringing. Then I worked in a bar, drank too much, got my act together and came home. There wasn't much to it. There isn't some exciting narrative.'

Rice said, 'What was wrong with your upbringing?'

Alistair fixed him with a stare. Gardner realised that it was the first time he'd looked antagonised. 'I don't want to talk about that. I'm assuming I don't have to?'

Rice looked at Gardner.

'No,' Gardner said. 'Not if you don't want.'

'Well, I don't, and it has nothing to do with Imogen.'

'I understand. What happened when you came back from Brazil? Why did you come here?'

'I folded a map in half. My parents were in the bottom half. I stuck a pin in the top half.'

Gardner nodded.

'That does take confidence,' Rice said.

'Didn't feel like confidence. It felt like self-preservation.'

'Do you think that you could ever heal this relationship with your parents?' Gardner asked.

'I'm going to stop it there,' Alistair said. 'My parents are irrelevant in all of this. I've lost the most important person in my life, and you want to talk about such painful things—'

'Okay, nothing more about your parents. I'm sorry, Mr Ashworth. Have you spoken to your work?'

'Yes... they know it is going to take a while to get back on my feet. They've got enough staff at the store to cover me.'

'Do you enjoy your job?' Rice asked.

'I stack shelves and work tills,' Alistair said. 'There's nothing to like, or dislike. I merely do.'

'You moved from law to retail?'

'Is all this really relevant?' Alistair asked.

Gardner didn't know. Until she had all the information, how could she ascertain relevance? Still, she wanted to keep him onside. 'Just a few more questions. Standard procedure around a sudden, unexpected incident. It is necessary to have a profile on all those close to the deceased for insurance, too. So, if you don't mind, why did you leave law?'

He sighed. 'Now, that was a dislikable job. I didn't want to commit every minute of my life to thinking about the plight and saviour of others. I wanted to spend my time thinking of Imogen, and the family we were planning to have. Is that enough for you?'

Gardner nodded. 'Thanks, Mr Ashworth. Yes, I believe we've talked about you long enough, and I can't thank you enough for helping us in building this picture of everything. Can I ask a few questions about Imogen, and then we'll be out of your hair?'

He gave a swift nod.

'How did Imogen seem recently?'

'Down. Very down.' Alistair rubbed his temples. Gardner allowed him time to develop his answer.

'Two months ago,' Alistair said, 'we lost our baby. A miscarriage.'

'I'm so sorry,' Gardner said.

'And, well, she found out that she couldn't have children... from the damage... you know. She felt hopeless. It's been an awful time.'

Gardner nodded. 'I imagine it has.'

'Still, we'd been considering adoption and so forth. In fact, just yesterday, she met someone about it. We went to the park last night, and were discussing it, when... well... you know. She just collapsed.'

'It must have been awful.'

He rubbed his eyes. 'It doesn't seem real. As we got up to leave, it just happened. I called an ambulance, but by the time they arrived, it was too late. I knew. They pretended there was still hope, but she was already gone. I could tell.'

His hands dropped away. His eyes were tinged red from the rubbing, but not from tears. Gardner studied his face, searching for genuine pain. There was something there, undoubtedly. But was it real grief or something else entirely?

The jury remained out.

'Why did you meet at Bebra Gardens?' Rice asked.

'If you must know, it's where we got engaged. I was trying to be romantic. I was trying to make her feel better. I took her a coffee... and... well... it all ended in a blur. Ambulances and hospitals.'

'And you were at work all day before that?'

Alistair narrowed his eyes. 'Yes. Why do you ask?'

'Just for clarity.'

'Phone my manager. I'll give you his name. I went straight from work to Nero for a coffee and then to Bebra Gardens.'

'Of course,' Gardner said. 'It's just standard.'

'Then, I was with her...' Alistair said.

Gardner nodded. 'I know.'

'And I've been alone ever since.'

Gardner's heart fell.

What a mess this favour was turning out to be. Having to probe a potentially grief-stricken man less than twenty-four hours after his life fell apart! She silently cursed Marsh for putting her in this position.

'Did Imogen have any other health issues you were aware of?' Rice asked.

Alistair shook his head. 'Surely you'd have those details? But no... nothing. She was the picture of health, until she wasn't. Recently, she was struggling with her mental health for the reasons I gave you.'

'And your relationship was good?' Gardner asked.

'Perfect. We were happy. We had plans, dreams. A future.'

Gardner nodded. 'Financially?'

'The mortgage on this place is nearly paid off. I have savings. She has a good job. Money has never been an issue.'

'Mr Ashworth,' she said. 'Is there anything else you think we should know? Anything at all about Imogen, about your life together, that might be relevant?'

For a moment, something flickered in Alistair's eyes – a mix of emotions Gardner couldn't quite decipher. But then it was gone, replaced by the same calm detachment he'd shown throughout the interview.

'No,' he said firmly. 'Nothing.'

Gardner nodded, closing her notebook. 'In that case, thank you for your time, Mr Ashworth. We appreciate your cooperation and again, I'm so sorry for your loss.'

'Yes,' Rice said, standing. 'I'm very sorry.'

As they made their way to the door, Gardner paused. 'One last thing, Mr Ashworth. If you need anything, or if you think of anything else, please contact us.'

Alistair nodded, his hand already on the door handle. 'Of course... but I'm not sure what I could give you.'

As the door closed behind them, Gardner and Rice exchanged a look. They walked in silence to their cars, both lost in thought.

12

They both got inside Gardner's car. 'What do you think?' Gardner asked.

'At first, I wasn't convinced. I mean, he communicated clearly for someone in the depths of despair. Different from the norm, I guess. But overall, he seemed on the ball. Gutted. Down. Jaded. I mean... good on him for answering our questions. I'd have shown us the door straight away.'

Gardner sighed, rubbing her temples. 'I don't know. It wasn't the same for me. I was never convinced. He's an intelligent man, too. He'd know that showing us the door would arouse suspicion. Something feels off.'

'Grief hits people in different ways, boss. Like a packet of Revels, you never know what you're going to get. When my mother died, I got all the worst possible ones. Coffee. I was throwing up all the time. When my father died, I got the tasty ones with peanuts in... Boss? Why are you looking at me like that?'

'Because I can't believe you just used that analogy.'

'I hated my dad.'

'Yeah... still. Anyway, Phil, we're losing focus.'

'Sorry.'

'I'm not stupid regarding grief,' Gardner said. 'But come on, there was something odd in there.'

Rice nodded. 'Well, it was odd, no question. My point is... wasn't it going to be odd one way or another? And also what would be his motive? They owe so little on the mortgage – insurance will pay that off. There was no critical life insurance – we checked. They'd been married a short time. I mean... what does he even gain? A house all on his own? Is it worth killing someone?'

'True,' Gardner conceded. 'Maybe you're right. Maybe Roy's suspicions are colouring my judgement.'

She thought to herself: *And all the other shit in my head right now.*

Of which, there was lots.

She checked her watch. 'Shit.' She started the car. 'I've got to be somewhere.'

'Is that your polite way of saying "get out", boss?' Rice snorted.

'Yes.'

'Where are you off to?'

She paused, wondering if she should tell him. He could, in his own way, be a reliable confidante. Still, she just wanted to get it all over and done with, and didn't have the time, anyway. 'Tell you another time. Hop it. And don't speak to Marsh. That's on me.'

He opened the door, stepped out and leaned in. 'How did I do? With the leash? How many times did you have to tug it to keep me in line?'

She laughed. 'You did well... but no plans to loosen it off just yet, I'm afraid.'

'This is animal cruelty.'

'Shut the door, Phil.'

13

Tracing the aggravated scar tissue on his ear, Alistair observed the two detectives through his lounge window.

Both were in the same car, deep in conversation, their body language expressive.

Probably dissecting every word he'd said, no doubt. Every micro-expression he'd shown.

A low growl echoed in his mind. He turned, expecting to see Clive, the Rottweiler, sitting in the room's corner, stringy flesh caught between its teeth, staring with unblinking and soulless eyes.

He saw only his empty room.

The police stopping by for a conversation wasn't entirely unexpected.

It hadn't been pleasant, but he was confident he'd handled it well.

Alistair moved to straighten the cushions the detectives had disturbed, aligning them with military precision. Each change was deliberate, measured. The world might be chaos, but here, in this space, he could maintain control. He smoothed out the indentations left by their bodies, erasing all evidence of their presence. Like erasing footprints in sand.

Satisfied with the room's restored order, he made his way to the kitchen. The hardwood floors creaked softly under his feet, a reminder of the house's age despite its modern facade. He paused at the entrance, surveying the gleaming countertops and stainless-steel appliances. Everything in its place, everything serving a purpose.

As he opened a drawer, his hand closed around a small booklet. He withdrew a Canadian passport, its deep blue cover embossed with the country's coat of arms. The cool, textured surface felt familiar in his hands. He ran his thumb over the gold lettering, feeling the raised edges of each character...

Then, a memory hit him like a physical blow, distracting him from his irritated ear, but launching him back into a time he had no business revisiting.

He shouldn't be here.

The office smelled of leather and cigar smoke.

Ahead, his father's desk shimmered under a glare of sunlight through open curtains.

Heart pounding, he circled the desk, nudged the chair aside and opened the drawer. The soft scrape of wood on wood in this small room was like thunder.

What was he searching for? Something to understand his father better? To make sense of the man who was more ghost than parent?

He saw his father's passport and took hold of it.

Heavy... weighty... He flipped it open and traced his finger over the photograph. Strong jawline, piercing eyes.

His mother had once called his father an assured man.

Was this his destiny, too?

To be assured? To have a strong jawline and piercing eyes?

He flipped through the pages. Each foreign stamp hid a story he didn't know, but wished he could.

When he heard footsteps outside the room, his chest went cold. He slammed the drawer and ducked under the desk, the passport clamped between clammy fingers.

He waited.

Nothing.

Pulse roaring in his ears, he hoped it was his imagination.

The door opened. He heard his father's voice. Also, Ms Redmond's voice. His father's personal assistant.

He liked Ms Redmond... she brought him presents, mainly colourful stationery, but once she'd given him an old computer console that her son didn't need any more.

He listened to the door shutting and looked at the passport in his hand.

How could he have been so stupid?

What did they say? Curiosity killed the cat.

He waited, but there was no more talking. Just rustling, and occasional groans.

He may only have been eight, but he recognised the sound of kissing.

He tried covering his ears, but the sounds broke through, and they seemed to go on and on.

It then sounded as if Ms Redmond was in some pain. Should he check on her? He stayed put out of fear.

The desk above him creaked and moved.

Ms Redmond's moans intensified, punctuated by occasional gasps from his father.

He closed his eyes, held his ears and tried to think about his new Nintendo console, about the games he could play, about anything but what was happening above him.

When the silence finally fell, he freed his ears but remained motionless, afraid to even breathe. He heard his father's voice, low and tender in a way it rarely was with his mother. He struggled to hear the whispers. Eventually, his father spoke louder. 'Go first, Sarah. I'll follow in a minute.'

The door opened and closed a first time.

He counted to one hundred.

The door opened and closed a second time.

He emerged.

Ms Redmond's perfume was strong in the air...

The memory dissolved like smoke, leaving Alistair standing in his kitchen, the Canadian passport still in his hands. He flipped it open. The photograph was a good one. He'd tilted his head slightly, to draw less attention to his damaged ear lobe.

Once again, he reached into the drawer and this time pulled out his UK passport. He looked at the photograph. Although he was slightly younger, it was less flattering. He didn't look the best when unshaven.

Another memory crashed through him, this one sharper than broken glass...

He may have been young, but he wasn't ignorant.

His father and Ms Redmond were doing things they shouldn't have been doing.

Through the window, he watched his father leave with Ms Redmond. Then he headed downstairs, passport in hand. His mother was asleep on the sofa. A bottle of opened wine on the table in front of her.

The blender.

He'd seen his mother and father use it.

He knew how it worked.

With shaking hands, he opened the lid and dropped the passport inside.

His finger hovered over the power button.

To anyone else, their lives looked perfect. His mother and father always made sure of that.

But it was just another lie.

He pressed the button.

He wanted the passport to be confetti, but it merely chewed at it. Tearing pieces off it, but mainly just scratching and damaging the rest.

The clunking of the struggling blades filled the kitchen.

When he was certain that the passport was now unusable, he pulled the plug and stared at the mess he'd made.

He felt sick, and tears sprang up in his eyes.

What had he done?

Panic rising, he hastily emptied the chewed passport and the torn paper into the bin and scrubbed the blender clean, erasing all evidence of his act of defiance. His heart pounded.

He imagined his mother waking up, coming up behind him and slapping his head. He thought of his father driving home and catching him...

But no one came. The house remained silent.

The years fell away as Alistair shook off the memory. His hand hovered over the blender in his kitchen. Without hesitation, he flicked it on and fed the UK passport in. The machine growled. The blender was more powerful than the one he'd used as a child. It struggled for a couple of seconds, but then it fed on its gift.

The pieces swirled. A kaleidoscope of what he was leaving behind.

Imogen's face flashed in his mind – her smile, her trust, her dreams, like his, of a family. For a moment, his hand twitched over the power button, a fleeting impulse to stop, to cling to what had been.

But the moment passed.

Then, as the last pieces settled, Alistair felt the familiar sense of calm wash over him. The man who'd loved Imogen, who'd dared to dream of a normal life, was gone.

He emptied the blender's contents into the bin, then meticulously cleaned the appliance until it gleamed. No evidence, no traces.

He picked up his Canadian passport, ready to start again.

He noticed his damaged ear had stopped itching.

14

Jack's lean frame, stripped of excess by prison food, sat perfectly still, the closely shaved head emphasising sharp cheekbones and a jawline that seemed carved from stone.

Considering the recent threats against his life, her brother looked remarkably calm and composed in the passenger seat of Gardner's car.

Nothing new there, then, Gardner thought. *Calm and composed while the world around him went to shit.*

Her stomach constricted when she observed the prison shrinking away in the rear-view mirror.

'You look good, Emma.' Jack's voice was smooth. To anyone else, it may have just seemed pleasant.

But she knew him better than that. 'Save it, Jack.'

'Thank you for coming to get me.'

'Thank you?'

'Yes.'

'Okay, first rule: let's keep all of this bullshit-free.' She indicated to come off at a roundabout.

After straightening the car, she glanced at him. In profile, he was barely recognisable with his shaved head. Still, when he'd climbed into her car before, and she'd looked directly into those eyes, a void absent of warmth, she'd recognised him well enough.

'Shall we start with your relationship with Neville Fair-weather?'

He didn't respond.

She glanced at him again and saw that he was staring out of the side window. He would not answer her questions.

'When are you planning on telling me what's going on?'

She caught him turning to her from the corner of her eye.

'I really appreciate everything you've done with Rose, Emma.'

'You're swerving the question, then?'

'I've missed her, but knowing that she's safe with you has enabled me to—'

'Sorry, Jack,' Gardner cut him off. 'Am I speaking in a different language?'

'—keep my peace of mind. She really is everything to me.'

She grunted. 'You're being ignorant.'

'Or, maybe you are? After all, you're asking me questions I can't answer.'

She glared at him briefly, before looking back at the road. 'Why not?' She negotiated several lanes on the motorway.

His silence spoke volumes. The conversation, in its present form, was a dead end.

She tried to ease into his conversation, see what he'd reveal. 'It was never a choice, Jack, with Rose, as well you know...' Gardner said. 'You must remember telling me so. Admitting to manipulating me?'

'I never remember saying that. I remember telling you I knew you'd feel obliged. Even with obligation, you've a choice.'

'So, you were relieved when I did it?'

He didn't respond.

'You never thought there was any danger I'd say no?'

She caught him smiling.

'Idiot.'

Jack shrugged. 'Idiot? Really. To be honest, it's probably the wisest thing I ever did. Whatever happens next, she stays with you.'

The words sent a familiar surge of protectiveness through Gardner, the same fierce instinct she'd felt when Rose had first arrived at her door, confused and afraid. 'I considered no alternative.'

'I know. I imagine if I tried to take her from you now... it would be over your dead body.'

A chill ran down Gardner's spine. 'Nice.'

'That was a joke.'

'Yes... just what we need. Jokes. Not so funny when it comes from someone who once fractured my skull.' She indicated to come off the motorway.

'That—'

'Save it. That was a long time ago. You've changed. I know, I've heard it many times.'

'And it's always been true.'

'Whatever. Well, if you can't tell me what Neville has over you, and why your life is in danger—'

'*Was* in danger. Not any more.'

'Good. Well... at least tell me how long you're with us.'

'I don't know.'

'You must have some idea.'

'I don't... it's at Neville's discretion. It could be a day... it could be a month...'

'Longer?'

Jack shrugged. 'I just don't know. It could be a matter of hours. The ball is in Neville's court.'

'Strange deal, really. Neville has got some clout, hasn't he?'

'Yes... but I've been behaving myself, anyway,' Jack said. 'I would've been out sooner rather than later. It's been accelerated because Neville can't afford to lose me.'

'Why is that?'

Jack shook his head to show that he wouldn't be answering.

'So, you're safe now. *We're* safe.'

He nodded. 'I wouldn't be coming if I thought there was any risk. Rose's wellbeing is everything to me.'

'Who wanted to hurt you... in jail?'

He didn't answer.

'Were you scared?'

Jack's expression didn't change. 'I've never really felt unsafe, to be honest. I just took Neville's word for it.'

'So, how can we trust him? I mean, having met him plenty of times, I can give you several reasons not to trust him!'

Jack shrugged. 'His intentions are clear to me. So, I trust him.'

Gardner shook her head. 'Good for you. Well his intentions, or yours, make no sense to me, so where's my peace of mind?'

'You're safe.'

The words echoed hollowly, reminding her of Alistair's equally measured responses just hours ago. Two men, both wearing masks of normality that never quite reached their eyes. She'd only been with Jack for fifteen minutes and she already felt exasperated. 'Okay, Jack, if you're going to be staying with us, we need to set some ground rules. I mean, last time you stayed, you knocked my colleague, Lucy, unconscious.'

'Unfortunate.'

'Yes, very. She's a close friend and...' Gardner took a deep breath. Better to just get it out there now. 'She stays over, sometimes, at the moment.'

'You're in a relationship with her?'

'Yes. That isn't a problem I hope?'

'Why would there be a problem?'

'Just be polite, please. And... non-threatening. Last time you were here, you beat someone half to death on my lawn... Now, I'm assuming prison has taught you a lesson?' She looked away so he couldn't see her rolling her eyes.

'You've nothing to worry about this time.'

'Good. So the ground rules. First, I need to know where you are. If you leave the house, you tell me where you're going and when you'll be back.'

Jack nodded. 'Reasonable.'

'Second, and most importantly, you don't take the children anywhere. I mean... nowhere.'

'Understood.'

'In fact, I'd prefer if you stayed in your room when the kids are home. At least until they get used to the idea of you being around, and then we may amend that slightly.'

'Whatever you think is best. I'll follow your lead.'

His easy acquiescence was typical. And, as it always had been, unnerving. It was too smooth, too perfect. Just like...

Gardner felt a sudden, overwhelming sense of déjà vu. The parallels between this conversation and her earlier one with Alistair were striking and immediately sent a shiver down her spine.

She came off into a rest spot on a country lane. She hit her hazards. 'Sorry just thought of something. Work related. One moment.'

'Of course,' Jack said.

She exited the car and phoned Marsh. As it rang, Jack's calmness, measured responses and focus on saying exactly what she wanted to hear, had her heart racing.

'Emma?' Marsh's voice came through, sounding surprised. 'You took your time... Phil has already spoken to me.'

'I told him not to. I needed time to think it over.'

'He seemed to suggest the interview went well...'

'Yes,' Gardner replied. 'Too well.' Her eyes darted to Jack in the car. He was sitting perfectly still, staring straight ahead. 'Alistair is similar to my brother, Jack, ma'am. *Too similar.* They both always know exactly what to say, how to act... They're both so skilful at wearing masks.'

'Okay... so what're you saying here?'

'I'm saying that I'd like you to order a full toxicology and post-mortem on Imogen Ashworth.'

Marsh sighed. 'Are you sure? This all sounds like a hunch and—'

Gardner's frustration bubbled over. 'You contacted me remember? I'm telling you. Alistair and Jack. It's like looking into the eyes of the same bloody person. The intelligence is there, but the emotion isn't.'

'Emma—'

'My advice would be a full toxicology, take it or leave it.'

The line went silent. Being too aggressive with Marsh was not advisable. She added a 'ma'am' to hopefully soften it.

'All right,' Marsh said finally. 'I asked you for help... you delivered. This is on me.'

'Thank you,' Gardner said. She was about to ring off, but then thought of Alistair and Jack, sitting there, unflinching, unconcerned, as the world burned around them. 'And... listen, ma'am... if it turns out to be something, then, well...' She stopped herself. What was she doing?

'You want it?'

She gulped. 'Yes.'

'Of course, Emma.'

After ringing off, she realised that was probably the worst decision she could have made right now.

'Everything all right?' Jack asked when she returned to the car.

As far from all right as it's possible to be, Gardner thought. 'Fine.'

When Gardner arrived at her home and they'd exited the car, she caught Jack looking up at Rose's bedroom.

'She's at school,' she said, finding her door key.

'I know. I'm excited about seeing her.' He said it with very little intonation, but Gardner heard the truth in it.

She unlocked the door, hoping that with the arrival of Jack and her offer to investigate Alistair, she hadn't just welcomed a storm into her life.

15

Gardner's hands were tight on the steering wheel as she drove to collect the children from school, rehearsing in her mind how to inform Rose and Ana about Jack's arrival.

It went as she expected.

Rose was excited, whereas Ana was nervous and full of questions. *Like mother, like daughter.*

As soon as Gardner pulled up in the driveway, Rose bolted from the car to the front door.

Gardner turned round and smiled at Ana. 'It'll be fine... I promise.'

Her daughter nodded. 'I know, Mummy.' Her voice was timid and full of trust.

Gardner gritted her teeth, praying that she wasn't about to let her down.

When they reached the house, Jack had already opened the door, fallen to his knees and embraced his daughter.

Gardner took Ana's hand and held back, allowing the father and daughter to be reunited.

She watched as Jack held Rose by the shoulders and said, in a gentle voice, 'I'm so happy to see you.' His usual mask of indifference had slipped. His eyes, typically empty, suddenly seemed warmer.

The scene before her betrayed everything she'd thought she'd known about Jack until his last visit here.

She'd believed he didn't possess feelings for anyone. With Rose, they seemed to overflow from him.

This moment, this genuine display of emotion, was the real reason she'd offered her brother sanctuary. *Please let this be real, Jack,* she thought. *Please don't let me be wrong about this.*

Jack stood and led Rose in. Ana tightened her grip on Gardner's hand. She leaned over and kissed her daughter reassuringly and then followed her brother and Rose into the house.

In the kitchen, Jack turned to Ana. He knelt, but didn't embrace her as he had Rose. 'How's my favourite niece, Ana?'

'You only have one,' Ana said.

Jack's lips twitched in what might have been genuine amusement. 'It's all I need.'

She nodded. She was quite a shy girl, especially around people she didn't know that well.

'Ana...' He smiled. 'I'm sorry for the last time, okay? It was disruptive.'

'I can't remember,' Ana said.

'Well, it was, and I'm sorry,' Jack said. 'Are you okay with me staying for a bit?'

She looked up at Gardner who gave her a nod.

'Yes,' Ana said.

'Thank you,' Jack said, offering his hand. 'Thank you so much.'

Ana shook it and then smiled for the first time.

Jack straightened and moved to the kitchen table, reaching into a plastic bag. He pulled out two colourful magazines, both with gifts glued to the front. He handed one to each of them. Their faces lit up.

Gardner felt her jaw tighten. He must have left the house in order to get those magazines. It'd taken him less than an hour to break the first of her ground rules!

The girls' excitement was obvious as they flipped through the pages.

Despite her anger, she kept her voice steady. 'Why don't you girls go upstairs and read those in your room for a bit?'

'Thank you, Dad!' Rose ran off with the magazine.

Ana, more reserved but clearly pleased, offered a quiet, 'Thanks, Uncle Jack.'

As soon as the girls' excited footsteps faded, Gardner turned to Jack. 'So, you went out?'

'Five minutes' walk down the road. Look, how could I turn up with nothing? I hope you understand.'

'I don't understand much of anything, which is a huge part of the problem... Jesus, Jack, I hope I'm not being duped in some way. That's *your* daughter up there.'

'I know. Relax, Emma. Everything will be fine.' His voice had that familiar, maddeningly calm quality.

She took a deep breath. 'Let me know before you leave, okay?'

'Of course,' Jack said, holding up his hands in mock surrender. 'Would it be all right if I went upstairs to sit with Rose for a while?'

Gardner hesitated, weighing the risks against Rose's obvious joy at having her father back. Finally, she nodded. 'All right but leave the door open.'

The moment Jack disappeared upstairs, Gardner sank onto the sofa. She pulled out her phone and called O'Brien who was keen to know about the reunion with Jack.

She wanted details.

'Details are the issue. I still don't have many,' Gardner said. 'He suggested his stay might be brief, which is something, I guess.' It was at this point that her voice cracked. 'I'm sorry.'

'Don't be. You've had a hell of a day.'

And wasn't that the truth? She'd still not communicated with Paul following his operation. Then there'd been a sinister meeting with the puppeteer Neville Fairweather, and then an emotionally draining interview with the bereaved husband, Alistair Ashworth, who was clearly hiding something.

To top that off was a reunion with the biggest enigma of them all: Jack.

She stopped to gather herself.

'Are you all right, Emma?'

Gardner took a deep breath. 'Just about.'

'I'll come over.'

'No... not tonight. It's too soon. I've told him about you, but remember your last encounter with him? Give him a day to settle, and then let's break you in more gently... but... shit... Lucy... this is going to sound weird.'

'Go on.'

'I need a favour.'

'Of course, anything...'

'I can't leave the house tonight, obviously. Could you go over and see Paul at the hospital? You don't have to stop for long. Just five minutes to say hello and apologise for me. Even if he's not awake, talk to him, in case he can hear. Don't mention Jack, of course, tell him I got waylaid at work. Lucy, I—'

'It's okay, Emma. Yes. Not a problem.'

Gardner closed her eyes and sighed. 'Thank you... and I know this is weird.'

'Stop it. I've said yes, that's the end.'

'Okay, I'll ring ahead to let them know you're coming. Then, tomorrow, I'll see him again while the kids are at school.'

After ending the call, she contacted the hospital to inform them of Lucy's visit. She also got an update. He'd been awake earlier, but had said little.

She leaned back on the sofa, closing her eyes for a moment. Upstairs, she could hear the muffled sounds of Jack and Rose talking, punctuated by occasional laughter.

All she could think about was the red wine in her kitchen cupboard. She hoped the craving would pass, but she was fairly certain it wouldn't.

The sound of laughter drifted down again. Normal, happy sounds that should've been comforting. Instead, they made Gardner's skin crawl. Everything about the last couple of hours felt wrong – having Jack here, asking Lucy to visit Paul, her request to lead an investigation into Ashworth...

She needed to be careful and vigilant.

Jack might seem calm, but masks could quickly slip.

And her wealth of experience kept reminding her of one clear thing.

Sometimes the storm could descend with no time to react.

16

Ahead, through the trees, Gouthwaite Reservoir glimmered in the late afternoon sun.

At Paul's feet, Colin crouched, hard at work.

'I had to wait until I was fourteen before my grandad taught me this. So, at thirteen, Paul, you're a lucky boy.' His father smiled up at him. 'You've that maturity about you.' His weathered hands worked a length of wire. 'The key to a good snare itself isn't the contraption...' He shaped the snare into a loop.

Paul nodded. 'It's in the placement. You've to set it in the right place.'

'Exactly!' Colin said, beaming. 'You see things others don't, Paul. That's a rare gift.'

The words hit Paul like a physical blow.

A rare gift.

Something was stirring in his memory.

He'd heard those words before, but not from his father. The voice that had spoken them was different.

He closed his eyes, chasing the memory, but all he could

recall was how those words had made him *feel*. Special... unique...

Welcome.

Yes. That was the feeling. Like being chosen.

'See here,' Colin said.

Paul snapped back to see his dad gesturing to faint tracks in the soft earth. 'This is where they come through. So, we'll set it just...'

With the precision of long practice, Colin anchored the snare to a nearby sapling, carefully arranging it so the loop hung at the perfect height.

'Help me gather some twigs and leaves, son,' Colin said, standing.

Together, they gathered some and scattered them to disguise their handiwork.

'Remember,' his father said, stepping back to survey their trap. 'We don't want it to suffer. It is better to wait, and then when it springs... be quick.'

'But I thought we were going to eat it?'

Colin's eyes softened. 'That's up to you, lad. But whichever way you go, you must be quick... but then, I guess I don't need to tell you that. You're not like the others. You understand what needs to be done.'

Again, he flinched. The words were jarring, antagonistic somehow.

You're not like the others.

Other than his father, who else was talking to him? Or, at least, who else had spoken to him in another time, or place?

You understand what needs to be done.

As he settled in to wait with his father, he tried to remember but couldn't see the person speaking. He sensed the man was tall, and he sensed again all those same feelings –

welcome, warmth and guidance – but he didn't know who he was.

Over the next few hours, the light started to fade and the forest grew quiet, save for the occasional rustle of leaves or the distant call of a bird, and as he waited for his first kill, Paul lost himself to concepts that seemed beyond his years.

The nature of duty. Of sacrifice. A world that needed men willing to step into the shadows and do what needed to be done, no matter the cost.

Were these his beliefs? Or were they someone else's?

Did they belong to the man hidden in the mists of memory and time?

The one who'd spoken to him as if he was special.

'Dad?' Paul's voice was barely a whisper.

'Yes, son?'

'I don't always feel in control of myself.' The admission felt dangerous, like stepping onto thin ice.

Colin didn't respond.

'Sometimes I feel as if other things, other people, are moving me.'

His father was quiet for a long moment. 'Those are dangerous things to believe, son.'

Paul closed his eyes, and there he was again – tall and old, leaning on a cane. The man's voice echoed with sadness. 'I'm not sure how much of my life has ever really belonged to me.'

The sharp crack of a twig broke the silence. Paul's eyes flew open to find a rabbit caught in the iron loop. It struggled, terror evident in its wide eyes.

'Be quick,' Colin whispered, pride in his voice. 'Be kind.'

Paul approached the trapped animal, his movements mechanical, as if someone else was guiding his limbs.

'I don't know what to do,' he whispered, his voice trembling.

The rabbit's eyes found his, dark and pleading.

He wanted to retreat into those shadows again, to seek guidance from the old man with the cane, but something held him back. This moment belonged to him alone.

'What do you want to do, son?' His father's voice was gentle, free of judgement.

Paul's hand shook as he freed the knife from his belt. He looked from it to the struggling rabbit and back again.

'Have you decided, lad?'

'Yes, Dad.' Without hesitation now, Paul set the knife on the ground. 'I know what I want.'

His fingers were steady now as he worked to loosen the wire. The moment it was free, the rabbit bolted, disappearing into the underbrush with a flash of its white tail.

'Not hungry?' his father asked, though his smile suggested he already knew the answer.

'No,' Paul said, his voice thick with something that felt like victory.

'Aye,' Colin said, crossing to squeeze his son's shoulder, 'neither am I.'

When Paul closed his eyes this time, the shadowy figure was gone, as if it had never been.

The walk back was quiet until Colin spoke, his hand warm on Paul's shoulder.

'It's not just the placement of the trap on the path that's important, son. It's the placement of ourselves on it, too.'

His father's grip tightened meaningfully.

'And remember, Paul, if you ever stray from it, get back on your own path, not someone else's.'

A bush rustled to their right. Paul turned, hoping for one last glimpse of the rabbit he'd freed, but the forest had already reclaimed it.

17

Riddick's eyelids fluttered open. 'Emma.'

O'Brien leaned forward. 'Just me, sir... Lucy. How are you feeling?'

Riddick's eyes were glassy, unfocused. His lips moved, forming words too quiet to hear. She leaned closer.

'Emma... thank you for staying.'

O'Brien felt her chest constrict. The raw intimacy of the moment – one clearly meant for someone else – made her want to retreat. 'I'm *so* sorry, sir, but it's me, DC Lucy O—'

'I tied knots... made a raft.' His voice was stronger now but slurred, distant. 'Emma... I set a rabbit free.'

The guilt hit her like a physical blow – not just for being here instead of Gardner, but for all the complicated feelings tangled between the three of them. 'Emma isn't here, sir. Something important came up at work.' The lie tasted bitter, but mentioning Jack's return might only agitate him.

'I want to make things right, Emma.'

Riddick's hand twitched on the white hospital sheet, fingers stretching weakly towards her. Understanding, O'Brien took it, surprised by the fever-heat of his skin. His grip was fragile but desperate. 'Sir, you're confused. I'm not—'

'My father... I'm with him... I've missed him, but I've missed you...' He squeezed O'Brien's hand weakly. 'I've been blind.'

'She'll come tomorrow, sir. To see you in the morning.'

He mumbled something else. Something that sounded like, 'Path.' Then, his eyes fluttered and his hand went limp in hers.

'Sir?'

He was asleep again.

O'Brien sat back and pressed her fingers to her eyes.

She felt herself welling up.

She shouldn't have been here.

This had been their moment.

Something existed between her two colleagues. After that moment, after feeling his desperation to hold onto Gardner, O'Brien knew she couldn't deny it any longer.

They were going to be together.

Yes, Gardner may have denied that was ever going to happen, but she was either lying to O'Brien, or lying to herself.

Obviously, O'Brien hoped it was the latter.

Betrayal would be another bitter pill to swallow.

She struggled to stand and had to steady herself against the side table. Witnessing Riddick's raw vulnerability had shaken her to her core.

So, what did she do now?

Fight for Gardner, with everything she had, because she loved her?

Or did she let nature take its course? Because, right now, in this moment, it was clear to O'Brien that nature hadn't factored her into the plan.

The monitor's sharp beep cut through her thoughts like a knife. She glanced at the display, her police training kicking in as she noted numbers elevating rapidly. Her stomach dropped.

Something wasn't right.

She took a deep breath and went for the door to alert someone—

But the door was already opening.

The machine had summoned a nurse. A young man came in, his eyes quickly scanning the monitors. He frowned and moved to check Riddick's vitals.

'What's wrong?' O'Brien asked.

'One moment, please,' the nurse said, pressing his fingers against Riddick's wrist, counting his pulse and using the time-piece hanging from his uniform to count.

'Has he been awake?' the nurse asked.

'Briefly.'

'How was he?'

'Confused for a minute. He didn't recognise me.'

The nurse nodded; his expression was serious. 'His temperature has shot up. He's developing a fever. Is it possible for you to wait outside?'

'Of course.' O'Brien felt the blood drain from her face. 'Is he okay?'

'The doctor will look. Infections aren't uncommon. Hopefully, we can get on top of it quickly.'

In the sterile quiet of the waiting room, O'Brien pulled out her phone. She should call Gardner, let her know what was happening. But doubt steadied her hand.

The doctor may get on top of it and, if that was the case, was there a need to cause Gardner a sleepless night? She really needed that rest.

O'Brien pocketed the phone and settled into the chair, knowing that something had changed.

Not just in Riddick's health, but in her own life.

She lowered her head and cried.

18

Alistair's lounge was silent, save for his tapping on the laptop keyboard. Each keystroke brought him closer to starting over.

He glanced at the clock in the bottom right corner of the screen.

Eight a.m.

In less than twelve hours, he would be gone.

He reached for his glass and brought it to his mouth. Unlike his usually precise movements, he'd overfilled it and felt a splash of cold liquid on his legs.

Glancing down at the spreading damp patch on his trousers, he sighed.

He marched to the kitchen, intending to grab a dish towel. The wet fabric against his skin breached carefully constructed mental barriers. He closed his eyes and gripped the worktop, trembling with the effort of holding back the memory. It was futile.

He was back in his classroom, desperate to hold in his piss. But the warmth was already spreading out over his lap.

He tried his best to force back tears, but that was a battle. He was twelve years old, and his classmates were about to see that he'd pissed himself.

Hand thrust in the air, he caught Mrs Jenkins's attention. 'I need to see the nurse.'

'Why?'

'I feel sick.'

He expected rejection, but she gave a swift nod. Perhaps his tears and flushed cheeks had earned her pity.

He stood, trying to hold his bag over his crotch, and left the classroom.

His classmates sniggered. Had they noticed? He wasn't sure... They always laughed at him, regardless.

He begged the nurse to contact his mother.

In the car, his mother didn't drive straight away. She stared at him instead. She gripped his arm tightly, her manicured nails digging into his skin. 'How could you do that? What's wrong with you?'

He cried and shook his head. All he wanted was the safety of home, but even that was an illusion. Sitting outside the school gates was merely aggravating this awful situation.

'What will your father say?'

He apologised between mouthfuls of tears.

'Do you know how much we pay for that school? Do you not think the other children will tell their parents?'

'They didn't see.'

'They saw, all right,' she hissed under her breath. 'Those little shits see everything. They saw you piss your pants.'

A dog's distant bark shattered the memory, pulling him back to the present. Though the animal was outside and posed no real threat, it triggered another, more potent memory. He pressed his forehead against the cool wood of the cupboard door.

He'd been watching the next-door neighbour's dog from his bedroom window for as long as he could remember.

It fascinated him how much Clive, the Rottweiler, loved Mr and Mrs Armstrong. The dog was a bundle of excitement when Mr Armstrong came home from work each day.

Meanwhile, Mrs Armstrong was forever throwing balls for Clive and being rewarded with long licks to the face for playing.

How different would his life be if he, too, was loved as much? Maybe Clive would love him in the same way if he threw the ball for him sometime? Greet him with happiness if he popped by every day?

The thought gave him hope in his loneliness, and one morning, he slipped through the back gate and into the neighbour's garden where Clive waited.

The dog was immediately on his feet and moving towards him but was forced to stop by the length of the chain which was tethered to a stake.

He showed Clive the ball in his hand. 'Do you want to play?'

Clive growled. But Clive always growled when he played with Mrs Armstrong, so surely that low intimidating rumble was merely a sign of happiness?

It bared its teeth in readiness for the ball.

Of course, Clive couldn't launch when tethered.

'I'll let you off, first,' he offered.

Clive tensed as he approached. The poor dog really seemed desperate to play...

The Rottweiler lunged. The chain went taut with a clank. Teeth flashed, and white-hot pain exploded in the side of his head.

Crying out, he stumbled backwards.

Blood trickled down his neck, warm and sticky.

It was his ear... Something had happened to his ear...

There were hands everywhere and Mrs Armstrong was screaming.

Clive was barking, his teeth red and bloody.

He'd only wanted to throw the ball, and now his ear burned.

'What the hell are you doing?' It was his mother's voice, calling out

through the chaos. 'You just walked in here?' He cried, not just from pain, but also from sadness over disappointing his family again.

'You've been told... so many times...' What she said next was hissed, but he heard it. 'Stupid little bastard.' In the background, he could hear his father apologising to the neighbours.

When he was carried home, he tried to reach up to his ear.

'Leave it. The dog took a chunk of your ear.'

Later that night, after visiting the hospital for stitches, his mother came to his room. She swayed in the doorway, reeking of wine, her mascara smeared beneath bloodshot eyes. Her fingers brushed the bandage wrapped around his head.

'Your father blames me,' she slurred. He looked up and saw his mother's black eye. 'Why couldn't you just do what you're told? Do you see what happens to naughty boys?'

'Sorry—'

'Well I'm sure you will be. That scar will remind you what an idiot you've been.'

The doorbell rang, dragging Alistair back. He straightened up, and realised he was touching his damaged ear, tracing the familiar scar tissue.

The bell rang again.

Who was it? The police again? Roy?

Either would be inconvenient.

At the front door, he looked through the peephole. It wasn't Roy. But that didn't make it any less inconvenient.

19

Gardner listened to O'Brien's explanation in the waiting room at the hospital, her body shaking.

'If I'd told you last night, you'd have panicked about leaving Jack alone with Rose and Ana. And you wouldn't have wanted me to come and take care of them, considering what happened last time I crossed paths with him.'

'Yes, but...' She broke off. There was very little argument. She wouldn't have had a minute's rest.

O'Brien put a hand on Gardner's arm. 'So where would that have left you? Awake all night? You *needed* sleep.'

Gardner sighed. O'Brien was right.

It didn't help with the shock, though.

Things had been looking up...

Just thirty minutes ago, after dropping the kids at school, O'Brien's phone call had shattered that illusion. 'He's got some kind of infection... It's not good... I'm sorry, Emma.'

Now, in the waiting room, she embraced O'Brien. 'Thanks for staying the night here, Lucy—'

She heard the door and broke the embrace.

Dr Euan Gresham had entered, and Gardner's stomach clenched.

His face was ashen. 'Please sit down.'

Shit. The news was going to be bleak.

Gardner and O'Brien sat. She clutched her knees and took a deep breath.

'I'm afraid Paul has developed a serious complication.' He sighed and sat down alongside them, leaning forward so he could see both their faces.

'How bad?' Gardner asked.

'It's a concern,' Euan said. 'He's suffering from invasive aspergillosis. A fungal infection.'

'Jesus,' Gardner said, lifting a hand to her mouth. She didn't know what that was exactly, but it sounded horrible. 'Can you get rid of it?'

'It's treatable, yes, but it can be life-threatening in immuno-compromised patients.'

It was nearly impossible to keep tears from her eyes. She moved the hand from her mouth to rub them clear. The doctor's hand settled on her shoulder.

'The infection has spread to his lungs and potentially other organs. We've started him on a powerful antifungal medication called voriconazole, but the next twenty-four to forty-eight hours are going to be critical.'

She took a deep breath and fought for composure, fixing him with a steady gaze despite her blurry eyes. 'Is he going to die?'

Euan paused, but didn't break eye contact. He was choosing the right words.

'Doctor?' she pressed.

'You need to prepare yourself. He's very unwell.'

She dropped her hands back to her knees, clenched her fists

and stared down at the floor. 'What happened? How did this happen?'

Euan took his hand from her shoulder. 'Emma, infections happen. It's unfortunate that it's such a nasty one. But he's in the best possible hands and—'

She cut him off, her voice sharp. 'He might die!'

'Yes,' Euan said, 'but let's be positive. The mortality rate for invasive aspergillosis in transplant patients is high, but DI Riddick is younger than most transplant patients. We have him on the strongest antifungal regimen possible. Now, it's a matter of supporting his body's functions and hoping the medication can get the infection under control before it causes too much damage.'

'Can I stay with him?'

'You can see him, Emma, but only briefly, and I want you to wear a mask. We don't want to compromise him any further, and we want him to rest. We'll be monitoring him constantly.'

Gardner's voice was firm, almost challenging. 'I'll stay at the hospital until we know either way.'

'My honest advice, Emma, is not to do that. I'll keep you fully abreast of his progress, and if there are sudden changes, I'll contact you.'

Her eyes narrowed. 'Like you did last night?'

Euan took a deep breath. 'Your friend, Lucy, told me you were exhausted. She asked me not to wake you. I listened.'

Gardner's anger deflated slightly, replaced by a weary resignation. 'Well, please, next time...'

'You've my word. Any change, I'll phone.'

She swallowed hard, her voice barely above a whisper. 'Can I see him now, then?'

He nodded.

20

Cocooned in the small tent, Paul felt a strange mix of safety and vulnerability, as the rain hammered against the canvas. He may have felt dry and snug, but the crashing thunder and regular flashes of lightning which illuminated his father's face were a harsh reminder of frailty.

Paul's mind these last minutes had been preoccupied with peculiar thoughts. Memories of a family he couldn't have because he was far too young.

But when he thought of them, and *remembered* them, he felt another strange mix. This one of happiness and sadness.

He wondered whether he was feeling love, and also, the absence of it.

Paul knew his father wasn't asleep beside him, simply because he wasn't yet snoring.

'Dad,' Paul said. 'How did you first know you were in love with Mum?'

'What a question, Paul... You just know, I guess... You feel *better*.'

'Better? In what way?'

Colin laughed. 'Good lord! You're eighteen now, son! Haven't you been in love before?'

Another flash of lightning illuminated the tent, revealing his father had turned his head to look in his direction. They were barely half a metre apart.

'Wait for it...' Paul said. On cue, there was another loud blast of thunder.

His father laughed. 'Hope it settles. I can't sleep through that.'

Paul sighed. 'I know. It makes you want to head home.'

'Yes...' his father said.

'But I want to stay, I'm enjoying our trip.'

'I know, but you hit the nail on the head, Paul. I wasn't saying yes to heading home because of the weather. I was referring to love. Love is that feeling of coming home. Even though you may never have been to that place before. Feeling that you belong there. Home is your mother... to me.'

Paul smiled. 'Okay, that's enough. What have I done? This is going to make me throw up...'

Colin reached over, his fingers finding Paul's ribs in the darkness. 'Eh, fella. You're not too old for this.'

'Okay... sorry... I take it back...' He giggled, feeling like a nine-year-old boy again. 'Sorry... stop... I adore your love story!'

His father stopped.

'Home is where the heart is,' Paul said. 'I guess it makes sense.'

'Why were you asking, son?'

Lightning struck again, illuminating his father's inquisitive face.

'I had this dream,' Paul said. 'In it, I'd a wife and two daughters. For that short time, I felt so connected to them, as if they were part of me, or an extension of myself... or maybe I was an extension of them.' Paul paused to reflect. 'And yes, while I was with them, it did feel like home.'

'It sounds like a nice dream, son.'

'Yes, it was, but... well, this is going to sound odd...' He stopped. 'No, it's okay—'

'Go on.'

Paul sighed. 'Well, there was this indescribable warmth. I wanted to be in that moment forever. Together with them. Existing... but then... Well... it just seems to end, and then I feel cold. Colder than I've ever felt.'

A short silence fell. Paul wondered what his father thought of his strange tale.

He heard a strange snuffling sound. It was only when the lightning flashed again, illuminating his father's face, that he realised he was crying.

After the next crack of thunder, Paul put his hand on his dad's shoulder. 'What's wrong, Dad?'

'Nothing. It's a beautiful dream.'

Paul felt a lump form in his throat. He'd never seen his father cry before.

'But it's just a dream, Dad.'

He felt his father's arms encircle him, pulling him close. 'Maybe... Look, I just want you to be happy. You deserve that.'

Outside, the rain continued its assault on the tent, the wind howling around them like a mournful spirit.

'Remember, son, that love... *real love*... is as much about the pain as it is about the joy. It's about being willing to feel that cold when the warmth is gone, because you know how beautiful that warmth can be.'

This was enough to bring tears to Paul's eyes despite not really understanding why.

Then, in the darkness, the father and son slept, clinging to each other, both lost in the bittersweet echoes of dreams and memories.

21

Gardner slipped on the pale blue surgical mask and pushed the door open. A low, pained groaning made her heart sink.

Moving quietly, she approached the bed.

Riddick's face was flushed and glistening with sweat. The oxygen mask hissed and his eyes rolled beneath closed lids.

Gardner felt tears welling up, but she swallowed hard and maintained composure.

'Paul,' she said. 'It's me. Emma.'

Having already sanitised her hands, she reached out, her fingers brushing against his. 'I'm here to tell you that you've got this. They're confident. Me too. No one knows you like I do. No chance this is getting the better of you.'

Her eyes traced the maze of IVs snaking into his body, and she thought about how cruel it would be to lose him now.

Riddick, with all his flaws and strengths, his demons and his determination, had become an integral part of her life in ways she was only now beginning to fully understand.

When her five minutes was up, she squeezed his hand one

last time. 'I'll be back, Paul. Sooner than you know. Keep fighting.'

She left him to face the biggest battle of his life, her heart heavy with unspoken words and fears.

22

Alistair hadn't expected his next-door neighbours at his door this morning, though in hindsight, their visit felt inevitable.

Harry and Mathilda Banks stood on his doorstep like mirror images – both in their twenties with blond hair and green eyes, matching builds and identical glasses. Sometimes Alistair wondered if they were secretly brother and sister. Watching them clutching each other's hands only strengthened the unsettling impression. 'We just wanted to come around and say how sorry we are,' Harry said, drawing Mathilda closer as if death might snatch her away too.

'For your loss,' Mathilda added softly.

Alistair lowered his face. 'Thank you.'

'Anything you need, knock on the door. *Anything.*'

'Imogen was such a lovely person,' Mathilda said. 'She was always there for us... for anyone... Are you sure there's nothing we could do now?'

Fighting the urge to close the door, Alistair forced himself to maintain appearances. 'Would you like to come in?' After yesterday's police visit, he couldn't risk arousing more suspicion.

'That would be nice,' Mathilda said.

He stepped to one side and let them into his home. As he followed them, he watched their eyes dart around, searching, no doubt, for signs of disorder or neglect.

But everything was immaculate, of course.

Alistair wondered if perfect tidiness looked suspicious.

He decided not. He'd always been tidy, and they'd know that. To behave differently, now, surely would be *more* suspicious.

'Tea?' he asked.

Harry shook his head. 'Oh, no, we couldn't—'

'I was about to make some for myself anyway,' Alistair interrupted smoothly. 'It's no trouble at all.'

'Well, if it's Yorkshire...' Mathilda smiled.

'Of course.' As he turned towards the kitchen, something nagged at the edges of his usually ordered mind.

He'd only made it three steps before it hit him.

He swung back and saw the open laptop on the coffee table. *Incompetent.* The blue passport was laid beside it like a beacon. *Unacceptable.*

'Let me clear some space.' Alistair moved with practised calm, but Harry had already seen too much.

'You flying anywhere nice?' Harry asked, then reddened. 'Sorry... wasn't looking.'

Alistair considered admonishing him for invading his privacy, but what would that serve? It didn't erase what he'd just seen. A booking screen for an airline.

Alistair sighed. He rubbed his eyes. 'We had a trip arranged. I'm just trying to cancel it.' He let his voice crack slightly. 'I know it seems strange, focusing on something like this, but I thought... get the money back. For the funeral arrangements.'

He closed the laptop in his hands and placed it on the mantelpiece beside the pictures of him and his wife. When he turned back, Mathilda's eyes were full of tears. 'So sad. She never mentioned the break.'

His stomach clenched as Harry reached for the passport. Moving quickly, Alistair snatched it up, but not before Harry had registered its colour. 'Is that a Canadian passport?'

Shit.

He nodded, allowing a hint of vulnerability to creep into his voice. 'It is, yes...'

Alistair didn't have to work to keep his gaze steady. Shock was not something he really responded too, these days. Extreme emotions were something from his childhood... something from a life he'd left behind...

Still, this wasn't good.

His mind was quick. 'I have dual citizenship. My grand-mother was Canadian.' A complete lie. He placed the passport on top of the laptop on the mantelpiece.

'Fancy that,' Harry said.

He noticed Mathilda nudging her husband for being too positive. His face reddened. Alistair realised, with an inward sinking feeling, that this would make the conversation even more memorable to them when the police started making enquiries over his disappearance...

Alistair went to the kitchen to finish the tea.

He felt irritated and berated his incompetence.

In his mind, he always berated himself in his mother's voice, which worsened the situation further.

This was a catastrophic error. A huge complication. If the Banks mentioned the Canadian passport to anyone, the investi-gators would automatically turn their eyes in that direction, potentially messing up everything he'd planned for.

Two options presented themselves with stark clarity. Elimi-nate the witnesses – feasible but risky with the police already showing interest. Or abandon his carefully laid Canadian plans and forge a new path. Both choices grated against his need for order and control.

Damn, he'd been so distracted by those memories... those flashbacks...

He made his choice and then prepared their tea.

Setting three mugs of tea on a tray, Alistair reflected on how one moment of carelessness could unravel the most carefully woven plans. Still, adaptability was survival. His mother had taught him that too, though perhaps not in the way she'd intended.

He carried the tray into the lounge and saw Mathilda smiling up at him. 'I was wondering if you needed any help with the flowers. My sister would be available. I'd arrange a discount, and I'd be happy to help you choose.'

'That's very kind of you,' Alistair replied, placing the mugs of tea down in front of his guests.

23

Gardner was in no mood for this.

With a sharp kick, she sent a kitchen chair clattering across the floor.

'Where the hell are you, Jack?'

The bastard had violated her rules again!

With Riddick now fighting for his life, she really didn't have time for this bullshit right now.

Jack still hadn't acquired a mobile phone, so with no way of contacting him, Gardner's options were limited. She righted the chair, sat down and took some deep breaths, attempting to calm herself. Then, she got back up and put the kettle on.

The familiar routine of making tea offered little comfort.

She stared into her cup, feeling utterly adrift, when her phone rang. For once, she was happy to see Marsh's name. Any distraction would do. 'Ma'am?'

'Are you okay? I heard about Paul...' Gardner's brief hope for distraction crumbled. No respite here after all.

'I take it Lucy went into work then?' Gardner asked.

'Yes... why?'

'I told her to rest, ma'am. She was at the hospital all night.'

'What was she doing there?'

'A favour to me, ma'am. I wasn't leaving my kids at home alone with Jack all night, and Monika isn't back until later today.'

'I would've done the same. Emma... there's something else, too. You made the right call on Imogen. Toxicology just rang.'

Gardner's pulse quickened.

'Have you heard of digoxin?' Marsh asked.

'It sounds familiar...'

'It's a cardiac glycoside – a heart medication,' Marsh explained. 'The thing about digoxin is that its effects fluctuate wildly with only small dose changes. At therapeutic levels it helps with irregular heartbeats, makes the heart beat stronger. But at higher levels, it quickly becomes toxic and causes cardiac arrest.'

'And Imogen had no heart issues. Nothing diagnosed anyway.'

'That's correct.'

'So, she was poisoned?'

'It is looking that way,' Marsh said. 'The fact that it's digoxin is also particularly insidious. It is easily missed in post-mortem. Asking for a full toxicology screen, Emma, was a massive call. Well done.'

She was in no mood for praise. 'How was it administered?'

'Orally, possibly mixed into a drink. It's odourless and colourless, easy to disguise. The onset of symptoms can be rapid, especially with such a high dose. Nausea, vomiting, confusion and then arrhythmias leading to cardiac arrest. We're about to send someone to bring Alistair in for questioning,' Marsh continued.

Gardner's mind raced. 'Hold on that, ma'am.'

'Eh?'

'The cups,' Gardner said. 'Imogen died at Bebra Gardens.

Alistair brought her coffee. If they haven't been emptied yet, search the bins. If we find the cups, find traces of digoxin... then...'

'We'll have our smoking gun,' Marsh finished. 'Nice thinking. CPS will eat that up.'

'No need to just bring Alistair in for questioning then. Go straight for the jugular,' Gardner added.

'Excellent, Emma.'

Gardner stood. 'I'll head to HQ now.'

Silence filled the line.

'Okay, ma'am?'

'Are you sure? I know you said yesterday you wanted this case, but circumstances have changed with Paul's condition. Besides, this case is turning out to be open and closed anyway... Phil has a good handle on it.'

Gardner felt her chest tighten. If she couldn't sit with Riddick, then this case offered a lifeline, a chance to focus on something else. 'Ma'am, I'm good to make sure this goes smoothly.'

'Okay, your wish. Can't very well knock you back from the investigation after you breathed life into it. I'll get a team to search for the cups at Bebra. If we find them, and they test positive for digoxin, you and Phil can arrest him.'

Gardner ended the call and checked her watch, calculating the time until she collected Monika from the station. Five hours. Enough time to lose herself in the investigation, to push away the fear and uncertainty surrounding Riddick's condition and her brother's wayward behaviour.

24

'I'll be less than thirty minutes,' Jack said, stepping out of the taxi.

The morning air bit cold at Brimham Rocks, but Jack left his jacket unzipped. Cold had never really bothered him.

Before him, ancient rock formations loomed against the sky like giants frozen mid-battle. Despite millennia of erosion and weather's endless assault, these rocks remained steadfast. Jack inhaled deeply, savouring something he'd desperately missed in the oxygen: freedom. No more stale prison air recycling endlessly through concrete halls.

There were visitors about, but not too many. It was a school day, and it was still quite early. A handful of early morning hikers dotted the landscape, their forms dwarfed by the towering rocks.

During one of her visits to the prison, his daughter, Rose, had spoken of this place, having come here with his sister. She'd painted pictures with her words – stones like giant mushrooms, stacks of coins balanced in a giant's palm.

Jack smiled at the memory of his daughter describing one

formation as a turtle stretching its neck towards the sky, and another as a wobbling tower of marshmallows. She possessed something he'd never had – the ability to see beyond what caged us, to find wonder in a cold, unyielding world.

Jack followed the route as described to him by Neville several days before his release. The directions started simple before becoming cryptic.

'You'll see a horse rearing.'

Jack saw the formation now. The horse's stone mane seemed to flow in an invisible wind.

Leaving the main path, he picked through the undergrowth, navigating uneven ground strewn with rocks and tangled roots.

As the 'horse' formation's shadow fell over him, Jack spotted a familiar figure. Neville, immaculate in an expensive overcoat, his white hair secured in its neat ponytail, looked absurdly out of place in this wild setting, like a silk thread in burlap.

'Jack,' Neville said, his voice carrying in the still air. 'How was your first day of freedom?'

Jack stopped several feet from Neville. He didn't bother answering the question. 'This is a strange place to meet.'

'Why? We stand among rocks that have endured for over 320 million years, formed when this was all a river delta. They've weathered ice ages, seen empires rise and fall. Makes our little dramas seem rather insignificant, doesn't it? Coming here can help us both with perspective.'

Jack remained silent. Philosophical talk was Neville's comfort zone. Jack wasn't interested, but, of course, Neville knew that. The wily old bastard just wouldn't change for anyone.

'You've always been a survivor, haven't you?' Neville said, running his hand over the side of a smooth rock. 'Weathering whatever life throws at you, adapting, enduring.'

'It's time,' Jack said. 'Time for you to get what you want.'

Neville smiled. 'Straight to the point?'

'Yes.' *Because that's how I operate*, Jack thought. *That's my comfort zone.*

Neville laughed. 'You know we achieved something together.'

Did we? 'I don't really look backwards.' *Or forwards, usually.*

'Well, we're in the twilight years now, you and I. The finishing line is in sight, but with one small matter remaining...'

'It doesn't need an introduction,' Jack said. 'I don't find the situation grandiose like you. Just show me your end first, and then you can have it.'

Neville nodded, reaching into his coat pocket. The envelope he withdrew seemed too ordinary for its significance.

Jack examined the contents. The American passport felt solid in his hands. He studied his new identity.

Michael Anderson.

A 'Bank of America' card bore the same name. A mobile phone completed the package.

After a last check, Jack slipped everything back in the envelope and secured it in his inside pocket.

'I'll let you know when they're activated,' Neville said.

'And if I give you this name, how do I know you won't leave them unusable?'

'Trust?'

Jack snorted.

'We've come this far together, haven't we?' Neville said.

Jack weighed his options. Neville had proven reliable, if theatrical. There was no logical reason for betrayal now.

'Gregory Pendleton,' Jack said flatly, releasing years of carefully guarded knowledge.

Neville nodded, his face a mask of practised neutrality.

Jack had never seen genuine surprise crack that facade. He doubted anyone had.

'I thank you for your service, Jack.'

'You'd have left me to rot if I hadn't had this information.' He patted the envelope through his jacket. 'And the only reason that you'll come good on this is because my disappearance, and absence, suits you immensely.'

Neville smiled. 'Even after all this time, you still have me wrong. I'm fond of you, Jack.'

Jack shrugged. 'Anyway, how will I know when to book that flight?'

'Once we've acted on your information, I'll send you a message. You can then destroy the phone and book your flight.' Neville sighed and his gaze drifted to the ancient stones. 'Wind and water have left behind these remarkable shapes.' His eyes locked onto Jack's. 'Our relationship hasn't been smooth, but I like to think that the erosion has left something remarkable behind.'

Jack met the stare without flinching. 'Is that everything?'

Neville laughed, the sound bouncing off the rocks around them. 'Remember when I used to call you my teenage boy! So full of attitude. But look, now. You're still alive! You know the real reason I chose these rocks, Jack, for our final meeting. Because of the history. They've been landmarks for centuries. Smugglers, outlaws, people living on the edges of society – they've all found refuge here. Nothing felt more appropriate, more special, for our last time together.'

The wind picked up, whistling through the formations. In the silence between them hung years of manipulation, survival and mutual use. Jack nodded.

Neville extended his hand. After a calculated pause, Jack accepted it. The handshake was brief, businesslike.

Without another word, Jack turned away. The path back felt lighter, unburdened of secrets.

He glanced back once. Neville's figure stood beneath the looming rock, already looking like a part of history.

Farewell. And good riddance.

25

Neville's phone call wasn't a surprise. Brandon West had been expecting it.

The target, however, was a complete surprise.

Gregory Pendleton.

Brandon had always believed their final target would be one of three men.

One of the *fabled three.*

It was unbelievable really that Gregory Pendleton was not one of the fabled three.

A real curve ball.

But things sometimes happened this way.

Gregory Pendleton, then.

The last of the maggots.

Brandon lived by two trades – fishing and killing – and he knew that maggots always ended up on hooks, one way or another.

He reread the dossier on Gregory. It contained details on his location, his family, his comings and goings. There were thousands of dossiers of this nature. Brandon's team had built careers watching potential targets.

So, when the call did eventually come, as it had done today, everything could click into place.

Brandon left his home and began his careful approach, driving between several garages to change his registration plate, evade ANPR. He made four changes instead of the usual three – insurance against years of inaction. Better cautious than caught.

The journey took over an hour.

Gregory had taken early retirement choosing several acres and a farmhouse well away from prying eyes.

A good choice for peace and quiet. A poor choice when marked for death.

On the entry road to the farm, Brandon pulled over and donned his gear – balaclava, gloves, blue paper oversuit, plastic covers on his feet. The silencer twisted onto his pistol with familiar efficiency. Then, he drove into the farmyard and waited a short distance from the house so as not to be spotted.

He watched in his rear-view mirror, waiting.

Ten minutes passed before, right on cue, Ryan Pendleton strolled into view.

The thirteen-year-old was in his school blazer, walking with the casual confidence of youth, bobbing his head to music from his earphones.

Brandon checked his watch – his timing was perfect.

At the door to the farmhouse, Ryan knelt and retrieved a key from under a plant pot.

Amateur hour!

These wealthy folk lived charmed lives, blind to real-world dangers.

Brandon was out of his vehicle before Ryan had the front door fully open, and then crossed the ground in silent strides. As the door began to close, Brandon wedged his foot in the gap and pushed hard, sending the young kid sprawling to the floor.

Brandon looked down as the lad turned himself over. His face was pale and he looked terrified.

'Turn the alarm off,' Brandon said.

'Please... don't hurt me...'

Brandon crossed the space between them, grabbed the boy's arm and yanked him up. His voice hardened. 'Turn it off, *now.*'

Trembling, Ryan hit four numbers. The warning beep died.

'Good. I want you to go and sit on that sofa.' He gestured with his silenced pistol towards an expensive leather couch.

'I'm scared...' A dark patch spread over Ryan's trousers. 'Please...'

Brandon supressed a sigh. 'Sit.'

Once the boy was seated, Brandon stood over him. 'When are your parents back, Ryan?'

'You know me?'

'*When?*'

He stuttered as he spoke. 'Soon... four... today...'

Later than expected, then. 'Where are they?'

'Max has a hospital appointment.'

Max was another curve ball. 'Who?'

'My baby brother.'

Shit, he hated these curveballs.

Brandon sighed. 'You're thirteen.'

'Yes.' Tears ran down Ryan's face.

'Same age as my son.' *A shame.*

'Please, don't hurt me...' His eyes were wide.

'You should never have been born. That's the truth. What happens today should've happened long before you turned up. Before Max, as well. Before your father even married to be honest. Someone kept a secret for far too long. What happens to your father has been on the cards for a long, long time. It isn't down to me to rewrite history.'

'I don't understand...'

'In a roundabout way, I'm saying I can't apologise for this.' Brandon met his gaze evenly. 'Your father was a bad man.'

Ryan shook his head frantically, scrunching his brow. 'No... he's not... he's really not... He does things for charity and—'

Brandon shushed him. 'It's the truth.'

Ryan looked down at his sodden trousers.

'You don't deserve all this,' Brandon said, realising that this was going on far too long. That he was delaying the inevitable. This wasn't his usual style.

But thirteen!

That was a real bastard!

The boy's voice trembled. 'Are you going to kill my dad?'

Brandon nodded.

Ryan buried his face in his hands and sobbed. Less than a minute later, he lifted his head up, his eyes red. 'And me? What's going to happen to me?'

Brandon shot Ryan in the head.

26

Brandon peered through the curtains of the lounge, watching a Land Rover pull into the driveway.

The killer was surprised by how steady his heart was, despite his many years of inaction.

You never really lose it.

He glanced back at the sofa, on which he'd covered Ryan's body with a duvet bearing the Nottingham Forest emblem. He'd angled the shot down to minimise blood splatter. There wasn't too much on the wall behind.

Through the window, he watched Helen Pendleton emerge from the driver's side. She moved with the confidence of privilege. Navy turtleneck dress visible beneath her glossy Barbour coat. Behind her, Gregory, the maggot which had attracted the hook, was reaching into the back seat, presumably to retrieve Max, the baby.

Brandon positioned himself in the hallway through a door behind the sofa. He lingered near the stairs, silenced pistol ready.

He listened to the front door open.

'Ryan! What've I told you about leaving the door unlocked?'

Criticise the boy, yet leave the key under a flowerpot, Brandon thought. *Ridiculous hypocrisy!*

He tracked Helen's footsteps across the parquet floor as she entered the lounge. 'Ryan?'

He'd already estimated fifteen steps to the sofa. He counted each one.

'Have you fallen asleep or something?' she asked, obviously intrigued by the duvet.

He planned to spare the poor woman the experience of seeing her dead son.

'Ryan?' Her tone shifted, confusion evident. She gasped. He guessed that she must have seen a trace of blood splatter.

She came into view through the open door. He fired.

Shit!

He'd missed her head and caught her neck.

Not my sodding intention.

He stepped out and stood over her. She lay clutching her throat, blood pulsing between her fingers, desperate sounds bubbling from her lips.

'This is because of your husband,' he said quietly, and ended her suffering with a clean shot.

Moving swiftly, he returned to the front door. Gregory stood frozen two metres away, a car seat dangling from his fingers.

A baby, presumably Max, slept inside.

Gregory's eyes were wide and his face pale. 'Who are you?'

'Inevitability, Mr Pendleton.'

Gregory shook his head. 'I don't know what you mean.'

'Oh, I think you do.'

He gulped. 'Where's my wife... my son?'

'Inside,' Brandon said.

'Tell me you haven't hurt them.'

'I must insist you come in now and join them.'

'Are you going to kill me?'

'I'm afraid I'm only going to ask one more time. This is your last opportunity to be with them.'

Gregory started to sob. 'They're dead, aren't they?'

'You won't have to worry about that for much longer.'

'How could you? This was so long ago... so long ago.'

Brandon had no sympathy for Gregory. For the kid, and the wife, and Max, yes, he'd plenty... but not for the maggot. 'You knew the risks.'

'Still... my family?'

'You always knew how this worked, Gregory. We can't risk them carrying your ideology. Continuing things that you started.'

'Ryan is thirteen!' he shouted, spitting tears.

'We've seen them as young as ten.'

'We're not terrorists!'

'Are you sure?'

Still sobbing, Gregory looked down at the baby carrier. 'Max is six months old. Did you hear me?'

'Yes.'

'So what's your argument there?'

'I don't have one. I just have my instructions,' Brandon said.

'Six months old!'

Brandon felt his stomach turn. His first real sign of discomfort.

'It would make you a monster,' Gregory said.

Brandon shook his head. 'No, this is because of you. I'm going to count to three. Better you die with them. But three is my final offer. One...'

'Okay, listen... there's someone else. I'm not the last. Do you hear me? *Not the last.*'

'I don't believe you.'

'It's true.'

'Tell me who. Tell me, or I'll have to hurt you before—'

'No need. I'll tell you... on one condition...' He looked down at Max again.

'Is that your condition?'

'Yes,' Gregory said.

Brandon sighed. It wasn't his call to make, really, but it felt acceptable. After all, could a six-month-old have been radicalised? Better to get the name of the other maggot.

Or at least lie.

'Okay,' Brandon said. 'Tell me.'

Gregory gave him another name. Another surprise. Another man not one of the fabled three.

'How do I know you're telling the truth?' Brandon asked.

'It's the truth.' He gave him the name of a company. 'I think you'll be able to join the dots. The shares and the money will all link.'

If it was true, Jack Moss had lied, and there was a fourth. Neville would be unhappy.

'Okay, come in,' Brandon said.

Gregory placed Max down. It woke him. He started to cry.

Gregory walked towards the house. Brandon backed away, maintaining some distance.

When Gregory got to the doorframe and saw his wife lying in a pool of blood, he moaned and clutched his mouth. He staggered forward and went to his knees. He cupped her cheeks. 'God... no... no...'

He looked up at the duvet. 'Ryan... dear God. Ryan.' He stood and turned angrily towards Brandon. 'You monster.'

No, maggot. This is on you.

He shot him in the face and watched him fall backwards onto his wife.

Outside, the baby's cries continued unabated. He exited and closed the door behind him and sighed.

He turned, looked at the crying baby, and lifted his gun.

His promise to Gregory meant little. Neville had told him to make a clean job of it.

The child started to settle, and fixed Brandon in his gaze.

Brandon sighed.

He looked up. The sun was setting over the isolated farmhouse. It cast long shadows.

He had to have a line he wouldn't cross, though. He just had to.

With that in mind, he lowered the gun and left.

27

Gardner stared at the information concerning Alistair on the computer screen, but struggled to focus on it.

Every time her analytical mind threatened to spark, she saw Riddick lying in that hospital bed, flushed and moaning, and she heard the hiss of the oxygen mask.

She rubbed her temples. Was her decision to come here ridiculous?

When a steaming hot cup of coffee appeared in front of her, she almost jumped out of her skin. She clutched her chest and stared up at Rice with narrowed eyes.

'Are you okay, boss?' Rice asked.

She took a deep breath. 'Just a million miles away.'

He nodded down at the cup. 'You'll be pleased to know I ditched the sugar after your moaning session in Nero yesterday...'

'Moaning session? There's that infamous flair for exaggeration.' Gardner sighed. 'Though the way I'm feeling, a burst of sugar might be just what the doctor ordered.'

'Bloody hell,' Rice said. 'I stupidly figured I was getting a thank you. No winning with you!'

Gardner smiled. 'Please don't tell me you've only just figured that out...'

Rice sat down opposite her and regarded her in silence for a moment.

'That look! Out with it, Phil,' Gardner said. 'I can't handle when you go all serious on me.'

'Well, I know I said it last time and you chopped me down, but I'm really sorry about Paul. I just heard about the infection. You should've told me.'

'Why? I came here for a distraction, not to mull it over.' She wrapped her hands around the hot cup, then stared into it. Her tone softened. 'Okay, Phil...' She looked up at him. 'It's bad, really bad...' Her voice cracked. 'He could go in the next day or two.'

Rice flinched. 'Shit... that bad...' He slumped back in his chair. 'Sorry... I didn't know. I really hope that doesn't happen.'

'He's in excellent hands, though,' Gardner said, nodding. She forced back tears. 'He's got age on his side, too.'

'And he's tough. I mean really chuffin' tough.' He smiled and pointed at his mouth. 'I should know. I still can't chew properly.' He was referring to the scrap they'd had on a hospital roof the previous year.

Gardner straightened up in her chair. 'All right, help me focus.' She took a sip of coffee and pointed at the screen. 'Alistair Ashworth.'

'Firstly, good call on the toxicology, boss.'

She waved off the compliment. 'Just being cautious.'

'Nah... sharp instincts. I couldn't see my arse from my elbow.'

Gardner grimaced. 'Phil?'

'Yep?'

'Stop making me cringe.'

'Eh?'

'The compliments. It's disorientating. Be normal. This nice you is hard work.'

'Okay… fair enough. I was finding it hard work, too, truth be told.'

Gardner snorted. 'Yes, I saw you sweating. Just go back to being a miserable, argumentative bastard for now.'

'Default mode engaged.'

'Good. Okay, this is what I've digested. Alistair is currently working at Marks & Spencer in Harrogate, so I've put in a request to HR to see what comes back on his employment record. I've also filed for his medical records and, according to Home Office records, he flew into Manchester from Rio de Janeiro on 15 April 2023. He's from Surrey, so what drew him up to the north? And Harrogate in particular? He didn't know Imogen at that point.'

'April 2023? Must have been a whirlwind if they met after that and got married.'

'Yes,' Gardner said. 'They met in May and were together less than a year before marrying in April 2024.'

'Fast mover.'

Gardner nodded. 'According to Marsh's notes from her conversation with Roy, it seems Alistair was the one obsessed with settling down and having children. More so than Imogen.'

'That bucks the trend,' Rice said.

'There he is – the Phil I know and love, straight from planet eighties' male.'

Rice looked away, clearly unsure of how to take that. He eventually smiled.

'Roy was furious about how quickly their relationship moved,' Gardner said. 'He never really took to him.'

'Alistair told us as much,' Rice said. 'This is very strange, though. He adores her. Yes, he's going to get the house, but it's no great shakes, and he's not getting any insurance... If not for your built-in bullshit detector, boss – sorry for the passing compliment – the bastard could have easily just walked away. How did you know?'

'Because he's a sociopath.'

'I didn't know you were a trained psychologist.' His smile had an edge.

'I have a sociopath for a brother, remember? There was something about the way he talked... the way he looked at me... it was all too pragmatic and analytical. It lacked authentic emotion and he seemed very focused on himself.'

Rice nodded. 'I guess that makes sense. Good job Jack is somewhere he can't hurt anyone.'

Gardner nodded, hesitating. She needed to tell Rice about Jack's return but dreaded his reaction. He wouldn't be best pleased and would consider her foolish. Still, it was necessary. So, she'd do it before they left.

'There'll be a motive,' Gardner continued. 'But it won't be from aggression – this was pre-meditated. And prepare yourself. I suspect the motive will make little sense. Like my brother's behaviours, it might seem insignificant to us – maybe just having the mortgage paid off by insurance. His threshold to kill will be far below ours because of his lack of empathy or remorse. And sociopaths are often very charming.'

'Well, he did a good job of swooping that poor lass off her feet.'

'Yes. I think we should reach out to his parents in Surrey and find out what really drove that wedge between them. Also, it might be worth looking into his stint in Brazil—'

Her phone buzzed. Marsh. 'Ma'am?'

'We've recovered cups from the park. I've expedited the

testing process, but you might still have a wait. You still keen on waiting for that arrest warrant before talking to him?'

Gardner considered. 'No, I've changed my mind. If he's what I believe he is, then his arrest may provoke his inflated sense of self. He may sneer at us and refuse to talk out of arrogance. If we go around and invite him in for questioning, while we wait for confirmation on the testing, then I may spot cracks in his charming persona, work through them.'

'Good idea. He might trap himself. And if the evidence doesn't come through, you'll have a head start.'

Gardner ended the call and turned to Rice.

He'd overheard the conversation and was buttoning his coat, ready to leave.

Gardner stood. 'One last thing, before we go.' She shrugged on her coat. 'Jack is back at home.'

Rice stared at her, his jaw slackening. 'Eh? Your home?'

'Yes. He's been released on the condition he stays with me until his feet are on the ground.'

Rice's eyes widened. 'Jack... the sociopath... What the hell in a handbag have you done that for?'

'Long story.'

'No story is long enough to explain this madness.'

'Not now, Phil. I don't have a choice,' Gardner said, her voice tight. 'His life was in danger in jail. And despite everything... he's still my brother.'

'Have you completely forgotten what happened last time?'

She dropped her head. 'I remember.' Again, she had to fight back tears. She wrestled with whether to tell him the rest. When she met his concerned gaze, the words tumbled out. 'Neville Fairweather is involved somehow.'

'That prick from KYLO? The one that stalked you?'

Gardner nodded. 'He seems to think that Jack with me is the right move... and I don't know whether or not to trust him.'

'I know! You don't.'

She sighed. 'What alternative do I have?'

'There are always alternatives. I thought you understood sociopaths! So why are you welcoming them all in with open arms?'

She glared at him, unable to argue with his logic. 'Look, I think Neville has some kind of moral compass. But you're right, I can't see how something so secretive can be entirely legitimate. And I definitely can't understand how anything involving my brother can be good...' She sighed. 'You can see why I'm back in work now.' Her voice cracked. She took a deep breath. Rice stepped forward, arms rising for a hug.

She exhaled and brushed him away. 'It's okay.'

'Sorry...' His cheeks flushed. 'Just thought you needed it.'

Gardner laughed. 'Phil, I'd have to be near suicidal to let that happen.'

He looked startled, then burst out laughing. 'Jesus! If this is what I get for being nice, is it any wonder I'm always bloody miserable?' As they walked out of the office, Rice glanced at her. 'You know, if you need anything – regarding Jack or Paul or what-ever – I'm here, right?'

'Thanks, Phil, but I'd prefer you just keep me focused on the job at hand – which is rounding up this killer.'

28

Alistair checked his hand luggage again.

His passport and laptop were present.

He checked his watch. Twenty-six minutes to go before the taxi arrived to take him to the airport.

He looked around the room, expecting it to feel hollow now, but strangely, it didn't. He hadn't stripped away the life he'd carefully constructed. The snapshots on the mantelpiece still showed him and Imogen, larger than life, glowing in their happiness.

The place kept its warmth, somehow.

He tried to give Imogen some attention in these last minutes, to honour the memory of their brief life together, but he was struggling to shake Harry and Mathilda Banks from his mind. Since they'd left, he'd thought about nothing but his stupid mistake.

They'd come here full of sympathy and left full of questions.

Perhaps killing them would have been the better choice.

But he'd decided against it for two reasons:

First, the discovery had been his fault. His sloppy mistake

with his passport and laptop. He felt a sense of fairness – they shouldn't be punished for his moment of weakness.

Second, and the main reason, was that two bodies would spark a manhunt. Not the best move when he was trying to slip away unnoticed, to present the idea that he'd thrown himself off a cliff somewhere.

Still, the mistake had cost him dearly. His plans were in disarray. He'd have to act quickly when he landed. Such a shame – everything had been set, everything had been smooth. All that hard work wasted.

He reached up and stroked the irritated scar tissue on his ear.

The irritation was inevitable, really, considering how the situation had deteriorated.

A knock at the door interrupted his thoughts. Alistair checked his watch. Twenty-two minutes until the taxi.

If not the taxi driver, who now?

Harry and Mathilda would be at work.

Another knock echoed through the house.

Police would be problematic – they'd question him about his travel plans. And Roy would be just as bad, regarding him with that perpetual suspicion.

He stood, but the third knock was so loud and insistent that it thrust him into the past...

A knock at the front door threatened his concentration.

He tried to ignore it and focused on labelling his preserved insects. Each specimen on the wooden board required precise handwriting.

The second knock came louder.

Curious, he crept to the window and peered out. Two kids from a nearby estate, similar age: Jake and Butcher. Jake had a battered ball under his arm. Butcher, nicknamed for his Mexican father who worked for peanuts in an abattoir, sported a new crewcut.

He'd met them a week ago while walking to the shops for his mother. They'd offered him a cigarette, which he'd politely refused, but they'd ended up kicking the ball around together for a few minutes. He'd told them where he lived. 'Rich kid, eh?' Jake had asked.

He went down and waited, wondering if they'd knock again.

They did.

He opened the door.

'Shit... what happened to your ear?' Jake asked.

He reached up and touched the place where Clive had savaged him years before. He looked at his fingers and saw the blood there.

He must have been scratching at it again without realising.

'I don't know,' he said.

'It looks disgusting, dude!' Butcher said.

Both boys pretended to throw up.

'Cool though,' Butcher said, clearly trying to make things right.

'Seriously cool. We're heading out for a game,' Jake said, lifting the ball. 'You in?'

The invitation sounded good, but he knew better.

'I can't.'

'Why not?' Jake asked.

Should he tell them about his insect collection? About the precise rows of pins and careful labels?

No. Better not.

'I'm waiting for my mother.'

'She must have her own key,' Jake said and laughed. 'You lot are rich enough.'

He smiled. He liked them.

They were normal.

He wanted that normality, that easy friendship.

But it would go against his parents' expectations.

'When's she back?' Butcher asked.

'I'm not sure.'

'Sure you could manage half an hour, dude,' Jake said.

Maybe he could.

He opened his mouth to agree, but the words died as his mother's car pulled into the driveway.

She stumbled out, her designer handbag dangling precariously from one arm.

Jake and Butcher laughed.

'What you two shits laughing at?' His mother's words slurred.

He tried to assess what he was feeling. Embarrassment? Not really. Pity for his mother? That was absent, too. Lately, he'd been struggling to feel much where others were concerned.

His mother staggered closer. 'Who are you lot?'

Jake narrowed his eyes. 'We were just wondering if he wanted to come play ball. You can't talk to us like that.'

His mother's face contorted into a sneer. She looked them up and down, her disgust at their dirty, scruffy clothes clear. 'Ha... I can and I will!' She walked past them. 'He's not going anywhere.'

As she passed him in the doorway, she leaned in close. 'Get rid of them.' The smell of wine washed over him.

'I can't go anywhere,' he said. 'Sorry...'

'She's a rude, old drunk!' Jake said.

He started to push the door closed. 'Have a good day.'

'Get us some of that drink!' Butcher said.

The door shut with a soft click.

He turned.

His mother stood in the doorway to the kitchen watching him. 'Are you okay, darling?'

'Yes, Mother.'

'Come here.'

He approached. She placed her hands on his shoulders, her grip uncomfortably tight.

'*You're a star. A bright, glorious star. Your place isn't with them. Do you understand that?*'

'*Yes,*' he lied. He understood only that this was his prison.

'*Your place is with us. This is your constellation. I don't want you to open the door to those children again, okay?*'

'*Okay.*'

'*They're animals. When you think about going out... wandering... think about what happened last time. Think about what happened when you went next door to pet Clive.*' She pulled a tissue out and dabbed his ear.

He stepped forward and hugged her. '*I love you, Mother,*' he lied.

'*Now isn't that nice?*'

In his mind, he saw a star burning, his parents perched upon it, melting away as it consumed itself...

The fourth knock jolted him back to the present, more insistent than ever.

He approached the door and peered through the peephole.

Clive's eyes bored into him from the other side.

'What do you want?'

The Rottweiler bared his bloody teeth.

Alistair backed away, blinking.

This couldn't be real.

He thrust himself back to the peephole. Clive had gone.

But in his place stood a person whose presence here seemed equally impossible.

He looked away and back again, but the visitors' identity didn't change.

Their presence made little sense.

He backed away, glancing at his watch again: twenty-one minutes until the taxi arrived.

The carefully constructed world of Alistair Ashworth was

slipping away like sand through an hourglass. What were his options?

The letterbox flap suddenly sprang open. A voice, insistent, called out, 'I know you're in there. Open the door... or I'll call the police.'

There was no choice, really.

He gritted his teeth and unlocked the door.

29

As Rice and Gardner walked up Alistair's driveway, past the silver Audi, Gardner regarded the manicured lawn with its perfectly trimmed hedges. The immaculate presentation matched both the tidy home they'd encountered yesterday and what they now knew about Alistair's methodical nature. Even his approach to murder had been meticulous – if not for her hunch about his similarities to Jack, he might have slipped beneath their radar entirely.

She tried the doorbell and waited.

When no response came, Rice stepped alongside and rapped his knuckles sharply against the wood. The sound echoed in the quiet street.

'Car's here,' Rice said, nodding at the Audi.

'Yes,' Gardner replied. 'But something feels off.'

Rice moved onto the lawn to peer through the window. 'Boss...'

Gardner came up alongside him. Some pictures had been knocked from the mantelpiece and were on the floor. There was also a cushion on the floor.

'Not his usual tidy self this morning,' Gardner said. 'Shit. We should've pushed harder for that warrant.' She scanned the interior. 'Can you see any movement?'

'No.'

Gardner pulled her phone out and called Marsh about expediting the warrant. Even with the chief constable's intervention, they were still looking at a three-hour wait.

'Let's check round the back,' Gardner said.

They made their way down the narrow path that led to the rear of the house. The backyard was as impressively maintained as the front, with a small patio area surrounded by potted plants arranged with military precision.

Rice moved towards the kitchen window, cupping his hands around his eyes to peer inside. 'Shit...'

She saw him go rigid. 'Phil?'

'You need to see this.' His voice was tight.

Gardner hurried over. When she looked through the window, her breath caught in her throat.

There was a body sprawled face down on the kitchen floor, surrounded by a dark pool of blood. 'Christ.'

Rice tried the back door. 'It's unlocked,' he called, pushing it open carefully.

'Wait.' Gardner's heart quickened. She pulled out her phone. Her hand trembled slightly as she called for backup and an ambulance. She watched from the doorway as Rice explored, regardless of her order.

After ensuring the space was secure, Rice knelt beside the body. His face was grim when he looked back at her. 'It's him... and we're too late. He's dead.'

'How?'

'I don't want to move him, but it looks like a cut on the side of his neck. I think he's been stabbed.'

The words hit Gardner like a physical blow. Suddenly she was back in that school corridor, all those years ago, in Salisbury, confronted by a violent witness. Again, she felt the knife slide between her ribs, puncturing her lung. The familiar cold sensation spread across her chest, and she stumbled towards the door, fighting for breath.

'Boss, you okay?'

'Just... give me a minute.'

She pressed her back against the wall, forcing herself to take slow, measured breaths. The panic began to recede, replaced by the calm detachment she'd learned to summon in crisis situations.

When she felt steady again, she straightened and returned to the kitchen. 'Let's secure the scene.'

Rice stood and sighed. 'Don't think that warrant would have helped after all.'

30

Gardner winced when they flipped Alistair. The wet sound of flesh peeling from the floor tiles made her stomach turn, as did the bloody strings that grew between his face and the floor.

With Alistair on his back, his half-open eyes seemed to stare past them into nothing. Rice had been right about the neck wound.

Robin Morton, a forensic pathologist who Gardner had worked with previously, knelt beside the body, her experienced eyes darting this way and that, cataloguing details.

'They'll never get the blood out of the grout,' Rice said from beside her.

Gardner shot her white-suited colleague a withering look.

'Just saying,' Rice said.

They stepped away from the body to speak privately.

'So, do you still think Alistair killed his wife?' Rice asked.

'Why wouldn't I?'

'Looks to me like someone killed him to shut him up about something.'

Gardner considered it briefly, but shook her head. 'Toxicology on the cups will show he killed her.'

'Okay, say it does... then, that leaves one obvious explanation?'

Gardner sighed.

'Marsh isn't here so we can say it...' Rice said.

'I admit, Roy Linders should be on the radar, but Phil, really? Would he be this stupid? A decorated copper.'

'A devastated, decorated copper...'

'I don't know... it just feels too... suicidal? He'd know we'd look at him first.'

'This man just lost his daughter,' Rice said. 'Thinking rationally is not a given.'

Gardner had to concede the point. Apart from Roy, who else did they have?

'Stab wound to the carotid artery here in the neck,' Robin announced, her voice steady and clinical. 'It wasn't professional. His throat wasn't cut. It came from a thrust, and the blade went deep. He would have died quickly. Based on blood coagulation, this didn't happen long ago. The angle of the wound suggests the attacker was right-handed and of similar height to the victim. There are other cuts on the victim's hands and forearms. He was defending himself.'

Rice moved through to the lounge and Gardner followed him in.

'Look at the coffee table,' Rice said. The table, which was being dusted for prints, had been knocked askew. 'It wasn't just the pictures from the mantelpiece.'

Gardner looked between the lounge and the kitchen. 'The confrontation started here, bounced around the room and then ended in there, then?'

Rice nodded. 'Makes sense.'

Fiona Lane, the chief forensic officer, approached. 'Emma,' she said, her professional tone tinged with personal concern. Their friendship had cooled recently, particularly after Gardner had begun dating O'Brien. 'Quite a mess you've got here.'

'Good to see you, Fiona,' Gardner said.

'Even if we only seem to meet under such bloody circumstances these days.'

Gardner caught the edge in her voice but ignored it. 'Anything of note yet?'

'Early days but oddest find so far is a shredded British passport in a bin liner in the kitchen. Looks like he was about to take the rubbish out.'

'How did you know it was a passport?'

'It didn't chew the cover up completely, and we can just make out the royal coat of arms.'

'Was it Alistair's?'

'We can't tell, the interior has been destroyed.'

Gardner filed that detail away for later consideration.

Fiona stepped closer, her voice softening. 'I'm sorry to hear about Paul.'

Unbelievably, she'd not thought about him in a couple of minutes. Of course, her intention had always been a distraction, but having achieved some, she felt a wave of guilt.

'How is he?' Fiona continued.

'Not good,' Gardner admitted. 'The operation went well until he picked up an infection.'

Fiona nodded sympathetically. 'If you need anything... time to talk, or just a drink, let me know.'

Gardner squeezed her friend's arm. 'Thanks, Fiona. I really appreciate it.'

Her phone rang. Her heart stopped when she saw Dr

Gresham's name. She excused herself and hurried outside. She answered the phone.

'Emma.' His voice was grave.

She felt as if a hand had taken her by the throat.

'I'm afraid Paul's condition hasn't improved,' Euan continued. The hand started to squeeze.

'In fact...' The pause stretched like an eternity. 'He's marginally worse. Would you like to come and see him again?'

She forced herself to breathe, checking her watch. She had just enough time before she needed to collect Monika. 'Yes. I'll come now.'

As she ended the call, Rice emerged from the house. 'Boss?'

Gardner steadied herself. 'I'm sorry, Phil. I need to go see Paul. Can you handle things here?'

'Is he okay?'

'Not really.'

'Think nothing of it, boss. Roy Linders?'

She sighed. 'Yes. Take Ray with you. A cool head for balance.'

'Shall I run it past Marsh first?' Rice asked.

'Yes... out of respect. She won't stop it. But handle it sensitively. He's not a suspect yet, just a person of interest.'

She turned towards her car, stripping off her white overalls as she walked.

Rice called after her, 'Give him my best, okay?'

She couldn't find her voice to respond.

In the car, Gardner rubbed her temples, wondering how much more she could take.

She felt like a pinball, ricocheting violently between Jack, Paul and now Alistair's murder – each crisis another blow. Worst of all, every single problem felt like it stemmed from choices she'd made.

31

The granite wall was a tapestry of jagged edges and narrowed crevices.

Paul climbed two metres before his father's voice cut through the air. 'What do you think you're doing? You daft apeth!'

Paul looked down. 'I can do it.'

Colin rapped his head. 'Are you soft in here, lad? Get back down before I drag you down.'

'I've free climbed before...' Paul rode a familiar rush of defiance.

'And don't I bloody know it, son? Don't we *all* bloody know it?'

Paul opened his mouth to argue further but stopped short as he caught sight of the genuine concern in his father's eyes. It was a look he'd seen before, not just from his father, but from others. Faces flashed through his mind. Faces of people he was yet to meet.

He scurried back down and stepped away from the rock face.

Colin's face softened with relief. He began unpacking their

gear, explaining each piece as he went. 'This here's your harness. It's your lifeline, son. Never climb without it.'

As Colin helped Paul into the harness, checking and double-checking each buckle and strap, Paul couldn't shake all those faces.

Their concerned eyes.

Hands reaching out to him.

'Now for the rope,' Colin continued, threading it through Paul's harness. 'This catches you if you fall. It's not a crutch, mind you. It's a safety net. You still need to climb under your own power, but this ensures you live to climb another day if things go wrong.'

Paul nodded. The rope was heavy and strong.

With their gear secured, father and son began their ascent side by side. The summer sun beat down on them as they climbed, their progress marked by the scrape of shoes against rock and the rhythmic clinking of carabiners.

The climb with his father felt more methodical than he was used to. Each movement felt carefully considered. He tested every hold before giving himself over to it completely.

'Fantastic, son,' his father called out, his voice carrying easily in the still air. 'I'm proud of you.'

Paul grinned, a bead of sweat trickling down his temple. 'You too, Dad. For an old man you climb well.'

As they climbed higher, Paul opted to look down. The ground seemed impossibly far away, the trees below reduced to mere specks.

Vertigo suddenly replaced his confidence.

'You're all right, son,' his father said. 'Just keep your eyes on the rock in front of you.'

Paul's heart thumped.

'One hold at a time,' Colin added.

Paul took a deep breath, forcing himself to focus on the present moment, on the rough texture of the rock beneath his fingers. It was a technique someone had taught him in another time.

He heard a voice in his head, recognised it, but again it was from another time, so the name evaded him: *Try and stay present, Paul. The here and now. A potential future full of disaster is merely an irrational fear.*

With both sets of advice, he found his rhythm again, and his movements quickly became more fluid and confident with each passing minute.

'Look at me now!' He looked right and grinned at his father.

'Focus, son...'

'I am. I'm a natural.' He moved quickly.

'You sure? You're starting to show off again. Slow down.'

He reached for a promising hold, fingers curling around the jutting piece of rock. 'No need.'

Paul shifted his weight, trusting it to support him, when the rock crumbled beneath his grip.

He lurched backward, his stomach dropping as he lost contact with the rock face.

Suddenly weightless, he felt a surge of terror.

But then he felt it – the sharp tug around his waist, arresting his fall. He swung in the air, his body colliding with the rock face with enough force to knock the wind out of him. A small price to pay for survival.

'Paul!' His father's voice rang in his ears. 'Are you all right?'

Paul hung there, his heart racing. 'Yeah... I think so...'

'Can you get back on the wall, Paul?' His father's voice was tight with concern but steady, grounding him.

Paul took a deep breath, steeling himself. 'Yeah, I think so.'

With trembling hands, he reached out for the rock face,

fighting against a feeling of another time he couldn't remember… a time when he'd dangled helplessly. He found a new handhold and pulled himself back into a climbing position.

He heard another voice in his head: *If someone offers a hand, no matter who, or why, always take it.*

With shaking hands, he attempted to move.

'You sure you're okay to continue, son?'

He glanced at his father again and gave him a swift nod. 'Yes. I understand now.'

He really did.

And it felt completely reassuring not to be facing the challenge alone.

Since kicking alcohol three years ago, Daz Horne had built up resilience and determination in many other areas of his life.

One of those areas was in the consistency of his emotions, and the way he presented himself to others.

Though his stomach had clenched at the sight of his friend's grey pallor, he kept any grim expressions from his weathered face.

'How do, buddy?' he asked softly, pulling up a chair. The legs initially scraped against the linoleum floor, but he quickly lifted it to avoid aggravating his friend. 'Your sponsor here.' He nodded and smiled. He looked up at the IV bags, and the tubes that wound their way into his friend's arms. 'I guess talking you out of the drink is irrelevant now, mate. Looks like they've already got you on a cocktail that blows anything that tempts us alcoholics out of the water.'

He reached out his large hand adorned with faded tattoos, and settled it on Riddick's limp fingers.

'Doctor told me it's a severe infection,' Daz said and laughed. 'Told him to stop exaggerating! Severe? The infection really has no clue how severe its target is, does it? Bastard bag of germs doesn't stand a chance, eh?'

He chuckled. When his friend's face didn't move, he forced back a sigh. He'd promised to keep himself upbeat, but his attempts at levity would fade shortly. Nobody could sustain such a sad sight for too long.

Daz shook his head. Why did you run and hide, buddy? We had it under control, didn't we? We could have kicked out your demons good and proper...

Daz lowered his head, listening to the monitor's beep as he gathered his thoughts.

Shooting up heroin again? Getting yourself stabbed? What a way to walk back into hell...

He gently squeezed his friend's fingers.

But you'll think it was all worth it, won't you? Getting those kids out?

'And you wouldn't be wrong, mate. You're a fucking hero. Nothing can take that from you.'

But knowing this gave Daz little peace. He'd rather have his friend back than say farewell to a hero.

We had your demons, fella. If you'd have stuck with me, you could have booted those bastards through the door.

'Life was never meant to be tackled alone, Paul.'

He closed his eyes, recalling the last time he'd said it to Riddick: *You rolled your eyes and said, 'I'm sure you use the same line every time I see you, Daz...'*

Always a bloody smart arse!

'How about some variation then? Same concept... If someone offers a hand, no matter who, or why, always take it.'

Then, he felt tears in the corners of his eyes.

Crap... he'd let his guard down now!

He wiped at his eyes with his sleeve, forcing back the

emotion. 'That's all you get, fella, because you're waking up, Paul... sooner rather than later. Okay? No more of this bullshit. It's time for you to live... really live... not just survive. Look at the state of me. If I can do it, then anyone—'

He heard a noise and turned.

Gardner was at the door.

'Sorry, Emma. Just took five minutes. They said it was okay.' He looked back down at Riddick. 'So many hands, fella. Enough is enough now. Stop being so bloody stubborn. Take hold of all these chuffin' hands!'

He released Riddick's fingers, stood and turned.

Gardner had stepped forward, and she now embraced Daz. 'You can stay.'

Daz stood back, looked at her and smiled. 'Nah, he doesn't want me hounding him while he's kicking the shite out of this infection.'

'Nonsense. He'd love having you here.'

Daz sighed and winked. 'Both of us would be overwhelming.'

'We're both his friends...'

'Friends?' He grinned. 'Is that all you are to him?'

'I don't know what you mean.'

'You know full well what I mean.'

'What did he say to you?'

'I'm his sponsor! Can't be breaking his trust.' He tapped his nose.

Gardner held his gaze, trying to draw the truth from him. He almost broke.

He'd told me once, Emma... Told me straight, that he'd never believed he could feel again what he'd felt for his wife... but then he met you, and with you, he felt something...

He let his hand settle on her shoulder. 'Just let him know

you're here, Emma... that you want him back.' He took a deep breath. 'And then I think he can do this.'

Feeling himself welling up again, he went for the door, turning at the last second. 'Shit... he will do it. Don't doubt it for a second. Okay?'

She nodded and then went to Riddick.

I love you, buddy, he thought.

33

Gardner could see the deterioration in Riddick since her last visit. A sickly, greyish pallor had replaced his flushed skin. The oxygen hissed steadily, but his breathing seemed more laboured than before.

Euan had insisted there were still reasons for hope. Intravenous antifungal medications sometimes took time to take hold. But his suggestion to visit now worried her. Was he expecting something to happen? The unthinkable?

She'd searched the heart surgeon's eyes for answers, but he'd maintained his professional mask.

They'd given her ten minutes. Five remained.

Could these be her last moments with Riddick?

With trembling fingers, she took his limp hand, her eyes filling with tears. She pressed his hand to her damp cheek and closed her eyes as memories washed over her: the raw vulnerability in his voice when he'd shared details of losing his family, the quiet reverence as they'd sat together in that chapel garden while he showed her the memorial for his children. In those moments, she'd seen past his gruff exterior to the wounded soul beneath.

You should've let me all the way in, Paul... If you had, perhaps things would have been different.

But there had always been obstacles.

The drinking, the violent outbursts... the orchestration of your family's murderer's death in prison.

That had been beneath you, Paul. So far beneath you. It was something I'd expect from Anders, that bastard of a mentor, who'd spent years manipulating you... grooming you... blowing smoke up your arse...

Gardner realised now that despite all these distractions and barriers, her feelings had only grown stronger.

How could that be?

Why would that be?

Movement at the door caught her eye. O'Brien stood there, raising her palm in silent greeting. Gardner still had Riddick's hand pressed to her cheek.

O'Brien dropped her gaze and pointed down the corridor, showing she'd wait for Gardner there, then walked away.

Gardner gently placed Riddick's hand back down on the bed, wiped her eyes and checked her watch. Time was up.

She stood and leaned over, desperate to kiss his forehead but knowing she couldn't remove the face mask.

Instead, she touched his hand once more and whispered, ensuring O'Brien wouldn't hear if she lingered nearby, 'I love you... Don't go anywhere... I'll be back when I can.'

34

Outside, in the car park, Gardner and O'Brien embraced.

Gardner kissed her on the forehead. 'Thanks for being there. Always.'

'Dr Gresham phoned me,' O'Brien said. 'Mentioned you might need some support.'

'I'm okay...'

O'Brien drew back and fixed her with a knowing stare. 'I don't think you are.'

Gardner looked away.

How could she deny it? She was clearly teetering on the edge – to suggest otherwise would be complete lunacy. 'Okay, shall we talk in the car?'

'My car or yours?' O'Brien asked and winked.

Gardner wiped away her tears and smiled. 'Yours... you have heated seats.'

Once they got into the car and cranked up the heat, they held hands and sat in silence for a while.

'Are you okay?' O'Brien eventually asked.

'Yes,' Gardner said. 'Can we just sit like this for longer?'

O'Brien nodded.

Gardner tried to resist falling into self-pity, but her thoughts inevitably turned to the mess her personal life had become. Especially since she'd left Salisbury initially to find peace. Back home, on the back of a crumbling marriage and a near fatal injury, she'd lost good friends. Collette, and before that, DI Mark Topham. By leaving Salisbury and eventually divorcing a husband who'd been cheating on her, she'd been quietly confident of turning a corner. But life, as always, had other plans.

And now here she was – embroiled in a relationship with a younger female colleague that seemed destined to fail, while hopelessly falling in love with a damaged, dying male colleague. And to top it all off, her sociopathic brother had returned just when she'd thought he was gone for good.

'None of this is fair to you, Lucy,' Gardner said, eventually.

'Don't be silly,' O'Brien said. 'I know what I signed up for.'

Gardner regarded her. Did she really?

And had she really signed up? They'd never actually spoken about their relationship and where it was going. They'd merely let it happen and evolve to this point.

Gardner stared out the window at the hospital, where Riddick was fighting for his life, and sighed.

'Listen... I know what I want,' O'Brien said, squeezing Gardner's hand.

'Now that's without question...'

The ensuing silence suggested O'Brien wasn't sure how to interpret that comment. Gardner herself wasn't certain what she'd meant by it. Had it been mere humour, or something more pointed?

'I want to stay with you tonight,' O'Brien said.

Gardner continued to stare at the hospital. Her feelings for O'Brien were strong, they really were, but were they as strong as her feelings for Riddick?

Right now, they paled in comparison. Yet she had to wonder – were her feelings for him being magnified by his current vulnerability?

She felt too tired to reason anything out.

'It's not a good time,' Gardner said, pulling her hand from O'Brien's. 'My brother... and Monika returns later, too. It's going to be a busy evening, and I may have to return here at a moment's notice... and... well—'

O'Brien cut her off. 'I know what I want, but the question is, do you?'

Her frustration wasn't surprising. What was surprising was how long it'd taken to burst through.

And who could blame her? Being forced to play second fiddle to a chaotic man who'd left nothing but destruction in his wake. A man who couldn't – and probably wouldn't – offer happiness to anyone, yet somehow commanded all of Gardner's time and attention since she'd arrived in Knaresborough.

O'Brien was young and beautiful. Compassionate and talented.

Why would she tolerate this?

'I'm *so* sorry, Lucy. I am.'

'For what?' Her tone of voice was sharp.

Gardner looked at her. 'For not being there for this. For us.'

O'Brien closed her eyes and took a deep breath.

She then exhaled while opening them. 'I can be patient... I have been patient, but...' She broke off. 'It's okay.'

Gardner took her hand, disappointed to see O'Brien retreating into passivity. 'No. You're right. This isn't fair. I don't know what I want. And you must be pissed off, but don't want to say how you really feel because I'm vulnerable. And you're right. I'm a mess! And can't deal with it right now. It's so, so unfair. Lucy, I'm sorry. All I can say, is when this is all over, I'll make it up to you somehow.'

O'Brien shook her head. 'I don't want to pressure you. Let's leave it tonight.'

Gardner squeezed her hand. 'Look at me, Lucy.'

O'Brien did. Tears glistened in her eyes.

'I think we both know that we have to cool this for now.'

O'Brien shook her head again.

'Just until everything is clear again. And I'll make it up to you. It sounds like an excuse, saying it just isn't fair to you, but that's the reality, and I can't stand to—'

'But I want to help!'

'I know. But it would also help if I wasn't driving you to despair.'

O'Brien's eyes narrowed. 'Are you in love with him?'

Gardner flinched. The question landed like a physical blow.

She looked at the hospital again. She wanted to be honest, but couldn't bring herself to speak the truth. 'I don't know.' Cowardly. A lie. She loved him. 'I have feelings for him.' Better. Closer to honesty. 'You know that already, though.'

'I didn't know you wanted to be with him.'

'I'm not saying I do.'

'Because, deep down, you know that's impossible. Even if he recovers.'

The truth in those words stung.

Gardner opened the door and stepped out. She leaned in. 'I'll speak to you later when we're both calmer, okay?' Gardner said.

'Okay,' O'Brien said without meeting her eyes.

'I'm sorry, Lucy.'

She looked like she wanted to explode, to tell Gardner to get out of her life for good. In a way, that might have been easier. The finality would have felt more appropriate. But O'Brien, as always, chose kindness over anger despite her own pain. She merely said, 'Okay, Emma.'

Gardner closed the door, choking back a sob.

35

Gardner collected Monika Kowalska from the train station. She'd already warned Monika that her brother, Jack, would stay with them for a time. Having not met Jack before, Monika had asked a lot of questions. Gardner had been completely open and honest with her, stopping short of his involvement with Neville Fair-weather because she didn't really know how to explain that one away.

Monika had saved the most obvious question until last. 'Am I in danger?'

Gardner had told her the truth. That she didn't think so but couldn't guarantee it. This had been enough for her petite dark-haired au pair, with the warmest smile known to humankind, to return. 'Also, if there is any trouble,' Monika had said, 'I'd hate to think that I'd left those two beautiful girls alone with it.'

Despite feeling grateful for Monika's loyalty, Gardner couldn't help but detect a fiery edge to the comment. Was her au pair suggesting that Gardner was being irresponsible, leaving her with no choice but to return and protect the children? Gardner would be lying if she said she hadn't considered that herself.

On the drive home, Gardner filled Monika in on Riddick's progress and his latest condition. This saddened Monika, likely because she'd witnessed Gardner's growing feelings for him over the past months. Gardner then attempted to lift the mood by enquiring after Monika's family. It worked. Monika had had a fun-filled week away in Poland.

When they were back home, Monika sat in the lounge, while Gardner went upstairs to get Jack for introductions. She knocked on his door.

Jack opened it, nodded, turned and went to sit on his bed. She noticed a mobile phone on his pillow.

'New phone?'

He nodded, without making eye contact with her. 'Neville gave it to me.'

Gardner's eyes widened. 'Has he been here?'

Jack shook his head.

'Where then?'

'It doesn't matter, Emma.'

'But it does because you promised to stay...'

Jack looked at her. He looked drained, the prison pallor still evident in his face. 'Failing to meet Neville carries greater consequences than breaking your rules.'

'Nice to know where we stand, then.' Her tone was more weary than accusatory.

'Anyway,' Jack said, his face returning to its usual impassive self. 'You'll be pleased to know that it's over... I won't need to see him again.'

Gardner raised her eyebrow. 'Really? That was much quicker than I expected. What happened to staying a while?'

He nodded at the phone and shrugged. 'He will let me know when I can move on...'

'You don't look so happy about it?'

He paused and sighed. 'I'm going to miss her.'

Gardner nodded. 'And she'll miss you, but...'

'It's for the best.' He finished her sentence and then turned and tilted his head, studying her face. 'You've been crying.'

The observation caught her off guard – it was rare for Jack to notice, let alone comment on, others' emotional states.

'One of my good friends is in the hospital. It's touch and go. I'm hoping he pulls through.'

Jack nodded. 'Why don't you go and be with him?'

'It's not like that. He's in the ICU being monitored and resting. But I'll visit again soon.' God willing, Gardner thought. 'I've also picked up a case at work... but it's looking difficult.' She looked at him awkwardly. 'What with everything else going on.'

'I told you. The issue with Neville is finished. You can relax. You'll hardly know I'm here...'

'You said that last time.'

'Still, this time, I mean it. I want my daughter to be happy. I want her to stay with you, Emma.'

Gardner nodded. 'Well, I could do with going back to work, but Monika, our au pair, has returned. You're going to have to meet her. She's downstairs now. Please be polite.'

He stood and stretched out. 'Just polite... or charming, too?'

Gardner sighed. 'I've warned her about you. Be polite and stay out of her way. Don't make her feel awkward, and don't ask her for anything. She's going for the kids shortly. Let her handle everything, and then, when Rose is ready, she can spend some time with you.'

Jack nodded. 'Fair enough.'

36

Gardner hit the windscreen wipers to fend off a light drizzle. It was a moment's distraction from glancing at her phone suspended on the dashboard, wondering if it had lit up with a message from Dr Gresham. That familiar mantra again: *no news is good news*, she thought, repeatedly. Each time, the words felt more and more hollow.

As she neared HQ, that familiar feeling of being a pinball ricocheting between crises settled over her again, so she tried to reassure herself with some wins.

At least Monika's presence would provide an extra layer of security, another set of watchful eyes on Rose and Anabelle. Not that she didn't trust Jack with the children. She knew he would never hurt them. It was simply that his presence, his very existence, had always been a magnet for some kind of trouble. And despite his assurances, memories of his past actions weren't fading fast, and his assertion that Neville Fairweather was no longer a presence in her life carried no weight whatsoever.

Like death and taxes, Neville would be back, Gardner thought. As sure as the sun would rise tomorrow.

Still, she had another potential win. One that involved that sinister prick.

A week back, Tanya Reid, a podcaster and ex-girlfriend of the late Collette Willows, had been in touch. Tanya knew Collette had been Neville Fairweather's biological daughter, but this had not held her back in investigating him.

Tanya was planning to air a podcast on defence companies contracted by the government. Some of these defence companies had shadowy pasts, to say the least. Rumours of illegal arms deals, money laundering and even a suspicion of having connections to human trafficking rings.

Tanya had tugged on a thread, revealing Neville's potential past actions, but out of respect for Collette's memory, she didn't want to expose anything until she was certain.

Gardner had been planning to follow up with Tanya before Riddick's deterioration. If she could get something, anything, on Neville, and he returned, then she would use it to be rid of him for good.

The shrill ring of her mobile startled her from her reverie. Her heart leapt, but it wasn't Euan.

'Phil. I'm on my way back.'

'I don't think that's a good idea.'

'I do.'

He sighed. 'How's Paul doing?'

Gardner swallowed hard. 'The same,' she lied. The truth – that he was slipping away – stuck in her throat.

'Marsh is going to take you off the case.'

'She's the one who wanted me on it!'

'I know, but she acknowledges now that you're going to be distracted with everything that's happening with Paul. And I agree. Sorry, boss. She said if you show, I need to contact her, immediately.'

Gardner shook her head. If she couldn't be at Riddick's bedside, she needed this case to keep her mind focused. 'Just update me, Phil.'

'Boss...'

'Now.'

She heard him take a deep breath. 'Well, it wasn't Roy. He was with his neighbour, Elaine Holbrook. Apparently, they're quite close. Not a relationship, like, at this stage, but both widowed and enjoying each other's company. She's his shoulder to cry on. Her thirty-one-year-old son, Tom, was also there. Roy has got an alibi for the two hours leading up to the moment we found him.'

Gardner was relieved. Roy had already lost his daughter – the thought of him throwing his own life away would have been too much to bear. 'Has the team expanded?'

'Yes. We've got two murder enquiries now. So, Ray and Lucy have joined us.'

She flinched. After their conversation at the hospital, O'Brien's presence could complicate things further. 'What else?'

'Ray and I notified Alistair's parents. Gerald and Margaret Ashworth.'

'And?'

'They're distraught, of course. Margaret was inconsolable. In the end, we had to end the call. They've since confirmed they'll be up tomorrow morning to identify the body, but they're willing to speak with us via Zoom before then, if we require.'

'Yes, we do. Can we set that up for when I arrive?'

'Boss, I—'

'I'll speak to Marsh. You can rest easy, Phil. Set it up, please. I'll be there in ten.'

After Gardner had made Rice promise not to speak to Marsh before her, she rang off and switched on the radio for the news.

There had been a triple murder on a farm near Swindon – not too far from her old stomping ground. The victims' names hadn't been released, but a thirteen-year-old boy and his parents were said to be the unfortunates. A baby boy was found alive at the scene.

The news hit her hard – another family destroyed, another child left alone in the world. *Awful*, Gardner thought, *just bloody awful.*

37

As Gardner entered the incident room, DS Ray Barnett approached. Despite his tall frame and broad shoulders, Ray's gentle demeanour and kind eyes always put people at ease. Unlike Rice's abrasive personality, Barnett was a rock, not just physically, but emotionally, and he had the most impressively analytical mind in the room.

'Boss,' he greeted her. His warm smile lit up his sharp African features. 'You look well.'

'Sorry... one second... you just sent my bullshit detector wild.'

Barnett laughed. 'Well, I'm pleased to see you, whatever...'

'Better.' She touched his arm. 'Good to see you, mate. Has Phil got you up to speed?'

'Yep. He's also given me a pile of emails from Alistair to his parents to sift through.'

Gardner looked at Rice. 'Generous, as always.'

'Well, I'd have done it,' Rice said, 'except you asked me to set up another interview with the Ashworths.'

Gardner felt the weight of O'Brien's gaze before she saw her.

When she glanced over, O'Brien quickly looked away, busying herself with her computer screen. The tension from their hospital conversation still hung heavy in the air.

She inwardly sighed. The guilt over their relationship threatened to overwhelm her. 'Okay, what's with these emails, then?'

'It seems Alistair was exaggerating. He wasn't completely estranged from his parents,' Rice said. 'The emails were pretty constant for most of his stay in Brazil between 2022 and 2023, and even continued after he returned home, albeit far less consistently.'

'When was the last one?' Gardner asked.

'Three months back,' Barnett said.

'Did his parents know that he'd married?'

Rice shook his head.

Gardner turned back to Barnett. She winked at Ray. 'Best man for the emails; nothing will get missed in those. How's the door-to-door on Alistair's murder? Neighbours saw any comings and goings before we arrived?'

'Most were out at work. Picking a few up as they return home,' Rice said. 'We've got nowhere as yet. We've reached out for CCTV footage around the area, too, and video footage from any active doorbells.'

'Okay,' Gardner said. 'Let's see what else the parents can tell us.'

'I was very gentle,' Rice said.

She raised an eyebrow. 'Unusual for you.'

'Made no difference. They were inconsolable. Hence the reason I got little back from them.'

'Hopefully, they've had enough time to settle,' Gardner said. The words felt hollow – how could anyone settle after news like that? 'Is the Zoom call set up?'

Rice nodded.

Before leaving the room, Gardner caught O'Brien watching her again. She offered a conciliatory smile and nod, but O'Brien turned away, the hurt evident in her rigid posture.

But Gardner didn't feel she had the time, or the energy, to deal with it right now.

38

Gardner and Rice sat in an adjacent conference room. A large screen displayed the waiting call.

'What did Marsh say?' Rice asked.

Gardner took out her notebook.

'You didn't speak to her!' Rice said.

'I will after,' Gardner said.

'Shit! She's going to hang me from a meat hook by my knackers!'

Gardner screwed her face up. 'Did you really just use that image?'

'Yes... because you need to understand the pain you've caused me.'

'Not as much pain as that picture you painted has caused me! Do you think I can ever be rid of that?'

'Good. After I've been put to rest, you can think about it all night long, and hear the bloody hook creak as it swings—'

Gardner rolled her eyes and clicked a button, connecting the call before Rice could elaborate further on his graphic metaphor.

Margaret and Gerald Ashworth sat on the sofa. Despite

their earlier distress when Rice had called, they appeared composed, having apparently collected themselves for this conversation.

'Mr and Mrs Ashworth,' Gardner began, 'I'm DCI Emma Gardner, and this is DI Rice, whom you spoke to earlier. Thank you for speaking with us during this difficult time. First, I'm so very sorry for your loss.'

The silence that followed felt heavy with grief. Gardner waited patiently, understanding the weight of the situation. She was about to check if they were on mute when Gerald broke the silence with a swift nod. 'Thank you, DCI Gardner.' His voice cracked slightly. 'We appreciate your efforts in trying to understand what happened to Ali.'

Margaret lowered her face. Gerald hooked an arm around her, pulled her closer and kissed the crown of her head.

'We told DI Rice earlier that we didn't even know he was back in the UK... and we certainly didn't know he was married...'

'Poor girl.' Margaret lifted her face. She looked drawn and exhausted. 'A heart attack in someone so young. What a tragedy! Ali must have been in pieces... Ali...' She broke off and looked away. 'I wish I'd known... I wish we'd known...'

Gardner hesitated. The truth about Imogen's death – that she'd been poisoned with digoxin – would have to wait. These grieving parents had enough to process without learning their son was likely a murderer.

'You said you last saw him in 2022. Is that correct?' Gardner asked.

'May 15.' Gerald's voice was heavy.

'And how was he?'

'Fine...' Gerald said. 'Then... Well, I mean, he was off to Brazil, and that was a big thing, so he was slightly nervous, I guess...'

'Okay, when did your issues with him actually begin?' Gardner asked.

'Hang on,' Gerald said, raising the palm of his hand. 'We'd no issues with Ali. His issues were with us.'

Gardner leaned forward slightly. 'We saw Alistair yesterday,' Gardner said. 'Prior to what happened. He said you were estranged... I took that to suggest you weren't in contact. Yet, now we have emails suggesting that the relationship was ongoing...'

Margaret gave a small moan and then dabbed at her eyes.

'Mrs Ashworth?' Gardner prompted.

'He used to be such a lovely boy... I mean... wonderful, good-hearted. Something happened to him. Changed him. But we don't know what... Who would hurt Ali? Who could hurt our sweet young man?'

Gerald rubbed his wife's back. 'Look... we haven't seen Ali since 15 May when he left. That is how we choose to remember him. Those emails, beginning in 2023, were confusing. They made little sense. Something was up with him.'

'Thank you for providing those emails. Hopefully, they shed some light on what may have happened,' Gardner said.

Gerald rolled his shoulders and sighed. 'As I said to your colleague, DI Rice, none of what he said is true. Those things. Such hurtful things.'

'Horrible things,' Margaret added.

Gardner noticed Rice making notes beside her as Gerald continued. 'We didn't do any of it. And we'd no idea that he thought those things... and we certainly had no idea he would never come back to us. Not until he told us he wouldn't.'

'He told us he would never see us again,' Margaret added. Her voice cracked with emotion. 'My boy, Ali, said that! He wasn't like that.' She looked into the camera with an incredulous look on her face. 'Had never been like that.'

Gardner made a few notes. She kept her voice gentle but firm. 'We will get to the emails, but could you tell us, in a nutshell, what he was accusing you of?'

'Complete bollocks,' Gerald said. 'Excuse my French. But it was. Absolute bollocks. Complete fabrication.' He pointed at his head. 'Something had gone wrong here. Something... they often talk about men's mental health now... and I tell you, Ali would've been a prime candidate. I mean, where would these ideas come from? If only we could have got to him. There's help with these things now.'

Gardner fought to keep her expression neutral despite her growing frustration at their evasiveness. 'So, what did he accuse you of?'

Gerald said, 'Please... I don't know if Margaret can bear to go through it all again.'

Gardner felt Rice shift beside her, likely sharing her impatience.

'Gerald,' Margaret said. 'No. We need to tell them. We want to help.'

Gardner straightened in her chair.

'Ali was always a bright boy, curious about everything. From a young age, he had this restlessness about him, wanting to explore, to push boundaries. We never held him back. We accepted everything. Allowed him this freedom... but...' Margaret put her tissue to her mouth to stifle her sob. 'Maybe it'd all been a mistake. Maybe we should've seen it then, for what it was. An illness.' She dabbed her eyes with her tissue. 'He said that we used to hit him. Hurt him...'

'Unbelievable!' Gerald grunted.

'Keep him locked up inside,' Margaret said.

'Not let him play with his friends... as if!' Gerald said. 'He was always out with his bloody mates.'

'He even accused me of drinking too much...' Margaret said. Her voice trembled with indignation. 'I hardly touched a drop... I swear.' She stared at the camera. 'You have to believe that.'

'And he flat out accused me of having affairs!' Gerald said.

Gardner thought of Alistair's damaged ear and his obsessive tidiness. 'And you don't think there was any truth in anything he said?' Gardner asked.

Gerald slammed his fist on the table and the image on the screen shook. 'No, there bloody wasn't. Are you not listening?'

'Yes,' Gardner said. 'But I want to be thorough.'

Gerald narrowed his eyes. 'How's this for thorough? He accused us of damaging his childhood.'

Margaret flinched, stood and walked out of the camera shot.

'Now look,' Gerald said, running his hands over his balding head.

Gardner exchanged a glance with Rice. His subtle head shake confirmed her own assessment – this interview wasn't yielding the clarity they'd hoped for.

'I'm sorry, Mr Ashworth. Would you like to go and talk to Margaret?'

He sighed. 'No need. She'll come back. Let's carry this on. Like we said, we do want to know who did this to our boy.'

Gardner nodded. 'Okay... so why do you think Alistair said these things to you in his emails?'

'As I said before, mental health. There's no other explanation. It was completely out of character.'

'Did he have a history of mental health issues?' Gardner asked.

Gerald shook his head. 'No... he always seemed well-rounded. Curious, adventurous, ambitious.'

Margaret reappeared on screen, her eyes red-rimmed but her composure somewhat restored. 'Sorry about that.' She was still dabbing at her eyes with that tissue. 'Something came back... and it knocked me for six. When he was about seven, he found an injured bird in our garden. He was so determined to nurse it back to health.' She nodded and gave a sad smile. 'He was a compassionate child. A kind child. Can people change so dramatically?'

Gardner thought of her brother Jack, of Alistair's carefully constructed facade, of how sociopaths could present completely different faces to different people. 'You say that there were no mental health issues, but did you notice any significant changes in his behaviour while he was growing up?'

Gerald's brow furrowed. 'Normal stuff, I suspect. Nothing unusual. Ups and downs. The teenage years had their moments. A few groundings here and there. But certainly nothing out of the ordinary... or so we thought. Nothing to damage a childhood!'

Margaret sighed. 'Well, there was a period when he was fifteen and sixteen.' She broke off, deep in thought.

'Mrs Ashworth?'

'He became more withdrawn. Spent more time in his room, less time with us. But we just wrote that off as normal teenage angst.'

Gardner made a note, though she shared their assessment – it did sound like typical adolescent behaviour. 'What did you do?'

'We just gave him space and let him work through things on his own terms.'

'And regardless of what those emails said, we certainly never stopped him doing what he wanted to do!' Gerald jabbed his finger towards the camera. 'And we certainly didn't beat him black and blue!' He glanced at his wife, who nodded in agreement. 'In fact, we gave him too much freedom – at least, that's how it seems now! He always had an urge to travel and experience the world so we encouraged it. And we supported his decision to live in Brazil, we really did. I told him we wanted him to spread his wings... wanted him to find himself. Looking back now, it does feel rather odd. Out of the blue, maybe? Brazil! I mean why Brazil? Why not Europe?'

'He was so excited,' Margaret added. 'Said he'd met someone at a travel expo who'd told him about volunteer opportunities in Rio. It all happened quickly after that. We were so supportive.'

'Did you have any concerns about him going?' Rice spoke for the first time, his voice carefully neutral.

'Of course. What parents wouldn't? But we discussed it and stuck by our beliefs in giving him space to grow, to make his own choices. We didn't want to change the way we'd raised him. It certainly won't feel that way when you read those emails,' Gerald snorted. 'But it's the truth.'

'What happened after he arrived in Brazil? How did the fall out between you all suddenly come about?' Gardner leaned forward slightly, sensing they were approaching something significant.

Gerald placed a comforting hand on his wife's shoulder as she gathered herself to continue. 'At first, everything seemed fine,' Gerald said. 'He'd email us regularly, full of stories about his work, the people he was meeting. He sounded... happy. Fulfilled. But then there was a change. A sudden change. The first email of this nature was angry and aggressive. In fact, they all were that day forth.' His face darkened. 'But this one really sticks with me. He began it by telling us how ashamed he was to have Margaret and me as parents. That we'd filled him with pain and anguish during his childhood.'

Margaret opened her hands to the screen. 'But we'd done nothing to him. Nothing!'

Gardner's detective instincts tingled at the abrupt personality shift they described. It reminded her of a case in Salisbury involving multiple personalities, though it was far too early to draw such conclusions.

'Did you address this accusation in your response?' Gardner asked.

Margaret nodded vigorously. 'Of course we did. We emailed, tried to call. You have our emails too! We tried to call, but he wouldn't answer. He just wouldn't engage. We were desperate to know where these fanciful ideas had come from! But then, we received another email, and...'

'It was even more hostile...' Gerald rubbed his balding head again. 'It continued this way for a time, then all correspondence stopped for a few months. It was awful.'

'Some of the worst months of our lives,' Margaret added.

'We were planning to hop on a plane—'

'We should've done,' Margaret said. Her voice thick with regret. 'We really should have.'

'But we didn't even know where he was. If he was even still in Brazil! We didn't even know the name of the bar, so we were unable to ask them if he still worked there.'

The rest of the interview continued with similar emotional intensity, Gardner noting how the Ashworths' grief seemed genuine, even as certain details about Alistair's behaviour raised red flags. Gardner sat back in her chair, her mind working to reconcile the loving parents' account with what she knew about their son's final days.

As the call wound down, Gardner couldn't shake the feeling that there was more to Alistair's story than met the eye. The disparity between the loving son the Ashworths described and the man who'd so thoroughly rejected them was stark. It reminded her, again, uncomfortably of Jack. What had transformed Alistair so completely? And how did it all connect to his death?

'Mr and Mrs Ashworth,' Gardner said, her professional composure masking her churning thoughts, 'thank you for speaking with us today. I know how difficult this must be for you. Please know that we're doing everything we can to understand what happened to Alistair. I believe you'll be up here tomorrow?'

Gerald nodded. 'I've a flight booked for us in the morning. We don't drive. Dizzy spells...'

'We shall see you then,' Gardner said, her heart sinking as she realised she would soon have to break the devastating news that Alistair was likely a murderer. 'And once again, I'm so sorry for your loss.'

39

As Gardner left the conference room, her mind whirled. The stark contrast between the loving son the Ashworths had described and the man who'd so thoroughly cut them out of his life was jarring.

In the incident room, she smiled at O'Brien and was relieved to receive one in return. Then, she approached Barnett, who was busy working on a computer. 'How are you getting on with those emails?'

Barnett looked up, his dark eyes reflecting the screen's glow. 'Interesting reading. Although, I feel like I need more context to make sense of it all...'

'Okay.' Gardner rolled over a chair and sat down beside him. She stole a quick glance at O'Brien again, but the young detective's attention was now fully on her computer screen. Gardner pulled out her notebook and went through the conversation she'd had with the Ashworths.

Barnett nodded throughout and, at the end, said, 'Yes... that's the pattern I have. Alistair's early emails from Brazil throughout 2022 are chatty and full of details about his life in Rio. Also very regular. There's even mention of a girl, Beatriz. This all changes on 18 February 2023.' Barnett consulted his notes. 'The emails slow down. The tone becomes cold and accusatory. He starts referencing childhood traumas, but it's all very vague. No specific incidents, just general accusations of neglect and emotional abuse. Things like... "you never let me socialise with other children"; "you were embarrassed if I showed emotion in public". That kind of thing... The parents are stunned... they express confusion... they don't understand. They want Alistair to come home. There are other patterns I'm picking up on.'

Gardner leaned in, studying the emails. 'Other patterns?'

Barnett nodded. 'Yes. The aggressive emails come in clusters, usually three or four over the course of a week. Then there's a long gap – sometimes over a month – before another burst. And each cluster follows a similar structure: anger, accusations, then a threat warning them never to look for him, or he will never speak to them again, or even commit suicide.'

'So... he's reminding them he's still out there, but doesn't actually want any contact?' Gardner asked.

'Exactly,' Barnett agreed. 'Then there's a long time between April 2023 and October 2023 when he simply doesn't write, despite his parents emailing him regularly. There are a few more towards the end of the year, which again, are merely warnings for them to back off.'

'What do you reckon to all this?'

'Well,' Barnett said, 'I'm no professional, so I'd definitely get someone qualified to take a look. The writing style is just not consistent. The original emails are flawless, while I notice grammatical errors and odd phrasing in the later ones. It could mirror a loss of emotional control?'

'Or multiple personalities?' Gardner asked.

'Possibly. Either that, or it's from a different person entirely.'

Gardner chewed her bottom lip. That was a very real option. There were too many discrepancies.

'What're you thinking, boss?'

'I'm thinking that if you're right, Ray, that the body in that morgue belongs to someone entirely different, then this investigation just became even more complex.'

Rice, who'd slipped up behind them and heard the end of the conversation, added, 'Aye. Because we'll need to find out what the hell happened to the original Alistair... a third murder, perhaps?'

Gardner's stomach clenched.

40

Jack listened to the front door close. He went to the window and watched as Monika drove away in his sister's second car to collect Rose and Ana from school.

Drawing back from the window, he hesitated only briefly before going into his daughter's bedroom. He ran his fingertips over the pink walls and the Taylor Swift posters and then sat down on her bed. Smiling, he flicked a switch, and a string of fairy lights draped across Rose's headboard glowed warmly.

He picked up the book beside her bed. *Diary of a Wimpy Kid.* He leafed through it. According to his sister, Rose was an exceptional reader.

At the far end of the room, above a small desk, was a board, pinned with drawings, school certificates and photographs. He'd noticed it yesterday, and it was the felt-tip drawing of a tall man and a small girl, holding hands, that had caught his attention then. And the words beneath it.

Me and Daddy.

The unfamiliar tightness in his chest returned, just as strong as yesterday.

Over at the windowsill, he regarded a collection of small potted plants – succulents and cacti in various stages of growth. She'd developed an interest in gardening.

She was nothing like him.

And would grow to be so different from him.

He reached up and touched the smile that had yet to fall from his face.

His phone vibrated in his pocket.

For fear of sullying such purity, he left Rose's room, before checking it.

There was only one person who'd text him on this phone.

> Unforeseen developments. Secrets and deceit breed consequences. Meet again tomorrow morning. Same time and place. Destroy this phone immediately.

Jack stared back into his daughter's room, and reached up to his face again, hoping for the smile, but confirming that it'd fallen away.

Are these developments really so unforeseen? He'd always known this moment might come.

Jack had known the risks. Chanced on keeping the secret that Gregory Pendleton wasn't the only name that he'd carried with him all these years.

The cryptic message could mean only one thing – something had happened to expose the second name.

Should I have the opportunity all over again, you think I would've done anything different?

Gregory is one name, but the other, well, the other... that one is too close to home.

I'm ready for your consequences, Neville.

He went back into his daughter's room, wanting to rediscover that fleeting moment of pride over the individual she was becoming. Instead, he went over to a shelf of trinkets, stuffed toys and a single picture of him and Rose, taken just before his incarceration.

They were at a park. Rose was beaming at the camera.

Jack stared at his smiling self. He wanted to know how real that smile had been. Was it reaching his eyes?

He looked at the way his daughter was leaning into him, her small hand clasped in his, which spoke of a connection he couldn't deny.

Yes, that happiness had been genuine. It had been very real.

Secrets and deceit breed consequences.

Could he really take any more risks?

Neville was not a man who tolerated being kept in the dark, especially by those he considered in his debt.

Jack's fingers tightened around the phone.

What could he offer to counterbalance his deception? What could he give that wouldn't compromise the fragile safety he'd built for Rose?

Neville was a man who had everything. Such a man fed on only one thing.

Commitment.

Subservience.

Those willing to walk through the flames on his watch.

If that was Neville's price, then Jack had little choice but to pay it.

His eyes drifted back to the photograph, to his daughter's smiling face.

She was free from the shadows that had defined his own existence, and that was how she would stay.

Jack took one last look around the room, checking he'd not

missed anything. He wanted every detail in his memory banks when he finally left.

The colourful bedspread, the half-finished puzzle on the floor, the little ballet shoes tucked in the corner.

With a deep breath, he stepped out of the room, closing the door quietly behind him. He made his way to the bathroom, where he methodically disassembled the phone. He flushed the SIM card down the toilet and broke the phone under his heel.

A broken phone was just the start, he realised.

After tomorrow's meeting, lives would have to be broken, too.

41

After another disappointing update on Riddick's condition, Gardner made her way to Marsh's office. There were several things she needed to beg for. First, to stay on the case despite the distractions; second, to ask for more personnel; and third, to spare Rice's anatomy from the meat hook after he kept her secret.

She smiled over this last thought, remembering their earlier banter, and then her phone rang.

'Robin?'

'Emma, we've found something odd,' the pathologist said. 'Alistair's medical records show that his appendix was removed when he was twelve.'

'There's no scar, is there?' Gardner felt her pulse quicken with the confirmation of her growing suspicions.

'No... I see you're not surprised.'

Gardner explained what they'd discovered about the emails.

'Any idea who this body belongs to then?' Robin asked.

'No... but let's confirm we have our facts straight first.'

After ending the call, she turned around and headed back to the conference room where she'd recently spoken to the

Ashworths. She contacted Gerald directly by phone. He sounded unsettled at hearing from her again so soon.

She apologised for the sudden return call. 'I'm sorry, Mr Ashworth. I'm aware this question might sound odd, but how old was Alistair when he had his appendicitis?'

'Twelve,' Gerald said. 'One of the worst nights of our lives. I'd never seen him in such pain.'

Gardner's stomach tightened. Alistair's medical records hadn't been wrong, then.

'Why?' Gerald asked.

'We wanted to confirm the medical records were accurate... Mr Ashworth, do you have an email address?'

'Yes, why?'

'I'm going to email you an image now... I want you to tell me if you recognise this person. Can I have your email?'

Gardner pulled up the passport photo Rice had obtained from the Home Office. Careful not to reveal too much too soon, she cropped out everything but the face before sending it to the email address Gerald just gave her.

'Okay,' Gerald said. 'It's come through. One moment... okay...'

'Do you know that person?'

The pause that followed felt endless. 'No... I really don't recognise him.'

Confirmation. Their worst fears realised – someone had stolen Alistair's identity.

'Shall I ask Margaret?' Gerald asked.

'That's not necessary.' Gardner pressed her fingers to her temples, feeling the weight of what she had to tell him.

'Who is it?'

Good bloody question!

She had to word her answer carefully.

Yes, it meant Alistair wasn't Imogen's murderer, but the implications were devastating.

The real Alistair was almost certainly dead.

She couldn't build false hope, but she had to be gentle.

'Gerald. The body recovered today isn't Alistair's. There's no appendix scar. However, this person has been using your son's identity.'

'Good lord.'

Gardner waited, letting him process the information.

'So, the photo you showed me... that's the dead man?'

'Yes,' Gardner said.

'So where's Alistair?'

'I'm sorry, Gerald, I don't know.'

The phone went silent.

'Gerald?'

'Yes, I'm here. Is he alive?'

Probably not, she thought, but said, 'I really don't know. But can you see how it maybe explains those emails you were sent?'

The silence stretched out between them.

Eventually, he said, 'They weren't from Ali, were they?'

'It looks that way,' Gardner said. 'I'm sorry.'

'Why? That could be good news.'

Yes, if they could ignore the darker implications.

There was another silence before, 'What vile bastard would do that to us?'

'We're going to try to find out.'

She heard something being thrown, followed by, 'He deserves to be dead. That bastard deserved it. All this time...' His voice grew quieter. 'All this time...'

Gardner waited, hearing his ragged breathing on the other end. The silence was painful.

'I'm going to speak to my team now, Gerald, but please,

cancel your flight for now. Stay with Margaret and show her that picture, too, see if she recognises him. I promise to keep you updated. And can you send us some photos of Alistair – as recent as possible?'

'Yes... and...'

She waited.

'DCI Gardner?'

'Yes.'

'Please find my son. He may still be alive.'

Gardner closed her eyes, hating what she had to say next. She didn't want to take away his hope. But, deep down, knowing what this impersonator had done to Imogen, how could Gardner suspect any outcome but the worst? It was only fair to warn him.

'We'll try, but please temper your expectations, Gerald. I'm sorry, but I don't think you've heard from your son in over a year...'

She listened for his response, but there was only the sound of muffled sobbing. She stayed on the line, a silent witness to a father's grief, until he finally hung up.

42

Gardner rushed back to the incident room, nearly colliding with Rice at the door.

'You smoothed things over with Marsh?' he asked.

'Sorry... I had—'

'Boss!'

'More pressing issues. Plus' – she nodded down at his nether regions and grinned, sheepishly – 'you're too old to have children now, surely?'

'No problem, then, hook them up and bring on the pain. Bloody hell. What was so important, anyway?'

'I'll tell you all,' Gardner said, striding into the incident room, calling everyone to attention.

The team looked up – Barnett, O'Brien and Detective Constable Suggs, who'd joined them less than an hour ago.

'I've confirmation that the man in the mortuary isn't Alistair Ashworth. Alistair mark one has an appendix scar. The victim doesn't. I've confirmed it with his father, Gerald. At least this explains the inconsistent emails.'

'So Alistair mark one is a goner, then,' Rice added.

Gardner turned to the board which Rice had meticulously arranged in her absence. She tapped a photograph of the victim. The same passport photo Gardner had sent to Gerald. 'So we need to know who Alistair mark two is... then maybe we can figure out what happened to the original, and also why he killed Imogen. I've got images coming from Gerald of the original Alistair, and...'

O'Brien had her hand in the air.

'Lucy?'

'Just pulled one up from the internet. Oxford University... a graduation photograph. Same colour hair and eyes as the impersonator, but the similarities end there.'

Gardner crossed to O'Brien's desk, conscious of the tension between them as she leaned in to study the image. She nodded. 'Good work, Lucy.'

'Boss,' Barnett said.

She looked over at him and nodded.

'I've been sifting through the earlier emails, before the abrupt change in tone in 2023. He never mentioned the name of the bar he worked in. However, at the back end of 2022, Alistair regularly discusses the area, Lapa. A vibrant nightlife district popular with expats in Rio. A few times, he mentions a João Oliveira, who gave him a job and treated him well. I linked the name to a bar in that area. Samba Nights.'

'Sounds like a place with my name written all over it,' Rice said.

'Not if they want to continue turning a profit,' Gardner said. 'Well done, Ray.'

'I'll get on the phone,' Barnett said, 'and find out what happened regarding the original Alistair. Remember, he was also involved with a woman called Beatriz for several months. No surname unfortunately. But I'm wondering if we could find her, too.'

Gardner glanced at her watch, aware she needed to get to the hospital soon to make visiting time and request some minutes with Riddick. She looked at Rice. 'Phil, are you able to get in touch with the Brazilian embassy? We need their cooperation to investigate Alistair's disappearance in Rio... there might be some unsolved crimes... unidentified bodies.'

Rice nodded.

Gardner then looked at their newest team member. 'Welcome aboard, Detective Constable Suggs. I want you to carry on looking through all the CCTV footage we have close to this imposter's home and speak to neighbours about him. Did anybody have suspicions over this man, think he was peculiar, perhaps?'

As everyone set to work, her phone buzzed. The email from Gerald Ashworth had arrived with several attachments.

The first photo captured Alistair and his father working on a classic car, both covered in grease, but laughing heartily. The scene was so at odds with the broken, serious man they'd interviewed yesterday that it felt like looking at a different world. The bond between them was palpable, a shared passion bridging generations.

The second photo was a candid shot of Alistair and his mother in the kitchen, flour dusting their faces as they attempted to bake. The love and warmth in their eyes as they looked at each other was unmistakable, a testament to the deep connection they shared.

Gardner felt her throat tighten. She spoke to her team again. 'Gerald and Margaret had been through unbearable pain. Years of believing that the child they adored had come to despise them.' She paused and looked between their faces. They were all nodding. 'The height of cruelty... and now they've no idea what happened to him. I couldn't imagine their confusion.'

They were a good team.

She could trust them to uncover the truth – to find out who'd destroyed not just one family, but two.

'Let's put this right,' she said.

43

Dappled sunlight filtered through the canopy, creating shifting patterns on the forest floor. Paul spotted the ground sloping downwards into a small clearing and felt drawn to investigate.

'Careful, son,' Colin called from behind.

As Paul descended, he noticed the distant sound of birdsong and a strong odour of rotting leaves. Something about the combination felt wrong, making him stop in his tracks. He looked around, his father's lessons about reading nature's warnings echoing in his mind, before deciding he was being paranoid.

He took another step forward, his feet crunching dry leaves beneath them—

The birdsong cut off abruptly, replaced by an ominous buzz.

He turned and saw his father at the clearing entrance...

And then pain exploded across his face and hands. He screamed.

Through the agony, he heard his father shouting, but the angry buzzing of the hornets drowned out the words. He closed his eyes and rubbed at his face, desperate to wipe away whatever was attacking him.

Terror rising, he lunged forward. He made it a few steps before catching a branch and going to his knees. 'They're all over me, Dad!'

He swatted frantically at the surrounding air, each movement bringing fresh waves of pain. His skin felt like it was being pierced by hundreds of burning needles.

'Paul!' His father's voice cut through the panic. 'Stand up and run!'

Fighting against the pain and fear, he willed himself to his feet and lunged again.

'Back up the slope!' his father cried.

This time his legs held firm, and eventually he found his father's hands pulling him to safety, away from the hornets' territory.

44

After spending almost an hour beside Riddick, she was unsurprised to see that she'd picked up several voicemail recordings after leaving the hospital.

One was from Monika informing her that Rose had spent some time with Jack, and now she and Ana were settled and ready for bed.

The other three were from Rice, and Marsh and Barnett, the latter two requesting phone calls. Marsh was insistent that Gardner returned her call. The edge in her voice made it clear she was intending to ask her to take a step back.

Rice's message informed her that the Brazilian embassy had been receptive. Someone was going to dig around and be back in touch within twenty-four hours. He also clarified that one of the coffee cups recovered from Bebra Gardens contained traces of digoxin. The lab was now testing the DNA on the cups alongside the DNA of the man in the morgue to confirm that he was Imogen's killer. Unfortunately, this DNA was not in the police database, so identifying him was still no further along.

Barnett, like Marsh, had requested a call back.

When she was back in her car, she opted to phone Barnett first.

'I got in touch with João Oliveira, owner of Samba Nights in Lapa. He spends most of his time servicing expats, so he spoke very good English. He remembers Alistair very well – referred to him as *Ali.*'

Gardner recalled that this was exactly the way his parents had referred to him.

'Said he was cheerful and hardworking. Sounds like they were rather good friends. I sent João the images from Gerald Ashworth via email. João confirmed it was Alistair. He sounded downbeat. Apparently, Alistair left his job rather suddenly. Didn't even turn up for his shift and emailed in a resignation. He claimed his mother was sick, and he was heading back to the UK. He promised to email again, which he did. The second email simply said he wouldn't be returning to Brazil with an apology, not much else. João has forwarded the emails. Alistair missed his last shift on 16 February 2023. His previous shift was two days before. Gerald and Margaret Ashworth received that first cold email on 18 February 2023.'

Barnett allowed Gardner to digest the information. 'So... his identity was stolen between the shift on 14 and 16 February 2023?'

'Seems that way, boss. Doesn't look good for Alistair, does it?'

'No, not at all.' She thought about Gerald and Margaret Ashworth, who were soon to experience the news that they'd lost their son all over again.

Yes, they could argue that there was still hope, but the sense of inevitability was now overwhelming.

'So this imposter,' Gardner said, 'put João's mind at rest with two emails, ensuring the bar owner never reported him missing.'

'Good thinking, really,' Barnett said. 'If João had contacted the police, the imposter would never have made it out of the country as Alistair Ashworth.'

Gardner sighed. 'Still... a forged passport? These days? Surely that's too bloody difficult? What with all the centralised systems—'

'It's still possible, boss,' Barnett said. 'With the right contacts and enough money. We have to assume our imposter is a man of means. Bribing individuals working in passport agencies to input you into the system wouldn't come cheap.'

'We've a lot of untangling to do,' Gardner said.

'Well, we could start with the woman he was seeing. João told me her full name. Beatriz Santos. I've tried ringing twice. No answer. I'll try again before I leave. Failing that, I'll try in the morning.'

'Brilliant, Ray.'

There was an awkward pause and then, 'How is Paul?'

Gardner swallowed. 'Not well, *but* there was more colour in his cheeks,' Gardner said.

And she believed that was true.

God, I hope it's not just wishful thinking...

'Marsh was looking for you. She looked... well...'

'On the warpath?'

'Something along those lines.'

'Thanks, Ray.'

After ending the call, she took a deep breath and called Marsh.

It was time to beg.

She didn't hold out much hope.

45

At home, Gardner tried to still her racing mind by watching television with Rose and Ana for an hour. She should've chosen an animated movie she was unfamiliar with. *Finding Nemo* was great, but she knew it back to front, so it offered her no relief from the day's turmoil.

At least Marsh had agreed to let her come in tomorrow. 'Only because you're so good, Emma, and we've only got this far because of you... but I'll check in with you, and Phil, hourly. If, at any point, he feels you're losing focus, then I'll be forced to act.'

'It won't be necessary,' she'd informed her superior.

After putting the children to bed, she lay with them for five minutes apiece, starting with Ana because she was the youngest. When she moved on to Rose, she hugged her tightly. *Would Jack change his mind and try to take her?*

Paranoia, surely?

After all, Jack knew leaving Rose here was in her best interests.

Not having heard from her brother since arriving back just

made her nervous, though. After leaving her niece, she sized up her brother's door, wondering if she should check in with him.

She couldn't bring herself to do it.

She was already emotionally drained, and all she could think about was a glass of wine.

It was quiet downstairs, and Monika had retired to her room to talk online with her boyfriend, like she did most evenings, so Gardner seized her opportunity for alcohol.

She was a quarter of the way through pouring a large glass of Merlot when she stopped.

What if the hospital called?

If she started drinking, she'd be in no fit state to drive.

She put the bottle down and regarded the quarter-full glass. Just a small one.

As she took a seat, her phone vibrated in her pocket.

She took it out and saw a text message from O'Brien.

I'm sorry for earlier. L x

She treated the sudden onset of guilt with almost half her small glass in a single mouthful, and then texted back.

Don't be. E x

Trying to make the wine last, she instead switched on the television with the remote as she waited for her reply.

The reply came quickly.

For being a selfish cow x

Don't be ridiculous x

> I wasn't compassionate. It is turbulent for you at the moment x

> You've been amazing. You're always amazing. I'm the cow x

Gardner couldn't hold back on finishing the glass.

She wanted O'Brien to be pissed off with her!

She deserved it!

Almost *needed* it.

She'd been so foolish in letting this relationship get out of hand! She'd known from the start how she felt about Paul. And she'd never been in any doubt about how old O'Brien was.

She texted:

> Please don't feel bad… none of this is on you. x

> I miss you x

> Let's wait until Paul is out of the woods and we can grab a drink? x

> Can't wait… let me know… x

She sensed movement behind her and almost jumped out of her skin.

Hand to her chest, she stood and turned to look behind her.

Jack.

Had he deliberately crept up on her, or had she simply been too engrossed in her guilt over O'Brien to notice him?

'You made me jump,' she said.

'Sorry.'

'Try not to do that.'

'Okay… how was work?'

'Do you care?' she asked.

He didn't answer, and she felt immediately guilty for her abrupt tone. After all, her anxiety wasn't entirely his fault. 'Sorry. It was okay. Work is a good distraction.'

He nodded. 'I see.'

His face was, as ever, impossible to read, but something was clearly troubling him.

'Everything all right on your side?' she asked.

He didn't answer.

'Jack?'

'There's been a hitch.'

Gardner's adrenaline spiked. She thought of Rose upstairs, remembering how just hours ago Jack had claimed he was almost out of their lives. 'What hitch?'

He shook his head. 'Nothing... at least nothing for you to worry about. It's a slight delay.'

'If it's nothing for me to worry about, why are you telling me?'

He shrugged. 'You wanted to know where I was going at all times, remember? Tomorrow, I have to meet Neville again.'

She couldn't resist a snort. 'Really? You've told me about none of your moves to date, and you suddenly feel compelled to tell me now! Why?'

He looked down.

'Well?'

He looked up. 'I was in Rose's room today, while you and Monika were out.' He stepped forward and gave her a swift nod. 'I appreciate what you've done for her. You've done something quite special. I'll always owe you for that.'

And just to think, Gardner thought bitterly, *if you'd swung that stone a little harder in Malcolm's Maze of Mirrors... then what? What would have happened to Rose then?*

'Why are you seeing Neville tomorrow?' she asked.

She didn't expect a response. Her eyes widened slightly when she received one.

'Because it is turning out differently to how I expected.'

'That makes no sense... but I don't like the sound of that... not at all.'

Jack shook his head. 'It's okay. For you, Rose and Ana... nothing changes.' He turned.

She thought he was going to walk away, but then he suddenly turned back. 'I love Rose... and I love you, Emma.'

The next time he turned, he walked away.

Her mouth hung agape. The words had felt so alien coming from him.

Guilt?

Sadness?

Emotions he wasn't capable of... unless...

Had she misjudged him all these years?

She looked at the empty glass of wine in her hand, wishing she could fill it, and ruminate on tonight's big question:

Were sociopaths capable of change?

46

Heart racing, Gardner fumbled on the bedside table for her ringing phone.

God, no, have I lost him?

She squinted at the unknown number and answered, trying to steady her voice. 'DCI Gardner speaking.'

'Emma, sorry to call early... it's Tanya.'

Tanya Reid – Collette Willows's ex-girlfriend and the podcaster who'd been investigating Neville.

She looked at her watch. 'It's the crack of dawn... what's happened?'

Tanya sighed. 'It's almost time to release the podcast. Look, this is hard... but I made a promise to inform you, first.'

She sat up straight in bed. 'What've you found out?'

'Too much! I must have a death wish! But it's my nature, see. Can't help myself.'

'I can relate.' Gardner took a deep breath. 'Talk to me, Tanya.'

'You haven't got long, Emma. I can only sit on this for another twenty-four hours. I was so close to running with it this morning, but I've been awake, all night, guilty over the promise I made to you and knowing that this is what Collette would want. There's a shock coming, a seismic one. A lot of people will be reeling. The police may try to cover it up. God, if Fairweather knew I had this, I'd be in danger—'

'Tanya. I'll make sure you're safe.'

'Ha. That's a promise you'll struggle to keep. Anyway, as you know already, Neville was a major shareholder in Aegis Dynamics, a defence company that worked on behalf of the government back in the early noughties.'

'Yes...'

'Aegis has been involved in everything from cybersecurity to drone development.'

'Let's not forget the multitude of clandestine operations...'

'Right.' Tanya went silent.

'Tanya? Have you found out what the operations were?' Gardner asked.

'Yes. Aegis worked on counterintelligence. Stifling the Russian threat.'

Although, it made sense. Neville's resources, his protection detail, his influence. 'So Neville is part of our national bloody security?'

'Yes. If it can be called that,' Tanya said. 'It's certainly *bloody*.'

'What do you mean?'

'I'll get to that in a moment.'

'Surely counterintelligence is a good thing, yes?'

There was a pause. 'At heart, yes. However, with great power comes great responsibility, don't they say? Seems that part went unchecked.' She sighed. 'I have access to redacted files that show that some of Aegis's employees were selling secrets and helping the Russians,' Tanya said.

'Traitors in Neville's company? Who? You've identified them?'

'No. At the time, they weren't identified, and they still aren't.

However, you know about the family that was murdered yesterday near Swindon, you hear about it?'

Gardner was confused. 'Of course, it was all over the news,' Gardner replied. 'But one had been a child.'

'Yes... The names of the victims were released to the press late last night. Gregory, Helen and Ryan Pendleton. Ryan was thirteen...'

'Awful. But I don't see—'

'Public domain records have painted Gregory as a retired civil servant. However, unredacted files show otherwise. I can't tell you my source, Emma. Gregory was a senior project manager at Aegis for a time. He was part of the counterintelligence strategy.'

Gardner felt her blood run cold. She knew it was coming. The suggestion that the traitor had been Gregory and his family paid the price.

'Ryan had a single gunshot to the head, Gregory, one to the face. The only anomaly from it being professional and organised was that Helen was shot twice. I suspect the assassin was off target just the once before finishing the job. Killing the whole family seems over the top, but then, I guess, where leaks are concerned, nobody likes to take any risks.'

'Shit.' Gardner swung her left leg from the bed, fighting a wave of nausea. 'You don't think...? Did Neville give that order?'

'I suspect so, but I can't say for certain. I guess it could have been someone in government who doesn't want to be embarrassed. Still, one thing is certain, no way this hit happened without Neville knowing about it.'

Gardner could feel her stomach somersaulting.

Was her brother involved in this somehow?

Gardner quickly calculated the timing. Jack couldn't have made it to Swindon and back during the few hours she hadn't seen him. That offered some relief, but just because he hadn't pulled the trigger didn't mean he wasn't involved.

'If you've figured it out, then won't the police?'

'The police will be forced to play ball by the government! They don't want embarrassing information about their defence companies leaked.' Tanya snorted. 'Sorry, Emma... but this will go nowhere. It'll be pinned on someone else. Without the leaked files and someone willing to speak out, Aegis, and Neville, will walk away from this.'

'Come on. I can't believe this. The police I work with have integrity. Like you. They'll be those—'

'Emma,' Tanya said, cutting her off. 'You've integrity and look what you've become involved with! When it comes to things like this, Neville and this lot have their ways. Insidious ways. Everyone has a price. Yours was your family's safety. How many people do you think have faced the same threat? But don't worry, they didn't count on me. I'll put it out. I've no family to worry about. These dickheads will pay.'

'And my brother. Jack. He's involved with Neville, somehow. Do you think he's involved with these assassinations.'

'I don't know. I'm sorry... I've seen nothing about that,' she said. 'But I thought you deserved warning, Emma, that I'm releasing this tomorrow morning. If your brother is involved in these murders, now is the time to distance yourself from him. Or rather distance *him* from you.'

'I understand that, but I don't know how I can do that. You know the situation—'

'Emma, I can't wait. Every second leaves me vulnerable to being taken out. Plus, we risk someone else, someone innocent, being hung out for the Pendleton murders... and my information will have less impact.'

'Okay... I understand... thanks, Tanya, for the heads-up, I'll—'

'Emma, are you listening? This is more than a heads-up. Could my warning be any clearer? Three dead people? Linked to Neville, who is connected to your brother. You need to put an end to this. Get Jack out of your house, now, but you can't tell him how you know. If they know the information is leaking from me, or my source, then... God... I don't even want to think about what they're capable of.'

'No one will hear it from me,' Gardner said. 'Thank you for the time, Tanya.'

After ending the call, Gardner sat as the sun rose outside her home. Despite this light, her world seemed to be growing ever darker. What kind of monster had she allowed back into her life? Into her home with her children?

Gardner threw on a dressing gown and padded down the hallway to Jack's room. She knocked softly, conscious of the early hour and not wanting to wake Ana and Rose.

She'd tell him to leave immediately. If he refused... well, shit would have to hit the fan. She felt capable of anything to protect her girls.

When Jack didn't answer, she opened the door.

The curtains were drawn and the bed was made.

She checked the wardrobe and then under the bed. His belongings were gone.

Hand to her mouth, she turned and saw Rose in the doorway holding a letter.

'He's gone,' Rose said. Her eyes were puffy. 'He says he's proud of me, and that he loves me, but he's saying goodbye for now.'

Gardner stepped forward and embraced her crying niece, relief flooding through her even as her heart broke for Rose.

47

As Gardner showered, trying to wash away the anxious sweat that had started up the moment Tanya called her, those final words from Jack last night echoed in her mind: *I love Rose... and I love you, Emma.*

Now, she could recognise it for what it was.

A goodbye.

She thought about calling Tanya back and telling her that Jack was gone from her life, and that she could release the information now. Expose Neville. Bring down that parasitic, corrupted world that he ran.

However, after stepping out of the shower and wrapping herself in a towel, she decided to hold back from making that call.

Better to make absolutely sure he didn't come back, first. After all, Jack had spoken of hitches and unforeseen circumstances the previous evening. What if there were more complications in his meeting with Neville, and he came back here just as the scandal was breaking?

The twenty-four hours she'd been offered seemed a sensible

option.

As she dried herself, she cursed under her breath when she realised she'd not brought her phone into the bathroom with her. What if Euan was ringing to update her on Riddick? This morning's news had been one hell of a distraction, but she needed to get her head back in the game.

After returning to her room, she cursed again when she saw she had, indeed, missed a call.

She listened to the voicemail. It wasn't from Euan, but on behalf of him. A request for Gardner to come to the hospital and meet with him regarding Riddick's condition.

Not for the first time this morning, her blood ran cold.

Why? What was his condition?

She clenched her fists. Please don't let it get any worse...

After all, wasn't further deterioration just death?

She took a deep breath and held on to the next affirmation with all her heart – be positive; remember the colour returning to his cheeks. Maybe he's improved... maybe Euan wants to tell me he's out of danger?

She considered ringing back, but they were unlikely to tell her anything if the doctor had put some time aside to speak to her, and she'd be sitting on hold for nothing.

No. She had to get her arse in there.

Marsh wouldn't be best pleased. It would surely be the final nail in Gardner's coffin regarding this investigation if she wasn't running the briefing.

Having dressed, she went downstairs and found Monika preparing breakfast for the girls. Ana looked up from her cereal, her face brightening at the sight of her mother.

'Mummy! I love your hair!'

Gardner had taken no time over her hair whatsoever, so it probably looked different from the norm. She didn't know how to take the comment – had she been making it worse every day of her adult life?

She kissed Ana on the forehead. 'You got my back, pudding.'

Rose was looking down at the letter in her hands sadly. 'Why didn't he come and say goodbye, Auntie Em?'

She went over and kissed her niece on the crown. 'Because he didn't want to wake you.'

'When will I see him again?' Rose asked, looking up at Gardner.

She couldn't answer that question. Secretly, she hoped, never, but she wasn't about to say that. Rose needed support desperately, but Gardner was all over the place right now. She needed to buy some time before really being there for Rose. 'Soon, I hope…'

'Can I write a letter back to him?' Rose asked.

'Sounds lovely,' Gardner said.

'Do you have his address?'

Gardner didn't want to lie, so she gave a swift nod and then changed the subject. 'I've got to head out now to see Uncle Paul.'

She felt Ana's eyes searching her face. Her daughter could be very perceptive. 'You seem sad, Mummy. Is Uncle Paul okay?'

'I think so,' Gardner said. *I hope so.*

'He's got a new heart, Ana,' Rose said.

'And it's a strong one,' Gardner said, and winked. She patted her chest. 'Everything the Tin Man would have wanted.'

Rose laughed, enjoying the reference to her favourite film. This was one of the reasons she called Gardner Auntie Em.

Gardner turned to Monika. 'I'm not sure when I'll be back. I'll call.'

She considered taking Monika to one side and telling her not to let Jack in if he returned, but that would just fill her with dread, and she'd have to provide reasons. Reasons that were far from clear now. Instead, she leaned in and said, 'Could you let me know if Jack comes back?'

'That letter suggests he won't be...'

Gardner nodded. 'I know... but if he does, phone me, please?'

'Of course.'

Gardner nodded again. She'd have to break the rules and keep her phone on silent in the hospital. If Jack came back, then she needed to be back here within minutes.

Gardner headed out to her car. As soon as she settled into the driver's seat, her phone rang. Barnett's name flashed on the screen.

She took a deep breath, trying to refocus herself to the point yesterday when she'd last seen everyone at HQ.

Barnett's voice crackled with excitement. 'Morning, boss, I got in touch with Beatriz Santos! She was in a relationship with Alistair from July 2022 to January 2023.'

'So, they broke up before he disappeared?' Gardner asked.

'Yes, a few months before he returned home. She emailed me a photograph of them together. They looked like a nice couple.'

'Why did they split?'

'She got back together with an ex.'

'I see.' Gardner pulled out of the driveway, putting the phone on speaker. 'Did Beatriz have much to say?'

'Yes. She claimed to have serious feelings for him. Still does. She said Alistair was a very good man, and that they became extremely close in a short space of time. But she'd already had a child with her ex, and thought it better to try to make a go of it with him when he came back into the picture. She met Alistair at Samba Nights when he was working one night. They'd decided in January not to keep in touch, on account of the child. She said Alistair understood. Again, she stressed he was a good man. He wanted her and the child to have the best possible life.'

'So, did she not know he'd left?' Gardner asked.

'She knew, because she went back a couple of months later to try to see him. She was told that he'd upped and left because of his mother. Someone that worked there passed the email onto her and told her not to expect much in the way of a reply. She tried emailing in April, after she split from her ex. This time for good, she reckons. In May, Alistair, presumably the imposter, wrote back and told her he felt betrayed by her, and was never returning. She said it sounded out of character but took it at face value.'

Gardner sighed. Still no hope that Alistair may be alive. Just more evidence that he probably wasn't.

'There's something else though, boss. Beatriz mentioned that Alistair had a really close friend he spent a lot of time with. They'd go hiking together, spend weekends exploring. She wasn't a fan, said the man seemed very different from Alistair. Polar opposites in fact. More reserved. Serious. Beatriz said he always had this judgemental look in his eyes when he was talking to her.'

'Sounds more like the man who started emailing everyone.'

'Precisely. His name was Mark... no surname as yet—'

'Shame it's such a common name. Let's get that surname.'

'I'll keep trying. She said Mark was dual national. Half Australian and half Brazilian. I sent a photograph through of Alistair's impersonator, and she confirmed it as Mark.'

'Stellar work. So, Mark befriends Alistair, studies him, learns his life story, acquires his email and other details... then, he purchases a false passport... It's building. We need the embassy onside. How's Phil getting on with that?'

'Slow. Still waiting for them to get back. He's right next to me.'

'Hi, boss!' she heard him calling. 'I've your coffee, no sugar, ready.'

She smiled. 'Tell him to put some bloody whisky in it... and tell him to pressure the embassy. Actually, pop him on.'

'Boss?' Rice said.

'I'm not going to be at the briefing.' She explained about the meeting with the doctor.

'You think Paul is okay?'

'I don't know...' She passed through Starbeck. 'But I'll know soon. I think if it's any worse, we have to face facts... I won't be back. But let me speak to the doctor first before that's confirmed. Okay? Can I have another word with Ray, please?'

The phone switched hands again. 'Yep?'

'Something personal, Ray... can you pretend the call has ended and go elsewhere, so I can ask you for help with something?'

'Ah... okay... yeah.'

'A bit less obviously perhaps?' She rolled her eyes.

'Okay, boss. See ya!'

Bloody hell! She rolled her eyes a second time.

Barnett was back on the phone a minute later.

'I just went into an adjacent incident room, boss. How can I help?'

She filled him in on her early morning call from Tanya Reid, explaining the connection between the murdered family and Neville Fairweather's defence company, Aegis Dynamics.

'Jesus wept,' he said.

'He's not the only one weeping. I've been struggling to hold it together all morning,' Gardner said, indicating off into the hospital car park. 'Ray... okay... I need a favour. Look into Aegis in more depth. The way only you can. Employee records, government contracts, anything you can find. I want to be more informed. How far is my brother involved with this shit? But keep this under the radar, Ray, and don't neglect the Ashworth case. Maybe, look into it when you clock off? I only ask because I know you're good at it.'

Barnett assured her he'd be discreet. 'Where's Jack now?'

'I don't know... I think he might be gone. I really hope that's the case. There was something in his tone of voice last night; he also cleaned his room out and left a letter for Rose this morning saying goodbye.'

'What if he comes back?'

'Monika will let me know, and then I'll be home in a heartbeat.'

'Okay... and I'll be the first to know.'

'Yes... okay... you or Phil, whoever picks up first!'

'Promise?'

'I'm crossing my heart right now.'

'Take a photo and prove it.'

'Piss off.'

After ending the call, Gardner sat in her car for a moment, trying to collect her thoughts.

Eventually, she sighed, looked up at the hospital and opened the car door. She had a strong feeling that everything was going to change, and not for the better.

48

Jack had been at Brimham Rocks for several hours.

He'd watched, with interest, the sunrise, as it painted the rocks amber and gold.

Eventually, the light had become so intense that he'd sought refuge in the pools of darkness at the foot of the stones.

These shadows were where he belonged.

Where he would always belong.

When he heard footsteps approaching from behind, he didn't bother turning; instead, he pressed his back against the cool, rough surface of a rock. He wanted a few more moments of feeling grounded.

Everything was about to shift significantly.

'I see you're packed and ready to leave, Jack.' Neville's voice floated over in the morning air.

Jack stared down at his backpack – all of his belongings in such a small container. The most important possession was in the front pocket – that picture of him and Rose.

Those real smiles.

Jack turned as Neville approached. He wore sunglasses to

shield his eyes from the morning light. His white hair glowed. He stopped a metre away. 'It's beautiful and clear... are you not cold in the gloom?'

'I'm used to it,' Jack said.

'Why not step out into the warmth?'

'Not everyone was born for that.'

'Are you suggesting that I was?' Neville asked.

Jack shrugged. 'You always seem confident... at ease.'

'And do you always trust appearances?'

'No,' Jack said. 'But if I see it enough, then I think there may be some truth there.'

'See me a thousand times, and you'd still have me wrong.'

'Maybe.'

'You know of the story of Absalom from the Bible?'

'Is it necessary?'

'Absalom was the third son of King David. He deceived David by pretending to go to Hebron to fulfil a vow, but once there, he declared himself king and gathered a significant following, leading a full-scale rebellion against his father. Disastrous consequences.'

Jack shook his head. 'No, then. It's not necessary. And it's you who's being deceived by an appearance. I didn't betray you.'

'Are you sure?'

'Very. I don't want your throne. Also, I'm not your son.'

'You lied.'

'No. I simply omitted information.'

'Simply? You use that word simply with ease, yet you know the importance of what I deal with. Of what we deal with.'

Jack sighed and looked around. The rocks around him seemed to grow as their shadows lengthened under the continuing sunrise.

'Come out of the darkness.'

Jack obliged. Outside of the shadows, he squinted in the brightness. 'Happy?'

'I was always happy to see you, son.'

'I'd prefer it if you didn't call me that.'

'Is that all the thanks I get?' Neville replied, his voice sharp. 'For everything I did?'

'Everything you did?' Jack said. 'You've only ever pretended to free me from the shadows. Never have you had any intention of sharing the light.'

Neville pulled off his glasses. He didn't squint despite the sharpness of the sun. 'You deceived me, Jack. Why?'

'Because for once something suited me.'

Neville took a step forward. 'And you forgot your commitment to never behave in this way?'

'I didn't forget... I merely ignored. Besides, when did I ever commit to you really? Did I ever really make that decision?'

'Some commitments don't need to be aired, they simply are. Your daughter, for example. Was Rose someone you decided to commit to, or do you simply commit to her?'

'You've an answer to everything... plus, I really don't like to discuss my daughter.'

'You should be proud to discuss her.'

'I am. Just not with you. Listen... you had a child killed. I never committed to that.'

'And since when did you have such feelings, Jack?'

'Look, can we just cut to it? The man in the light talking to the man in the shadows – it was always, and will forever be, a waste of air.'

Neville's eyes narrowed, not because of the sun. His gaze was piercing. He seemed to hunch over, slightly, as if crushed by Jack's accusations. 'Don't judge me on a child, Jack. Gregory cost this country many lives. The poison within him could have been passed to his son...'

'You can't know that.'

'No. But I can't take the risk.' He paused, a fleeting shadow of something – regret, perhaps? – crossing his face. 'I accepted that the baby was spared.'

'You left him alone.'

'That isn't my fault.'

'Your words are hollow.'

'I agree. Words sometimes are. And in this instance, not just mine, either. You know you have to rectify the situation.'

Jack turned away. Silence settled. The only sounds were the whisper of the wind through the rocks and the distant call of a bird. Eventually, he said, 'I know.' Jack stepped back into the shadows and looked at Neville again.

Neville continued to stand tall and proud in the sunlight, carrying the demeanour of a man who believed himself righteous, justified in his actions no matter how questionable.

'The person you kept from us was someone I knew personally. I trusted him. In the same way I trusted you, Jack. With him, you can rectify your error.'

'The man died in 2015! So there seemed no point! I never told you because the information felt unnecessary.'

'No, Jack.' Neville's voice hardened. 'The information is necessary, because his relative isn't a baby and, as I'm sure you're pleased to know, not thirteen years old. He could have passed on this disease. And it is a disease, Jack, you must understand that. Anybody who is soulless enough to work with those who want us destroyed, is most definitely, diseased. Anyway... we digress... you know what you must do... you know how this works.'

'Are you sure about that? It always seemed quite changeable to me.'

'The only thing that's changed here is the fact that you omitted this name for personal reasons.' He paused, letting the accusation hang in the air.

Jack took a deep breath.

'And that's why I'll overlook your mistake... because I'm not what you think I am, Jack. I know, at heart, that you aren't Gregory Pendleton, poisoned and diseased. You'll rectify this, and I'll forgive you. This is no surprise, is it?'

Jack exhaled and shook his head.

'So... there's no need to talk this through any longer.'

Jack remained silent. Better to just forge on now. Get this done with.

Neville stepped forward and proffered a plastic bag. Jack reached out and took hold, but Neville didn't release it just yet. Instead, he inched closer, until he was in the shadows too. 'I never lie,' Neville said softly. 'When I told you how I feel about you, I didn't lie then. Your lie, your omission, as you call it, hurts. I want to stay loyal to you, Jack, but I need you to buy my forgiveness.' He released the bag.

Jack could feel the weight of the weapon inside.

Neville stepped back into the light. 'After, Jack, everything will return to how it was promised. Rose's and Emma's safety... your life in the states as Michael Anderson... our new lives apart from one another...'

'Everything but the ability for me to truly step out of the shadows,' Jack said, turning a glare onto him.

'You were lost in the shadows long before you knew me. I tried what I could, but you wanted to stay there.'

'Really?' Jack said. 'Still, maybe, I could have left with some dignity. Something for Rose to hang onto. Something for Emma to find just a modicum of decency in.'

'Omission was your choice. It was you that took away that

option.'

Jack looked around at the ancient rocks of Brimham, silent witnesses to bargains in shadows.

Neville pointed at the bag. 'There are two phones in there. One phone holds two numbers, simply tagged "A" and "B". A refers to one of Brandon West's burners. Phone him first from a payphone so he can give you any necessary information. After the job is done, the gun needs to find its way to the bottom of a lake. Then text me using the number linked to B, and then destroy the burner immediately. You'll find your passport and bank account activated not long after. On the second phone, there are no numbers, but there's a boarding pass...' He paused, took a deep breath and sighed. 'I can sense your bitterness, and I'm sorry it has to end this way between us.'

Jack grunted.

'I'll miss you... son.' Neville turned and walked away, his figure receding into the distance.

As the sun climbed higher in the sky, Jack remained in the shadows of the ancient rocks. The beauty of the morning continued to mock him now, the light and warmth feeling like things meant for others, not for him. He looked down at the bag in his hands and thought about using the weapon on himself.

He didn't fear death.

He didn't fear anything, really. But would his suicide offer anything but bitterness to Rose?

What he was about to do came with risks.

But if he was careful enough, if he stayed below the radar, then Emma and Rose need never know what he was responsible for.

With a deep breath, Jack shouldered his backpack and began to move, keeping to the shadows as he made his way down from the rocks.

He had a job to do. He had to address the poison and disease in Neville's tinpot world. He needed to protect the memory for his daughter as best he could before changing identity.

But, as he walked, he couldn't shake the feeling that no matter how far he went, the shadows of Brimham Rocks, and the choices he'd made, would follow him to the grave.

49

After a day of antihistamines, cooling lotions and painkillers, Paul sat with his father by Gouthwaite Reservoir.

He'd tried his best not to cry despite the agonising pain, fearing his father would cut their trip short and take him to the hospital if he showed too much distress.

'That was some bad luck, son, but you seem over the worst of it. You must have endured some pain.'

'Yes,' Paul said, his voice barely above a whisper. 'But it was nothing compared to how trapped I felt... that feeling I couldn't get away.'

Colin nodded, his eyes, as always, filled with understanding. 'I'm proud that you did... proud you got away and found me.' Paul winced as his father dabbed more lotion onto his arms.

Staring at the horizon, Paul felt himself being transported beyond the reservoir to another place where he was trapped, unable to escape.

There was a taste in his mouth he recognised – an acidic tang like the beer his father sometimes let him taste in the evenings.

'The hornets stung me, poisoned me, from the outside,' Paul said.

'What do you mean, Paul?'

'Somewhere out there, I poisoned myself from the inside.'

'I don't understand.'

'Look... I don't want to go back there,' Paul said. 'Okay?'

'Of course. We'll steer well clear of the hornets, son.'

'No, Dad. I'm not talking about the hornets. I'm talking about there.' He nodded over the reservoir. 'Do you understand?'

'Yes, son, I think I do. But I need you to remember something.'

'What do you want me to remember?'

'The rabbit...' Colin said.

A ghost of a smile crossed Paul's face. 'I remember.'

'You set it free.'

'Yes.'

'Never forget that moment of choice and control.'

'Dad, I dreamed I killed a man. It felt real.'

His father laughed. 'Don't be ridiculous, son. You're a child. You've killed no one!'

'I'm eighteen, Dad.'

'Okay, then, who did you kill?'

'I'm not sure. I only know it was someone who took everything from me. So, I took everything from him.'

Colin put the lotion down and gripped his son's shoulder. 'You need some rest. What happened has shaken you.'

'It felt real.'

'The rabbit, son. That's what's true. What's real. You letting it go. And that nest. You got away from it... you can go back.' He nodded at the reservoir. 'Over there.'

Paul sighed. 'I don't know what I want.' He closed his eyes, exhausted.

50

The walls around Gardner were pulsing.

She closed her eyes, trying to slow her breathing.

But Dr Euan Gresham's words had torn a path through her heart and her mind.

The doctor had given her a private moment to get herself together, but right now she was failing miserably, and it wasn't long before she found herself propelled back to that first connection with Riddick...

He led her down a path between rows of gravestones. Some of the stones were crumbling, and many were worn to the point of being unreadable, but that simply added to the beauty of the scene. Vines crawled up the stone walls that enclosed the resting place, while daffodils waved in the gentle breeze, and purple crocuses rested in the enduring quiet.

'I'm sorry, Emma...' Back in the pulsing room, Euan's words hit her again, and her eyes burst open. 'But the infection is too strong.'

She looked around desperately for the doctor, but of course, he'd already left.

Her breath now came in short, sharp gasps and the room started to spin as well as pulse.

Faster and faster... a dizzying carousel. She closed her eyes again.

He took her to the end of the path. The last of the gravestones. Up ahead were several rows of planted trees, all still in their infancy. Each tree came with a small golden plaque. She was too far back to read what was written on any of them.

There was a bench to their right. He sat down and shuffled along to make space for her.

She looked out over the trees, each one representing a life lived and a life lost...

Back in the spinning room, she stared down at her hands as she gripped the metal armrests of her chair. Her knuckles were white. But with all this movement, she needed to be anchored to something solid.

But was this possible? Everything was suddenly unreal. Maybe her hands would pass through the metal armrests. Maybe they weren't really there.

'He's too weak, Emma. Prepare yourself. I'm so very sorry...'

She couldn't breathe. The air felt thick, viscous, as if she were trying to inhale underwater. Drowning on dry land...

He pointed at the trees. 'Second row back, furthest right. That's Rachel. My wife. She was long-suffering as you can imagine. She was also the most beautiful woman I ever met... next to her, are my two little scoundrels, Molly and Lucy... Don't be fooled by the quiet. They were anything but...'

She looked at his profile. He was staring at the trees, smiling.

'I'm sorry,' she said.

'There's no need for you to be sorry. That's not why I brought you here...'

Flashes of colour burst behind her eyelids – vivid purples

and searing reds. The sensory overload was overwhelming. She opened her eyes, but the colours came with her. The waiting room was now an impressionistic swirl.

'I expect it will be some point today... I don't know when. Go, be with him... as long as it takes.'

She had to get to Paul. Had to be there.

But there was so much colour, disorientation and movement, and she couldn't stand...

I already know that if I want any chance at a life, I have to start letting go,' he said.

'Am I the right person for this?'

'I saw the way you looked at Bradley. I saw the way you felt *for the victim, how you championed him. I've seen the passion in your eyes, Emma, for justice.'*

'And I've seen those things in you too, Paul.'

'You made me remember what they were.'

Gardner was suddenly on her feet. Her breathing steadied.

Euan was right. If this was to be his last day on earth, then she had to be with him.

She went for the waiting-room door.

51

Paul listened to the whine of the Cortina's timing belt as his father pulled up to the kerb.

Then, after his father killed the engine, he listened to the soft tick as the metal cooled.

He looked out at their red-bricked terraced house and smiled.

He could see himself kicking the football over the narrow front garden, against the low weathered wall. Next-door's net curtains twitched as Mr Tompkins peeked outside. Above them, he spotted a new satellite dish poking awkwardly from the Victorian architecture.

'This is the end,' Colin said, putting one of his calloused hands on Paul's arm, while keeping the other on the steering wheel.

'Does it have to be?' Paul asked.

'Ha, son! Have you learned nothing? Everything ends.'

Paul nodded. 'Okay.'

'I hope our trip together gave you something.' Tears welled in Colin's eyes now.

'I'll never forget it.'

'I'm sorry I never gave you what my old man gave to me.'

'I think you always tried,' Paul said. 'In your own way.'

Colin smiled. 'You're kind, son. You always were a good boy. But don't make excuses for me.'

Paul nodded, swallowing hard.

'Maybe things would have turned out better for you if I had,' Colin said.

Through the window, Paul saw a child circling a garden on a space hopper. 'Maybe... but who knows? Could we not say that about nearly everything in life?'

They sat in silence for a moment.

Paul watched a lad streak past the Cortina on a BMX, pulling a wheelie, grinning.

He was wearing a Hypercolor T-shirt, the fabric changing hues with his exertion.

When he turned back, his father was pointing at their terrace. 'In there.'

'What's in there?'

His father shook his head. 'I don't know. The end, I think. The end in some way.'

'Sounds intriguing.' Paul reached for the door handle.

His father's hand was still on his upper arm. The grip tightened.

The gesture felt familiar to Paul. His father may have been absent most of the time, but when he was there, he could be an affectionate man. 'Please know that I really enjoyed this time with you.'

'I know.'

Colin's tears ran down his face. 'It means more than anything.'

Paul paused, his hand on the door. He smiled at his dad,

feeling his own first tear roll down his chin. He mimicked his father's strong accent, something he used to love doing. 'Aye, I know, Da!'

His father smiled through the tears.

They embraced and Paul whispered into his ear, 'I loved every second. Even when those bastards stung me.'

His father laughed.

Paul broke away and just as he was about to step out, his father reached out and stopped him again. 'Wait,' he said, reaching into the back seat. He pulled out a length of rope and, with practised ease, began to tie a knot. 'The bowline, remember?' He offered it.

'I remember.' Paul took the rope, feeling its rough texture against his palm.

He stepped out of the car and closed the door. He went to the kerb and turned back as the Cortina's engine roared to life. He waved and waited as the sound of its rattling exhaust faded into the distance, leaving behind only a faint smell of petrol.

Dandelions poked through the cracked path leading to his home. He worked the knotted rope between his hands. At the door, he let his father's gift fall to his side in one hand and, with the other, he knocked.

No answer.

He tried again.

This time the door started to open.

He smiled, expecting to see his mother.

When the door was open fully, no one stood there and, after taking two steps inside, he quickly realised that this wasn't his home.

The layout was different, and there was no wallpaper, no floral designs. Everything was cream, and the banister on the stairs sparkled white. The wood gleamed with gloss. A lemon scent filled the air, and the floor wasn't carpeted, just varnished.

Then realisation hit – he did know this place.

He'd lived here too.

Understanding struck like lightning.

He smelled her perfume and heard their laughter.

He called their names, but then everything fell silent again.

'No...'

He stumbled forward.

'Not again...'

A deep, twisting ache started in his stomach that threatened to bring him to his knees. He gripped the newel post. It kept him upright, but the pain climbed upwards.

He clutched his chest.

His heart burned.

52

After confirming with both Rice and Marsh that she would go off the grid for a while, Gardner checked her phone was on silent. She should really turn it off, but if Jack returned home, she needed to know immediately. She couldn't risk that man being anywhere near her children.

Then, Gardner went into Riddick's ICU room. Her heart was heavy with the possibility that this would be her last time here.

She scanned him, looking for changes. The extra colour in his cheeks the previous evening had clearly been false hope. Now, his face was definitely puffier. Apart from that, much remained unchanged. The hissing oxygen mask, the beeping monitors and the winding IVs all strengthened the sense of familiarity.

'I'm back, Paul.' Her voice wavered. She took a deep breath. 'For as long as you need me, I'm here.' She pulled up the chair, sat down and took his hand.

You won't face this alone.

During most visits, she'd remained quiet and stoic. She'd

spoken to him occasionally, but not at length. Finding the words had been hard, and part of her felt shy, almost embarrassed, about laying her feelings bare. But now, with the warning that the end was near and the ensuing despair and panic, such concerns melted away. The words tumbled out.

'I was thinking about when we first met... behind the castle keep? Don't act like you don't remember, either. Shit. That infernal attitude. I wanted to throw you over the side! I'd not even unpacked yet... and that was my welcome.' A smile played on her lips. 'Trust me to bring that up when you can't fight your corner... ha! Never mind, and don't worry, I saw through that bloody act of yours. Yes, you were wearing a mask, Paul, and you know it!'

She paused as a nurse wandered in. They greeted each other, and the nurse read the numbers from the monitors and made notes on the clipboard.

Gardner considered asking how he was getting on, but decided she didn't want to hear about his decline.

After the nurse left, Gardner leaned in, her voice softening. 'Behind the mask, there's compassion. I've yet to encounter so much in one person. That day, sitting next to you in that chapel... the trees... Rachel, Molly, Lucy... I think about it so often. No one knows you like I do, Paul...' She broke off, put a hand to her mouth and stifled a sob, steadying herself with a deep breath. 'The pain you endured... it's unbearable.' She shook her head. 'I hope you get the peace you want, you deserve, with them.'

She couldn't stop herself from welling up. She turned and pressed her sleeve to her eyes.

Despite what she'd said, she was desperate for him not to go.

She didn't want to say it though, in case it came across as selfish.

What she wanted to say was that she believed he should stay, that he'd so much more left to give.

To her... and to others, too.

But she didn't want to make him feel guilty about what was going to happen. Her shoulders shook with quiet sobs. She stood and moved away. She'd vowed to hide these breakdowns from him before coming into the room.

After composing herself, she returned to her seat. She had something to get off her chest. Something that had plagued her from the moment he'd first disappeared. 'An apology.' She took his hand again. 'Remember that night I came to you, after Si Meadows died... you'd lost control... you were drinking again.' She rubbed her temples. 'I stood that bastard up... Hugo Sands. Ed Sheeran concert, too! Anyway, while we were lying together on that sofa.' She paused, the memory vivid. 'You tried to tell me something... it was about Ronnie Haller, wasn't it? You tried to tell me what you'd done to your family's killer.' Her grip on his hand tightened. 'And it was me... my fault I didn't listen... I pushed you away. You were desperate...' She felt tears rolling down her face. 'You told me you were burdened. You needed me and I wasn't there. I held you at arm's length. I was afraid. Afraid of getting too close to you. I palmed you off until morning and then... well, then... you never told me. And now I can't get it out of my head. I've thought about it a lot recently. When I did find out, much later, I hit out at you for lying, took a holier-than-thou attitude, when I should've been helping you! I could have been there for you much earlier. I'm an idiot. A fool...' She leaned closer, her face inches from his, hearing his laboured breathing. 'I'm sorry, Paul. I'm so sorry. Are you here because I didn't listen then?' Her voice broke. 'Forgive me.'

Gardner sat back in her chair, still holding onto Riddick's

hand. She watched the rise and fall of his chest, willing each breath to be stronger than the last. She focused on the steady beep of the heart monitor, each sound a reminder that Riddick was still with her, still fighting.

53

O'Brien left Harry and Mathilda Banks' place, her mind buzzing with the oddities of what she'd just heard, and climbed into her car.

Gardner would be over the moon with these discoveries. Anything to cheer her up right now, to spark some kind of conversation. O'Brien pulled out her phone and saw a message notification on the screen.

She opened it and her heart sank.

> Paul has deteriorated. Euan thinks we might lose him today. I'm sorry – I won't be at work. I'll be with Paul as long as needed x

She sat there for a moment, processing the gravity of the situation. She knew Gardner would be distraught. Her sympathy was overwhelming, yet she couldn't deny feeling a twinge of irritation.

She shook her head and hit the steering wheel, admonishing herself for being so selfish.

The woman she loved was going through hell!

She took a deep breath. She would give Gardner all the space she needed. She would remain available for support if called upon. That was all she could hope for right now.

She called Rice and relayed what the Banks had told her.

'Maybe the imposter was fleeing to Canada?' Rice said.

'Yes,' she replied.

'This passport was never recovered,' Rice added. 'The house has already been searched top to bottom. They only found the British passport that had been destroyed and thrown away. Whoever killed Alistair's imposter must have taken the Canadian passport with them.'

'Do you think he was changing identities again, sir?'

'It seems the most obvious conclusion. He told them he was cancelling a trip...'

'That's right. They saw him on a flight booking page on the laptop...'

'Maybe he was checking in. Was it to Canada?'

'Harry Banks didn't get a long enough look.'

'Shame.'

'I've also spoken to another neighbour, Mrs Edith Thornton, who saw a taxi outside his home. It gave up and left about ten minutes before you arrived.' She gave the name of the taxi firm. 'Maybe the taxi was going to take him to the airport?'

'Brilliant work, Lucy. Okay, we need to get onto the taxi company and confirm an airport. If we manage to do that, we can identify any no-shows for Canadian flights after the time the taxi was sighted. I'll get Ray on this. Have you heard from the boss, Lucy?'

'Yes.'

'Are you okay?'

She fell silent for a moment. 'Yes, sir.'

'Sure?'

'Yes, really.'

'Just let me know... if... well, you know, you need some time.'

'I will, sir.'

O'Brien ended the call, surprised by Rice's unexpected show of compassion. She'd always seen him as gruff and difficult; this glimpse of empathy was a bolt from the blue.

O'Brien stopped for lunch, and then drove to HQ. When she entered the incident room, Rice immediately kicked off a briefing. She could tell by his expression he'd found more.

Looking around, she saw the team had swollen to about eight officers. Most were familiar to O'Brien, but there was a new young, female detective she didn't recognise.

Rice opened by explaining that Gardner wouldn't be leading the investigation for the foreseeable future, and he would be the SIO with Barnett as his assistant. He didn't explain why Gardner was off the case; those that knew her well already understood.

Rice briefed them on O'Brien's earlier discoveries, offering her small nods of gratitude that made her feel uncomfortable.

She felt extremely sensitive and any attention, even positive, was jarring.

'DS Barnett spoke to the taxi company. Can you fill us in on where that took you?'

'The driver was waiting to take him to Leeds Bradford Airport,' Barnett said. 'When he didn't show, the driver left. I've cross-referenced all the Canadian flights that day after that time. We have two. I've spoken to both airlines. Four people didn't turn up for their scheduled flights.'

'I requested passport images from the Home Office for all four,' Barnett continued.

Meanwhile, Rice clicked a remote to bring up an image on the large screen at the front of the incident room.

A passport photo of Alistair's impersonator appeared before them.

'This is the current Canadian passport photo for a man named Landon Thambley... issued a month back.' He clicked again, and a different face appeared. 'And this is the older passport image Landon Thambley used to get into the UK in 2020. Now, we're all aware that appearance can change in five years, but I think we can all agree, that for this to be the same person, they'd have to have had extensive, groundbreaking facial reconstruction surgery.'

'Or regenerate like Dr Who,' Suggs added.

'So, the logical conclusion is,' Rice continued, 'whoever stole Alistair's identity has now stolen Landon Thambley's.'

'But in this day and age,' O'Brien said, shaking her head, 'everything is computerised. How does someone apply for a new passport with a vastly different picture from their previous one? I can imagine all sorts of alarms going off in the digital world.'

'I'm with you, Lucy, but our eyes don't deceive us.'

Barnett added, 'Look, as I said before, it remains possible. With enough money, or contacts, this still happens. The Home Office confirms it. Either someone hacks the system, or pays someone working on the inside. As we don't know who our impersonator is yet, we can't rule out either.'

Rice jumped in. 'If he doesn't turn out to be Neo from *The*

Matrix, then I'm thinking a lot of money has changed hands here. Whoever this dead bastard is, he's not short of a bob... not if he can keep funding passports of this quality.'

'Can we not trigger facial recognition with his image?' O'Brien asked. 'We could find out how many identities he's had... trace back to the original.'

'I've made the request,' Rice said. 'But pulling information across the globe isn't quick. Different levels of approval and whatnot. However, we've made another step. Landon Thambley, who didn't show last night for his flight, resided in Leeds – or at least he did. He was in a relationship with Nathalie Blake, who he met while she was holidaying in Canada. I spoke to her before this briefing. She split from him in 2022 after he developed an alcohol dependency and started using drugs. She went looking for him in early 2023. When she finally found him, she barely recognised him and he didn't respond to her offers of help. Given what we know about this man, the death of Imogen, the disappearance of Alistair, we can't help but fear the worst.'

O'Brien nodded in agreement. It looked bleak for Landon.

'However, Ray spoke to the council a few minutes back, and... some déjà vu coming up for some of you... Bright Day.'

Several colleagues exchanged knowing glances. Bright Day had formed a large part of their last investigation. The facility was a state-of-the-art homeless shelter and rehabilitation centre, funded by KYLO Ltd. It had replaced the controversial Helping Hands shelter, which had been embroiled in scandals involving deaths and mistreatment of residents. Now, Bright Day offered comprehensive support services, including counselling, job training and healthcare, aiming to provide both temporary refuge and long-term solutions for homelessness. All resident records were kept in a centralised system with the council.

'Landon stayed there only a few days ago,' Ray said.

O'Brien felt her pulse race.

The investigation suddenly felt like it was moving at pace.

Gardner would be pleased, though it was unfortunate she had to miss out after raising those initial suspicions.

'Lucy and I'll head down there and see what's what,' Rice announced. 'Ray will be here, on hand, for the Brazilian embassy, who haven't been in any rush to get back to us.'

'I suspect it should be any year now,' Barnett said.

'Everyone else grab their tasks from the board. And listen everyone, we know this bastard's previous incarnation, and we know his subsequent incarnation. It's only a matter of time before we have him. He's dead... yes... and we can't look him in the eye, but it seems he's left a trail of carnage behind him, and if we can bring peace to a few by sullying the dickhead's memory, then we'll have to settle for that.'

Rice was relishing his temporary leadership role.

Outside, she said to him, 'You seem to be coming into your own, sir.'

He looked at her and narrowed his eyes. 'You didn't take it the wrong way earlier, did you?'

'What?'

'Me asking if you were okay?'

'No.' His question caught O'Brien off guard. 'Why do you ask?'

'Good. I just know how sensitive folk get about that these days, especially you young 'uns...'

She couldn't resist a laugh at this.

His cheeks reddened. 'Look, I know about you and Emma—'

'Maybe we should leave it there...'

He held up his palm and nodded. 'Yep. I agree. Just so you know that I know. So, there it is. Out there. Just want to make sure you feel okay.'

'There's nothing serious between us, sir.'

At least that's how it seemed to her now, she thought bitterly.

'Really?' Rice replied. 'Just that she never shuts up about you.' He turned away. 'Come on.'

O'Brien felt tears welling up in her eyes, but she blinked them back furiously.

55

Jack used a payphone to make the one required call to Brandon West before moving on the target.

The information hadn't been detailed, but it had been useful.

There was no alarm on the target's address, which would make access easier.

The property sat far from town – a quiet, affluent area with sprawling gardens and manicured hedges.

Hood up to hide his face from door cameras, Jack strolled down the residential street. His keen eyes scanned the home, noting every detail. No car in the driveway. Curtains open, but no signs of life within.

Brandon had already confirmed the house was empty. His access to intelligence data through Neville's national security connections had confirmed the target was at work.

Jack took a deep breath, feeling the gun shift against his lower back beneath his jacket. The silencer was cold and metallic.

Better to enter now and wait, he thought.

Head down to avoid cameras that would later be scrutinised, he veered off the pavement, slipping between two neighbouring properties. The narrow passage led him to the rear of the houses, where privacy fences separated the back gardens. Jack paused, listening intently for any activity.

Only a distant lawnmower broke the silence.

He ran his gloved hand over a weathered fence. Spotting an empty recycling box, he flipped it over. He pulled on his balaclava before stepping onto the box and hoisting himself over the fence.

Jack picked his way through the garden to the patio doors – locked from the inside.

Frustrating, but not unexpected.

Jack circled around the side of the house, staying low and close to the walls. He checked each window. Most were securely latched, offering no easy entry.

His luck changed on the other side.

A small window, slightly ajar, just above head height.

To his right sat a large plastic container with a lid, filled with cycling equipment.

Perfect.

He pushed it beneath the window.

The container creaked ominously as he stepped onto it, but it held his weight.

Now level with the window, Jack examined it closely. The gap was barely an inch wide. He pressed his gloved fingers against the glass, applying pressure. The window resisted at first, then slowly began to give way.

Though narrow, the opening would suffice.

Balancing precariously on the container, Jack gripped the windowsill and pulled himself up, the rough edge scraping against his gloves as he hauled himself higher.

A sudden, sharp pain shot through his lower arm as he squeezed through the opening. The unexpected jolt threw him off balance, and he tumbled through, landing heavily on the floor inside.

He cursed – so much for a silent entry – and he could already sense that his arm was bleeding.

He lay still for a moment, listening intently for any sound that might indicate Brandon had been wrong, that the target was here... and that his entry had been detected.

Satisfied by the silence, he pushed himself to his feet. He was in a bathroom. Looking down at his throbbing arm, he saw blood seeping through his torn sleeve.

Standing on tiptoes, he spotted the culprit – a nail beside the windowsill holding a wooden plaque that read 'I do some of my best thinking in here'. He'd caught it on the way in.

A few drops of blood stained the floor below.

Moving quickly, he found a bottle of bleach and using some tissue, cleaned the blood from the floor, and sterilised the nail for good measure.

He took some toilet roll and pressed it against the wound to stem the bleeding. The white tissue quickly turned crimson. After a few minutes, he checked the injury. The bleeding had nearly stopped, but he applied pressure for another minute before flushing the evidence.

He reached behind his back, drawing the gun and attaching the silencer with practised movements. Despite Brandon's intelligence, it was better to be cautious.

Jack moved to the door, pressing his ear close without touching it. Silence. Slowly, he turned the handle, easing the door open just enough to peer into the hallway beyond.

Empty.

He slipped out of the bathroom, gun held low but ready.

Though years had passed since he'd last held a weapon, the familiar weight felt natural in his hands. The hallway led to a kitchen. He moved silently, each careful step drawing on years of experience. At the kitchen doorway, he paused again, listening. The quiet hum of the refrigerator was the only sound.

Moving through to a spacious lounge, Jack's eyes scanned every detail.

Photographs lined the mantelpiece.

He sighed and suddenly felt quite hot.

Unconcerned about leaving hair evidence with his closely shaved head and trimmed brows, he pulled off the balaclava.

He sighed a second time, the gun growing heavy in his hand.

Today would hurt Emma.

Would break her heart.

He took a deep breath and thought of Rose, of the clean life he wanted for her – one untouched by the shadows that had defined his own existence.

For that, he had to fix things with Neville. There was no choice.

Jack's grip tightened on the gun.

Focus, he told himself. One final task and your freedom is secured. Rose stays safe.

But he had to be meticulous, ensuring nothing linked this murder back to him.

If Emma ever discovered the truth that he'd done this, it wouldn't just devastate her – it would destroy her. And Rose would have to live knowing her father was truly monstrous.

He looked at one photograph of the target, much younger and smiling beside his late mother. Their resemblance was striking.

He took a deep breath.

Time to dig in... and wait.

The house creaked and settled around him, broken only by the steady tick of a wall clock marking the seconds until he would take the detective's life.

56

Cinnamon and apples. Paul savoured that smell. He opened his eyes and smiled at Rachel. His wife. 'Mummy's apple pie is the best.'

She leaned over and kissed him, gently, on the lips. The tenderness of her touch felt like a distant memory.

The sensation took his breath away.

'My pie is the only thing that brings you home early from work,' Rachel said.

He rubbed his paunch. 'I think your plan is working too well...'

'Daddy, look what I made!' Molly burst into the kitchen, something colourful in her hands.

'What've you got there?'

Molly thrust a paper creation at him. 'A fortune teller! Lucy showed me how to make one.'

Paul took it and turned it over in his hands. 'What's in store for Daddy then?' He handed it back.

Lucy came in and sat opposite him at the kitchen table, watching eagerly.

'Pick a colour, Daddy,' Molly instructed.

'Blue.'

Molly giggled as she worked the paper. 'Now a picture?'

'It's supposed to be numbers,' Lucy said. 'I told you numbers.'

'I drew pictures,' Molly said. 'So, you can choose a rope... a raft... a bunny rabbit... a hornet... a rock face... and...'

Paul suddenly felt unsteady. 'Those pictures... why those pictures?'

Lucy laughed. 'From your story, stupid!'

'Yes,' Molly said. 'The one last night.'

A wave of disorientation washed over him. He felt, briefly, as if he wasn't really there. He stared hard at the images, desperately trying to ground himself. 'The pictures are so clear and detailed.'

Rachel's hand settled on Paul's shoulder. 'Did you tell them about your camping stories... with your father?'

He looked up at her, confused. Had he ever been camping with his father?

'Hurry up and pick one, Daddy,' Molly insisted.

Paul looked back at the images. 'Okay... rock?'

'Rock is four letters.' She manipulated the paper, counting to four. She opened the flap and read: 'Your heart stays with us... forever!' Molly announced triumphantly.

Paul felt his chest tighten with love when he saw his little ones so animated. 'I could have told you that without the fortune teller.' He hugged Molly close to him and kissed her on the head. Simultaneously, he reached over the table and took Lucy's hand.

Rachel removed her hand from Paul's shoulder. 'The future has been set then...'

'Yes, by our children, it seems...' Paul said.

'Was there anything about the pie in the future?' Rachel asked.

'Yes,' Lucy said. 'A massive piece with custard and another slice if required.'

Paul and Rachel laughed.

'Okay,' Rachel said. 'We best honour the fortune tellers then!'

While Rachel was cutting the pie, Paul stood and walked over to her. He wrapped his arms around her waist and breathed in the scent of her hair.

'That's disgusting!' Molly said.

Lucy pretended to throw up.

'Sometimes it all feels too good to be true, you know?'

'Did you get a pay rise or something?' Rachel said. 'You don't often come back from work glowing like this!'

'Sorry...'

'No need to apologise.'

He turned her around. 'No, I do... I won't ever take this for granted.'

'Glad to hear it. I don't either.'

They kissed.

'This is seriously disgusting,' Molly added.

A thud sounded from upstairs.

Paul looked up at the ceiling. 'Someone left the window open again?'

'Not me,' Molly said.

'Maybe it was Mr Snuggles?' Lucy said.

'Well, if it is Mr Snuggles, he's in trouble,' Paul said, heading out of the kitchen, especially if he's broken something.

Paul smiled as he headed up the stairs. Family pictures adorned the walls, and he reached out to touch them, as he so often did when climbing up.

Upstairs, he pushed open Molly's door. The window was closed. Nothing had fallen.

He moved along to Lucy's door and smiled to himself when

he thought of her stuffed bear, Mr Snuggles. He'd bring him downstairs and pretend to scold him – that would make them laugh. He touched the doorknob and a cold sensation spread over his body.

He yanked his hand back.

Something wasn't right.

He felt strangely disconnected tonight.

Not himself.

He sighed, opened the door and saw that the window was wide open.

Bloody hell, Lucy...

He moved into the room, noticing that the draught was only tepid. Yet inexplicable goosebumps rose on his arms. He looked down and saw what had fallen on the floor. Bending down, he picked it up.

It was a picture of him and his parents, taken the day he became a police officer. They looked proud.

Paul smiled, wondering how the picture had ended up in his daughter's room – he hadn't seen it for a long time. Maybe Rachel had taken it out of storage.

He closed the window and replaced the picture.

Remembering the guilty Mr Snuggles, he turned to grab him from Lucy's bed.

Someone was sitting there.

Her eyes were filled with tears.

She seemed familiar...

Yet even though he recognised her, he felt, at the same time, that he didn't know who she was.

Right now, he could be sure of only one thing: she was deeply sad.

So, he asked her why.

57

Rice drove down a street of boarded-up shops and graffiti-covered walls until he reached the Bright Day homeless shelter. The gleaming structure stood in stark contrast to its dilapidated surroundings, a beacon of hope amidst urban decay.

After parking, Rice glanced at O'Brien, and immediately regretted his decision to bring her along. She was as far from fine as she could be.

Her eyes were red-rimmed, and she'd barely spoken on the journey down. She kept checking her phone.

'Any news?'

O'Brien blinked, as if coming out of a daze. 'No...'

'You can wait here if—'

'I'm fine, sir.'

'Okay...' He reached for the door handle but paused before opening it. 'Just know that whatever happens, Emma will get through this. That lass is rock solid.'

O'Brien nodded.

'But I guess it's hard not to worry. I care about her too, you know. Between you and me, the boss gave me a chance when few ever have.'

O'Brien looked at him.

He nodded. 'Yes... she's one of the few who doesn't tell me I'm a dickhead...' He smiled. 'At least, one of the few who doesn't actually think I'm a dickhead.'

O'Brien smiled and reached for the door handle.

When they reached Bright Day reception, Rice recognised the security guard who approached to search them. 'Don't tell me I'm going to get frisked again.'

The guard looked confused.

'Last time you patted me down. You left no stone unturned, for want of a better expression. Maybe you can spare the theatrics?'

The guard shook his head. 'Sorry, procedure... plus, I don't recognise you.'

Rice sighed. 'And I thought we'd grown close...' He held up his arms for the search. 'I'm rather hurt.'

The security guard shifted uncomfortably.

Miranda Reikh, the facility manager, appeared at the door. 'No need, James. I remember DI Rice.'

Rice smiled and dropped his arms. 'See, James? I told you I was a friendly face.'

He could tell from Miranda's expression that she probably disagreed. He promised himself he'd be less abrasive this time – Gardner would want that. And he felt unusually warm towards his absent boss at the moment.

'Thanks for agreeing to speak to us,' Rice said. 'This is DC Lucy O'Brien.'

Miranda nodded. 'Always happy to help. As we were last time.'

Rice glanced behind him at O'Brien, making sure only she could see him roll his eyes.

As they made their way through the facility, Rice watched O'Brien look around, impressed. He'd felt the same way during his last visit. The dining area was bustling with activity, residents chatting over steaming plates of food. It felt like stepping from one dimension into another.

'It's quite something,' O'Brien murmured, her eyes scanning the room.

Rice nodded, his expression guarded. 'Aye, that it is.'

As they passed, residents turned to stare, curiosity and wariness mingling in their gazes. The atmosphere shifted subtly, an undercurrent of tension rippling through the room.

Miranda's office combined professional efficiency with personal touches. Framed awards lined the walls, interspersed with colourful artwork – likely created by Bright Day residents. Through the large window behind her desk, the urban decay served as a constant reminder of the world they were trying to improve.

Not wanting to waste time, Rice pulled out a photograph of Landon Thambley and put it on the table. 'Do you recall this man staying here recently? His name's—'

'Landon,' she said, studying the photograph. 'Thambley.'

'When did you last see him?'

'Not for a couple of weeks.'

'I see, but I take it he was quite regular?'

'Very... yes...' Her expression saddened. 'A kind soul.' She sighed and looked up. 'I won't lie, we're quite worried about him.'

Rice nodded.

Miranda looked at O'Brien. Rice followed her gaze. Whether it was concern for Gardner or Thambley's likely fate, O'Brien's gloomy expression was stark.

Miranda sighed. 'Something happened to him, then.'

Rice took a deep breath, drawing her attention back to him. 'Truth is, we don't know. We were hoping you could tell us more... places he used to go, outside of here? Or failing that, who he was spending time with?'

'I'm not too sure where he'd get to outside of Bright Day, but he did get rather close with another long-term regular. His name is Mathis Roux. As you probably know, Landon was French Canadian. Mathis was French, so they hit it off – spoke French most of the time.' She lowered her gaze. 'And I speak French too.' She shook her head. 'I often chatted to them both.'

Mathis Roux. Could he be Alistair's impersonator? Rice reached into his pocket for his phone to show her the picture of the dead man.

'Mathis is here today, actually...'

Rice froze, phone in hand. He pointed downwards. 'Here?'

'Yes, I saw him as we walked in. Would you like to speak to him? He thinks himself quite the gentleman. Very kindly spoken.'

'That would be great,' Rice said. 'Now, if possible.'

He caught O'Brien's eye. An interesting development. Maybe Mathis could shed some light on what had happened.

Miranda spoke into her walkie-talkie. 'Brad...'

After he responded, she requested he bring Mathis through to the office to speak to the police.

She put the walkie-talkie down. 'Won't be a minute.'

Rice showed her the passport photo of the dead impersonator on his phone. 'Do you know this man?'

Miranda nodded, and Rice felt his heart rate quicken. 'Who is he?'

'Thomas... let me think...' She clicked her tongue. 'Baker.'

Rice felt a surge of adrenaline.

'He's been here several times over the last four or so months. And he was close to Landon and Mathis. In fact...' She turned to the computer and began typing.

Rice looked at O'Brien. Her gloomy expression had lifted, her eyebrows raised. Rice wondered if she could see the sweat breaking out on his forehead.

'He was only here two weeks ago. The last time he checked in. He's not been back since.'

'And Landon,' Rice asked. 'When was he last here?'

She typed, her eyes widening before fixing Rice with a stare.

'That was the last time you saw him too, wasn't it, Miranda?'

She nodded.

Her walkie-talkie burst into life, crackling with loud voices. One broke through. 'We've a situation...'

It wasn't Brad.

'Sam?' Miranda asked.

'Mathis has gone haywire. He hit Brad with a tray, and now has a needle to his neck.'

'A needle! A bloody needle? How? How the hell did he get a needle in here?'

Rice shook his head. Apparently that doorman James wasn't so thorough with procedure unless it came to irritating police officers – rather stupid...

'I don't know... shit... he's at the door through to reception.'

Rice bolted into action, out the office door.

He could hear Miranda shouting into the walkie-talkie behind him. 'Don't let him out!'

Rice saw O'Brien running alongside him down the corridor.

What had happened to the gentlemanly Mathis with his kind manner?

A desperate, dangerous man could mean only one thing – he was either involved or knew what had happened.

Together, they rounded the corner into chaos and shouting. The calm facade of Bright Day had shattered like an egg, its chaotic contents spilling everywhere.

58

Paul sat beside the familiar woman on Lucy's bed.

At first he'd felt confused, but now he felt warmed by her presence.

She handed him Mr Snuggles, Lucy's well-loved teddy.

He stroked the soft golden-brown fur, worn thin in places from years of cuddling, and regarded the bear's mismatched eyes, one sitting slightly lower than the other, giving him an endearingly lopsided expression. He tugged at the frayed red ribbon tied around the bear's neck, testing it. The material held.

'His stuffing has settled,' Paul said. 'He's a lumpy thing, but Lucy says it makes him all the more huggable.'

He noticed the familiar woman was crying now.

'Are you okay?'

He waited for a reply, but none came.

It was as though she couldn't hear him.

Maybe I'm imagining her, he thought. Or maybe – and this thought made his blood run colder – it's me that's not really here?

He looked down at Mr Snuggles, considering whether to take

him back down to Lucy as planned, but instead, handed him back to the woman.

She looked like she needed him more than Lucy did right now.

He stood up and started to turn.

'How many times?'

He froze.

'How many times must I lose you?'

He turned back and looked down at her, pondering the strange question. He realised she wasn't addressing him; she was talking directly to Mr Snuggles.

He shook his head, again wondering if one of them wasn't really here. 'Are you here?' he asked.

She nodded. 'I'm here.' She stroked Mr Snuggles's arm. 'With you.'

That sense of familiarity grew stronger.

'I know you, don't I? It's me who wants you here, who brought you here... yet I can't remember who you are... not exactly. I have to leave now... I have to go back to them.'

When she didn't respond, he turned to the door.

As he stepped into the hallway, he remembered.

Emma.

The air rushed out of him like a punch to the gut.

Emma.

He took a deep breath, steadied himself and swung back, her name on his lips.

Emma.

He looked into the room.

59

'Emma.'

Her eyes flew open, and she sucked in a deep breath, angry at herself for almost nodding off. She was desperate to know if he'd spoken.

Riddick's eyes remained closed.

She leaned closer to his puffy face. The hiss of oxygen intensified.

Had she imagined it?

'Emma.'

Though little more than a croak, that his voice could be heard through his oxygen mask seemed significant.

She leaned forward, clutching his arm. 'Paul? I'm here. Can you hear me?'

She waited.

Nothing.

'Paul... please?'

She held onto hope for as long as she could, but then the moment – which had felt like she was bursting through the surface of water, gasping for oxygen after drowning for so long – was suddenly gone.

Had that been his final, desperate attempt to return?

If he couldn't break through now, was that it? Was this the sign that he was truly gone?

Forever?

She hunched over and cried.

60

After ending the call to the Brazilian embassy, Barnett's fingers hovered over the keyboard. His next move was clear, but he felt numb.

The embassy had confirmed that the passport used by Alistair Ashworth for his return flight from Rio to Manchester on 15 April 2023 had been different from the one he'd arrived with on the 15 May 2022. The images were of two completely different men. Barnett had confirmed that the person flying in had been the real Alistair, whereas the one flying out certainly hadn't been.

They'd indicated they'd open an investigation into Alistair's disappearance.

Barnett had expected this first confirmation, but what followed had left him cold.

He'd queried information about 'Mark' whom Alistair's former girlfriend Beatriz Santos had mentioned – the man Alistair had been spending so much time with. The embassy did a quick check on investigations conducted in Rio around the time of Alistair's disappearance.

A man called Mark Almeida had vanished in April 2023. The

case was initially investigated but quickly closed when it was determined that Mark had likely taken his own life. He'd been suffering from severe depression, having lost his wife, Camilla, to a heart attack just a week earlier. The loss had left him broken and distraught.

The similarities to Imogen Ashworth's death sent Barnett's head spinning. Mark was a Brazilian national who'd been living in Australia, so Barnett had requested the image from his passport when he'd returned to Brazil. Mark had arrived in Rio on 6 November 2021. By now, it wasn't really a shock when Barnett learned that the passport picture of Mark Almeida matched the man who'd flown to Manchester as Alistair.

If Barnett was right about Alistair being dead, then Mark Almeida was likely dead too.

How far back did this trail of identity fraud extend?

And how many women had been poisoned along the way?

There was only one way to answer these questions.

He'd have to continue following the trail backwards.

61

With O'Brien beside him, Rice moved quickly towards the commotion by the door to reception, his ID thrust out, so no one would be stupid enough to get in his way.

A wild-eyed man, in clean blue scrubs, had his back to the exit, his arm around the throat of a man far larger than him. 'Open the door!' His French accent was strong. 'Now!'

Once Rice was close enough to confirm there was a syringe held against Brad's neck, he shouted, 'Police! Mathis, put your weapon down.'

The man, his greasy hair hanging to shoulder length, shook his head. 'I'll stick it in his neck. It's been in my arm, already... do you want to make him sick?'

Brad was white as a sheet. 'Please... he's serious... I can feel it...'

'See?' Mathis said.

The door buzzed.

Bloody hell!

Mathis slipped backwards through the door, still holding Brad.

Rice pounced, shoving his way through the small crowd to follow.

Brad was lying in the centre of reception, holding his neck.

The automatic doors to Bright Day were just closing.

'You okay?' Rice asked.

'Yes... it didn't break the skin...' Brad kept touching his neck and checking his hand. 'I don't think.'

Rice had no time to respond. He was already through the half-open doors again. Looking right, he spotted Mathis across the road, sprinting.

'Mathis!'

The man looked over his shoulder, shouted something in French, and continued running.

Right then, old man, Rice thought, this is when you wish you'd taken the boss's advice about jogging to help with those anger issues.

As he broke into a sprint, he glanced behind him.

O'Brien was emerging from Bright Day.

Being younger and fitter than him, she'd probably catch up soon. Looking back, he saw that Mathis had gained even more distance.

Bloody hell.

Though he was slender and taller than Rice – and looked the favourite – the man shouldn't be outrunning him so easily. He was homeless; his health and diet surely couldn't be that good...

Then again, were Rice's any better?

Mathis passed some boarded-up shops before taking a swift left and vanishing from view.

Gasping, Rice pushed himself harder as he approached the ginnel's opening.

He could see Mathis ahead again, running God knows where.

The man would know these streets – Rice was at a clear disadvantage.

As Rice pounded down the ginnel, his knees ached. He winced. This reminded him why he hadn't taken up the running advice.

Bursting from the ginnel, sucking air, trying not to succumb to exhaustion, he saw Mathis dash across a road. He checked for traffic and followed.

'Sir!' O'Brien's voice came from close behind him now.

His quarry took another immediate left into a second ginnel.

When Rice entered this one, still panting heavily, he found it overgrown with shrubbery and badly lit. A bloody nightmare. And now he couldn't see Mathis.

Where had he gone?

He slowed, hearing the faint sound of flowing water. O'Brien reached his side.

He leaned against the wall, catching his breath, and pointed to a break in the ginnel where steps led downwards. 'Down there... the canal...'

'Let me,' O'Brien said.

'No...' Rice said. 'He's got that needle...'

'It's okay.'

'No,' he insisted, starting to run again. 'Have you called backup?'

'Yes,' she said, jogging alongside him.

'And you still caught... me up... bloody... hell.' He turned left and descended the steps at pace ahead of his colleague.

The steps wound down quite a way, and he was surprised he kept his footing at such speed – he felt a small sense of accomplishment when he burst out beside the canal.

Perhaps there was life in this old dog yet?

Though the burning in his lungs suggested otherwise.

He heard a thump behind him and spun around.

O'Brien had fallen on the final step, clutching her ankle.

'Are you... okay...?'

'Yes, go!'

He carried on. The murky water flowed languidly between steep concrete banks, reflecting the dull grey sky above. Cars rumbled across overhead bridges, their roads cutting through the urban landscape like arteries.

Ahead, an old stone bridge arched over the canal. Rice spotted Mathis fleeing towards it, his ragged figure disappearing into the shadows beneath.

He looked behind and saw O'Brien struggling to her feet.

With a groan, Rice forced himself into one final sprint. His legs felt like lead, each step sending shockwaves through his aching joints. As he reached the bridge, he stumbled to a stop, doubling over, gasping for air. His heart pounded furiously in his chest. For a terrifying moment, he wondered if he was about to have a heart attack right there on the towpath.

Then Mathis emerged from the shadows, brandishing the needle. Rice straightened up, forcing himself into a defensive stance despite his exhaustion. When Mathis lunged forward, Rice caught his wrists, twisting them to disarm him.

But Rice's strength was spent.

Mathis pushed back with surprising force, and Rice felt himself losing ground. His feet slipped on the damp stones of the towpath.

'Sir!' O'Brien's voice rang out as she finally caught up after her fall. She reached out to grab Mathis—

But it was too late. With a final shove, Mathis sent Rice stumbling backwards. His arms windmilled as he teetered on the edge of the canal. For a sickening moment, he hung suspended between land and water.

Then he was falling.

The shock of the cold water drove the remaining air from his lungs. He flailed, trying to right himself, but the weight of his clothes dragged him down. Water rushed up his nose, burning his sinuses. Panic set in as he struggled to find the surface, the murky canal closing over his head.

62

When Barnett knocked on Marsh's door and entered, she looked at him over her spectacles.

'Ma'am... sorry... it's important.'

'I guessed that by how quickly you entered. People usually wait until I give the all-clear. I hope it's going to be worth the sudden surge of irritation.'

'Yes, ma'am, it is...' He gulped. 'Because I know who Alistair's imposter is.'

At that, she pulled off her spectacles. 'In that case, sit down.'

He settled into the chair opposite her desk. 'I've spoken to the Brazilian embassy, the Australian embassy, and the US embassy... and... we've both serial identity theft and serial murder.' He took a deep breath, composed himself, and took out his notebook, opening it to a diagram.

'What's that?' Marsh slipped her spectacles back on.

'A timeline.'

'I know what it is... what's it for?'

'I work visually. Plus, it makes it easier to explain.' He tapped the name at the top. 'Our imposter is Rowan Sinclair, from Oregon. You want to go up or down?'

Her raised eyebrow suggested she couldn't give a shit, as long as he got on with it.

Moving his finger to the bottom of the diagram, Barnett explained, 'So Rowan Sinclair was posing as Alistair Ashworth when he married Imogen, and eventually killed her. He'd already arranged Landon Thambley's identity for his next move to Canada – which was interrupted, fatally, before coming to fruition. If no one had stopped him, Alistair Ashworth would have simply disappeared, likely presumed a suicide.'

Marsh nodded. 'So, who killed him?'

'That piece is still missing...'

'Okay,' Marsh said, nodding.

Continuing up the flowchart, Barnett said, 'Working backwards: Rowan was in Rio de Janeiro from November 2021 to April 2023, posing as Mark Almeida. There, he befriended the real Alistair Ashworth at Samba Nights before taking his identity. While living as Almeida, his wife Camilla died of a heart attack, just like Imogen. When he went missing, the police assumed Mark had killed himself from grief.'

Marsh's eyes widened. 'Shit... I see... why this pattern of killing wives?'

'I've a theory about that. But first, let me show you how he became Mark Almeida. That identity was stolen in Sydney, where the real Mark worked between 2018 and 2021. Mark must have come across someone called Donald Mitchell, Rowan's previous stolen identity. At this point, Rowan, as Donald, was married to a woman called Sarah Hope. This timeline all matches. When Sarah also died of a heart attack in November 2021, Donald went missing, presumably through suicide, while Rowan, now posing as Mark, set off to Rio.'

'This is unbelievable,' Marsh said, rubbing her temples. 'And I'm struggling to get my head around it all.'

'I know, but the evidence fits, ma'am. The embassy has provided passport records – this one man, Rowan Sinclair, is moving through identities.'

'So when did he become Donald Mitchell?'

'Back in his home country. America.'

Marsh sighed. 'This must be pathological.'

'Exactly. It's almost a routine. Serial identity theft combined with serial murder. The original Donald Mitchell was a wealthy businessman from Perth. He was estranged from his family due to being homosexual. He went to New York in 2016, and at some point, he must have crossed paths with Rowan. Mitchell's money likely helped fund Rowan's subsequent identity thefts. The passport records show "Donald Mitchell" returning to Australia in 2019 – but as I said before, the photo on the passport was Rowan Sinclair.'

'But officially, Rowan Sinclair has never left America? So, how do you know it is Rowan Sinclair?'

'Because the USA embassy ran his image and found a log of his actual passport. No one has ever reported him missing, despite him being off the grid since 2019. I've located his mother, Patty Sinclair, and I'm going to contact her.'

'It's difficult to take in,' Marsh said. 'How does someone get away with such an elaborate scheme?'

Barnett shrugged. 'Care and detail. Meticulous planning.'

'Has he done this for pleasure?'

Barnett considered this. 'Maybe. He obviously felt compelled.'

'Four identities!'

Barnett nodded. 'Yes... five if you count his own. Rowan

Sinclair to Donald Mitchell, then to Mark Almeida, to Alistair Ashworth, and, finally, Landon Thambley.'

'And you're certain about this evidence trail? It seems complex.'

'The evidence will align perfectly once I've put the pieces together.'

'The four men must be dead, or the cat would be out of the bag.'

'Yes... three dead women, and four dead men.'

'And the dickhead will never see justice.'

'At least we might find those who helped with the forgeries... though that's outside our jurisdiction.'

'What drives that need to keep changing identity? That compulsion to erase everything that went before?' Marsh was looking away, contemplating now. 'There must be something in his past.'

'That's where Patty Sinclair might help. I've done some background. She's an alcoholic widow, just out of rehab for the fifth time. When Rowan's father died in Oregon, he left Rowan a substantial inheritance – bypassing his wife completely. That money, combined with what he took from Donald Mitchell, could have funded this whole dark journey.'

'Yes, and with crypto, money is far easier to move these days.'

Barnett nodded in agreement.

'This is incredible work, Ray. Incredible.'

'I just followed the trail.'

She grinned. 'With your timeline? Bottom to top!'

'It works top to bottom too!'

She laughed.

He returned her grin. 'I should speak to Patty.'

'I'm amazed, Ray, well done... any news from the others on who has actually killed our serial killer?'

'No,' Barnett replied, checking his phone again. 'I still can't reach Rice or O'Brien.'

63

Mathis folded to the ground, sodden and shivering. His long hair clung to his face in wet strands, water dripping from his nose. The once-clean blue scrubs provided by Bright Day now hung dark and heavy on his thin frame.

Rice, meanwhile, was struggling to get his breath back, down on his knees, spluttering.

When he felt steadier, he glanced up at O'Brien, who was also drenched after diving in and pulling them both from the canal. 'This is a new bloody suit.'

'Well... you were pretty close to being buried in it.'

He laughed, coughed and spat out canal water. 'Thank you... both of you.' He looked up at the sodden man in his twenties beside O'Brien. The stranger had appeared out of nowhere to help O'Brien. He shifted from foot to foot against the chill, his high-tech running shoes squelching, the compression shirt clinging to his well-defined torso.

The runner nodded. 'Good training for my triathlon, though it isn't the warmest day for a swim... You should get yourself checked over, especially if you breathed in some of that water.'

Rice nodded. 'Good idea.' *Though I'll be doing no such thing*, he thought, rising to his feet. Swimming lessons, however, might be worth looking into...

The runner glanced at O'Brien. 'I could do with warming up.'

O'Brien nodded, spotting her waterlogged notebook floating in the canal. She sighed, then reached for the phone she'd tossed on the ground before diving in. 'Could I just take your name and number?'

He grinned.

'For official purposes,' she clarified.

His grin didn't fall.

Bloody hell, Rice thought. *You're definitely not her type.*

The runner gave his details and jogged away. Rice watched him go, not bothering with another thank you.

Looking down at Mathis, Rice saw the man had managed to sit up, hugging his knees. Mathis's eyes darted nervously between Rice and O'Brien, then down to the discarded needle on the towpath.

'Why'd you run?' Rice asked, his voice rough from the canal water. He coughed again, grimacing at the taste.

Mathis looked up, his eyes full of fear and something else – a deep, consuming sadness.

'Why?' Rice demanded, in no mood for games.

Mathis shook his head. It was impossible to tell if he was crying.

'What happened with Alistair Ashworth?' O'Brien asked, stepping forward. 'Did you go to his home?'

Mathis nodded, looking away.

'Why?'

'That wasn't Alistair... His name was Thomas...'

'Okay, what happened?'

'You know already. I killed him.'

Rice exchanged a look with O'Brien. They needed to caution him before this went any further.

After O'Brien had read him his rights, they took an arm each and led him back the way they'd come.

Sirens wailed in the distance as backup approached.

'Wait... stop,' Mathis said.

'Why?'

'I want to show you where Landon is.'

'What?' Rice released Mathis's arm.

Mathis pointed at the canal. 'He's in there... the bastard put him in there.'

Christ.

There was no doubt now – those were definitely tears streaming down Mathis's face.

64

After looking at pictures of the man posing as Alistair Ashworth, Patty Sinclair confirmed it was her son.

So far, Barnett had only told her that Rowan had been travelling the world using fraudulent identities. He'd carefully avoided mentioning the murders, wanting to keep her focused. If he revealed too soon that her son was likely a serial killer, he risked losing her to despair or denial.

Patty perched uncomfortably on a leather sofa, pastel artwork dominating the wall behind her. Years of alcoholism had left their mark – her hands trembled as they worried at her pearl necklace, and her gaze darted around the room like a trapped bird. 'Is he definitely dead?'

The body awaited formal identification, so Barnett chose his words carefully. 'We suspect so. And once again, I'm very sorry, Mrs Sinclair.'

She barked out a harsh laugh. 'Patty, please. God... you sound like one of my doctors. Mrs Sinclair this... Mrs Sinclair that... they never give me any peace.'

'They may be trying to help you, Patty.'

'The only thing that can help me is a long sleep, if you catch my meaning…'

Barnett made a mental note – potential suicide risk. Protocol demanded he report it.

'Shit, strike that. I don't mean it,' she backtracked, her fingers tightening on her pearls. 'Last time I said that – they put me in a special room in the rehabilitation centre and watched me even when I was taking a shit.'

'When did you last see your son?'

'2016. We'd buried his father at the beginning of the year, and he was gone by the end. Off to New York. Never heard from him since. Little bastard.'

Barnett watched her reach for a glass of water, noting how her lip curled at the clear liquid. Seven murders later, he thought, and here sits the beginning of it all.

'What do y'all want to know?'

Leaning forward, notebook ready, Barnett asked, 'Why did he leave Oregon?'

'He was ungrateful, I told you that.'

'Did he give you an actual reason?'

'Reasons?' She laughed bitterly. 'He was never in touch.'

'So, he left near the end of 2016 with no explanation?'

'Oh, he left explanations. Pages of them. About his "damaged childhood". About how we "stifled" him. His father never made it to a single school play or baseball game. And me? I was too busy with my social calendar to notice when he stopped coming to dinner.'

Barnett noted how her voice remained eerily detached as she recounted her son's accusations. 'Were you not worried? Did you contact the police?'

'Oh, I knew he was in danger all right. Rowan was weak-willed. Always had been. I knew he wouldn't last long.'

'Before he came home?'

'No, before he ended up dead. Of course. And here you are.'

The temperature in the room seemed to drop with each revelation. 'What makes you say he was weak-willed?'

'Because he couldn't accept his place. His role. He moaned about his childhood. About us... his parents. He thought his childhood was difficult. Ha! He should've tried mine on for size. Used to get a slap around the head every morning for breakfast. Whereas, Rowan, I treated him well... told him he was my star... my everything... but it was never enough for him.'

The pattern was emerging – a child desperate for genuine connection, trapped in a world of hollow praise and conditional love. It explained so much about the identities he would later steal, the relationships he would forge and destroy.

'Did you ever hurt him?'

Her smile was sharp as broken glass. 'Every child needs discipline. When he was punished, it was warranted.'

'Tell me about his father,' Barnett prompted, seeing her grip on composure starting to slip.

'Gerard wasn't perfect... Men with that power and influence rarely are, are they? He was tortured with intellect and responsibility... but he provided for us. Gave us this life, so...' Her voice cracked. 'So I forgave him his indiscretions.'

'He had affairs.'

A slight nod. Her hand went to her throat.

'And did Rowan know?'

Her silence was answer enough.

'Can you tell me more about Rowan's relationship with his father?'

'What relationship?' The bitterness in her voice could have stripped paint. 'Gerard was a busy man. He didn't have time for a child's neediness. And Rowan was needy, I can tell you. But the man deserves praise. He gave Rowan everything – the best schools, the best clothes, the best opportunities. And how does that bastard repay us? With this!'

She leaned forward suddenly, nearly spilling her water. 'You know what he did after Gerard died? Treated me like a prisoner!'

'A prisoner?'

'He controlled everything! The money, the house, even what I ate. Wouldn't give me money. Said I'd drink it away.' Her laugh held an edge of hysteria.

'How long did this go on?'

'Months. Then one day, near year's end, he just left. Left me with money and disappeared. Said he would never see me again.' Her fingers twisted the pearls so tight they threatened to snap. 'Said he was going to "create what I failed to". Can you believe the ingratitude?'

Barnett watched her carefully. 'Did he say anything else before he left?'

A shadow crossed her face. 'I used to tell him he was a star at the centre of my universe. My mother's words... they were supposed to make him feel special.' Her voice dropped to a whisper. 'He threw them back at me. Said, "Stars burn out... and then everything starts again."'

Like his victims, Barnett thought. Each identity burning out, each death marking a new beginning.

'You can't escape who you are,' she said, more to herself than to him. 'No matter how many times you reinvent yourself.'

Barnett had heard enough. The picture was complete – a childhood of emotional deprivation that had spawned a lifetime of desperate searching, each new identity an attempt to find the connection that had always been denied.

'Thank you for talking with us, Patty. We'll be in touch when we've confirmation.'

'Wait,' she called as he reached for the disconnect button. 'Do you think... do you think he ever found what he was looking for?'

Barnett thought of the trail of destroyed lives, each victim representing another failed attempt at creating the family he'd never had. 'I don't think he did, Patty. That's all I really know at this stage.'

After ending the call, Barnett sat back, letting the weight of it settle. The pieces had come together – a child starved of genuine affection, trapped in a world of appearances and expectations, desperate to create the family and love he'd never truly experienced. A deprivation that had sparked a chain of tragic events, each new identity an attempt to rewrite his story, each failure ending in destruction.

He typed up his notes and shared his findings with Rice, who was about to take a confession for Rowan's murder.

It seemed that everything was coming to a close so, sighing, he checked his watch, and turned his attention to Gardner's favour in researching Neville Fairweather.

Gathering his things, Barnett headed home. Something told him that unravelling that particular mystery would require a fresh perspective and a clear head.

65

Rice and O'Brien arrived at Leeds District Headquarters, Elland Road, where a desk sergeant provided them with dry police-issue clothing. While Mathis was being processed, Rice took a call from Barnett that left him stunned – the full story of Rowan Sinclair's murderous path across the globe.

After the call, Rice brought O'Brien into an interview room to explain what he'd learned.

'Seven people!' O'Brien said in disbelief.

Rice nodded. 'Maybe we should have Mathis knighted,' he said with grim humour. 'Stopping a serial killer is no minor accomplishment.'

'We'd have got him, anyway,' O'Brien said.

'Really? Are you sure?' Rice asked, lifting an eyebrow. 'He's been active since 2016, and evaded justice in three countries! Ours would have been the fourth if he'd made it to Canada... If that was the case, there'd have been more victims. Still Mathis won't be getting a thank you for killing him. The man is doomed. So don't go patting him on the back for a job well done.'

'I wasn't going to – you made the point first!'

Rice smiled and winked. 'You bite so easy...'

They found Mathis slumped in an interview room chair, now dressed in plain grey sweats. He'd already waived his right to a solicitor. After Rice introduced the interview for the camera, he began questioning.

'Today, when I asked you why you ran from the police, can you remember what you said to me?' Rice asked.

'*Oui*... yes,' Mathis replied. 'I told you I murdered Thomas.'

'Thomas Baker?'

'*Oui.*'

'Were you telling the truth?'

'*Mais oui*,' Mathis said, quietly.

'Did you know that Thomas Baker was not his real name?'

'I know now. Thomas Baker was a lie. I watched him for some time and when I finally confronted him, he told me he called himself Alistair Ashworth.'

'I see,' Rice said, making a note. 'Can I ask why you killed him?'

'This bastard admitted to killing Landon.' His face contorted with grief.

'How?' Rice asked.

Mathis flinched. He leaned forward and rubbed at his face. 'Landon...' he murmured, and went into a daze.

Rice looked at O'Brien, prompting her to try.

'Were you and Landon close?' she asked.

He broke from his reverie. 'Close?' Mathis gave a bitter laugh. '*Non*, more than close. *Je l'aimais*... sorry... *I loved him*. For two years, he was everything to me.'

Rice and O'Brien remained silent while Mathis wiped tears from his cheeks with shaking hands.

'*Pardonnez-moi*,' he said finally, clearing his throat. 'Let me explain from the beginning. When I first arrived at Bright Day... I was miserable, lost, and...' A ghost of a smile played on his lips. 'I saw him in the common area.' He looked between the detectives. 'He was trying to make these paper cranes, *mais mon Dieu*, he was terrible at it! His fingers were all clumsy with the paper.' He chuckled. 'When I laughed, the look he gave me! But then he surprised me, speaking in perfect French: "Do you find my artistic endeavours amusing? Perhaps a Frenchman could do better?" His accent was *parfait!*'

Mathis's smile faded as the memory passed. 'We had so much in common... not just the language. Both of us had failed marriages. We shared the same sense of humour – how he could make me laugh! And the books – his favourite was *Le Comte de Monte-Cristo*, mine *Le Petit Prince*. He dreamed of having a golden retriever one day...' His voice softened. 'Like sunshine, he would say. Me, I prefer *les bergers allemands* – German shepherds – but we'd joke about opening a shelter together, *après* we got clean.' He chewed his bottom lip, nodded and continued. 'That was our greatest battle, *notre plus grand demon*... the heroin. Both of us fighting it, falling, getting back up... I'm sorry,' Mathis said suddenly, turning to Rice. 'For pushing you into the canal. And for threatening Brad. I was... how do you say? Not myself. Terrified. But now I know this is right. *La vérité*... this is the truth. It's what Landon would want... the bridge by the canal was our place... where we'd go to shoot up together. When I reached the bridge today, running from you, I could hear Landon's voice in my head, telling me to stop running, to tell the truth.' He rubbed his reddened eyes. 'We couldn't take drugs into Bright Day, but when the need became too strong... impossible... that's where we'd go. It was a *cycle sans fin*. One would get clean while the other relapsed, back and forth, but we were always there for each other. "Nothing is harder than pulling back when you're at the edge," Landon would say. We might never have beaten it completely, but we worked as a team.'

'Did you ever tell him how you felt about him?'

'*Non.*' Mathis shook his head sadly. 'Once, he mentioned having had... *sentiments*... feelings for men in the past, but not for me. I was just his brother.' He took a deep breath. 'We had all these little jokes, these dreams. "*Un jour, mon frère,*" he would say, "we'll be drinking coffee in Québec, watching the world go by." But then everything changed.' Mathis's face darkened. 'Thomas Baker.' He spat the name like poison. '*Ce monster* appeared five months ago.' He pressed his hands against his face. '*Un moment, s'il vous plaît.*'

'Of course,' O'Brien said.

Eventually Mathis continued, his voice breaking. 'Thomas destroyed everything we had.' Tears spilled down his cheeks. 'I should've just gone into the canal with him... before... drowned. Been with him.'

Rice exchanged a glance with O'Brien. 'We've put in a request to have the canal dredged, Mathis. If he's there, we'll find him, I promise you that. Tell me about Thomas.'

Mathis nodded, wiping his eyes. '*Au début* he seemed kind, funny even. We'd see him occasionally at Bright Day, then more regularly. I should've known something wasn't right. He moved differently from other homeless people. Too confident. But there seemed no reason to question it. He became very close to Landon. And I... *mon Dieu*... I was jealous. Knowing Landon had felt things for men before... *la paranoïa* ate at me. I felt myself being pushed aside. But we still had our secret... our addiction. Thomas didn't use, so that was still just for us. But I was *si naïf.*'

'Sorry?'

'Naïve.'

'Okay... what happened?' Rice asked.

'Three weeks ago, everything' – he made a spiralling motion with his finger – 'went to shit. Landon needed a fix, and Thomas said he wanted to try it. To understand Landon better.' He clenched his fists. 'It was sickening. I thought perhaps they were falling in love. My mind was chaos.'

'And...'

'I went with them to the canal beneath the bridge. I couldn't leave them alone. We all took the heroin and...' His eyes locked onto Rice's. 'The things he said, they were wrong. So very wrong...'

'How so?' Rice asked.

'Well, his voice changed. I know I was high, but I'm certain he suddenly had an American accent. But that wasn't the worst.' Mathis shuddered. 'The nature of what he said... *mon Dieu*... I'll never forget it...'

66

Cocooned in shadows beneath the bridge, Mathis listened to the canal's soothing flow, remembering the lullabies his mother sang in Dijon so many years ago.

At the drug's peak, he closed his eyes, surrendering to the water's rhythm.

How simple life would be, he thought, to achieve such perfect calm and purpose. The canal didn't wrestle with addiction or loneliness – it simply flowed, eternal and untroubled.

When he opened his eyes, he studied his companions through the haze.

Landon lay there, face slack but beautiful, radiating a gentle peace that made Mathis's heart ache.

Thomas reclined nearby, his face pale and twisted. Though he'd become part of their lives, he remained somehow separate – more Landon's companion than his.

His mother's warning about his own absent father echoed in his mind: 'a charming man isn't always a trustworthy one.'

Who are you, Thomas? What do you want? Why attach yourself so desperately to Landon? Do you love him?

Could you ever love him as I do?

And worst of all – does he love you back?

Thomas's eyes fluttered open.

If not for the heroin dulling his reflexes, Mathis might have startled. Instead, he watched, transfixed.

Thomas stared at Mathis, his gaze seeming to look through rather than at him. 'Are you okay?' Mathis asked.

A tremor ran down Mathis' spine as Thomas spoke. 'I see you, Clive. I see you watching me.'

Was that an American accent breaking through?

Had the drugs twisted his perception?

Thomas's hand went to his ear. 'You've already taken too much of me.'

Mathis hadn't imagined it – American. It sounded natural, as if it had always been there...

'You can't have any more, Clive,' Thomas continued.

Who was Clive?

Mathis watched, horrified yet unable to look away, as Thomas's eyes began to dart around the shadowy underpass. 'Look,' he whispered. 'Watch... You can see him, too? Clive. Prancing in the shadows. Don't let him take from me again.'

Mathis forced himself to breathe slowly, steadily.

Thomas's eyes rolled back before closing, and Mathis dared to hope the episode had passed.

But Thomas's eyes snapped open again, and this time Mathis physically recoiled.

'You think I meant for him to eat me?' Thomas's voice cracked as he squeezed his eyes shut, rocking his head from side to side. 'I only wanted to share. That's all. Share what I have. There's warmth in sharing. Let me touch the faces of my children, let me warm them, and I'll show you that. Show you all what I have...' He stopped abruptly and took a deep breath. 'Sarah... I'm sorry... but you can't choose work over that warmth. How can we build if all you want to do is grow somewhere that will never thank you? All we have to give is here... is in our warmth... Camilla... forgive me... but you need to turn away... your mother can't strip you of what you're capable of, what we're capable of... our world must burn bright with new hope, and that same warmth, and not be lost in the shadows of the past... and my Imogen, my sweet Imogen, how cruel the biology... how nasty the hand of fate... but we must honour the choices the world has made, and if I can't build, then it must be so again.'

He opened his eyes and his gaze locked onto Mathis with terrifying intensity. 'We all may long to be stars at the centre of the universe... but a star without love and warmth dies... burns and dies... Look at me, Mom. See me. Try.' He put a hand to his chest. 'I am worthy... I am worthy... They'll see it. My family will see it. They'll love me. They'll free me.'

Thomas fell silent, his eyes drifting closed.

'But no matter... there's always a chance to go on... Stars burn out... and then everything starts again.'

Several minutes passed in oppressive silence before Mathis realised the strange confession was over.

Who was this man, really?

And what could Mathis do? How could he make Landon understand what he'd witnessed?

Would Landon even believe such a bizarre warning?

But Mathis had to try, because Thomas was a man consumed by fire, a dying star, and the Frenchman feared he would drag Landon, the man he loved, down into the inferno with him.

67

Mathis leaned forward, his eyes intense as he continued his story. 'The next morning,' he began, hands trembling slightly, 'I followed Thomas. *Mon Dieu*, I was desperate to know the truth. I saw him get on a bus, and, without thinking, I climbed on too. I sat at the back, my heart pounding the whole time, *terrifié* that he'd turn around and see me.'

Rice nodded, encouraging Mathis to continue.

Mathis wrapped his arms around himself, as if seeking comfort. 'The journey felt like it took forever. Every time the bus stopped, I was sure Thomas would get off, that I'd lose him. But *non*, he didn't. We rode all the way to Knaresborough. Can you imagine my shock? Here was this man we thought was homeless, travelling to *un quartier chic*... sorry... a nice posh area.' His voice dropped to barely above a whisper. 'I followed him down these streets... always keeping my distance. And then, he just walked up to this house. A normal, everyday house. He had keys. He went inside like he owned the place... which, *bien sûr*, turns out he did!'

O'Brien leaned in, her pen poised over her notebook. 'And what did you do then?'

'I stood there for a long time, just staring at the house. I felt sick to my stomach. Everything we thought we knew about Thomas was a lie. He wasn't homeless. He'd been deceiving us, deceiving Landon, this whole time.' Mathis ran shaking fingers through his hair. 'I wanted to tell Landon right away, but... *comment expliquer*? How? "Hey, Land, I followed our friend home like some kind of stalker, and guess what? He's not who he says he is." I was afraid Landon wouldn't believe me, that he'd think I was just jealous or paranoid.' He rubbed his temples.

'And?' Rice prompted.

'Nothing. Then... I decided to confront Thomas at Bright Day. Get the truth from him directly. But we only saw him once more at Bright Day. There were people around, staff, other residents. I lost my nerve. *Pathétique, non*? I didn't want to cause a scene, didn't want to risk Landon turning against me. Each time I saw Thomas with his wife – *oui*, his wife! – I backed away. Then Landon disappeared. Just... gone. He never came back to Bright Day, never showed up at our usual spots. For ten days, I hoped he'd return with some explanation, but hope turned to fear.'

Mathis's voice cracked. 'And then, several days back, full of despair, I went to Thomas's home.' He pointed at Rice. 'I saw you and another woman there. Official looking. So I left, but suspicions grew. *J'étais fou d'inquiétude...*' He shook his head.

'Sorry?' Rice asked.

'I was... mad with worry. So, yesterday I went back, I banged on the door, demanded he open it, or I'd call the police and tell them he was a liar. He opened of course.' He paused, dabbing at his eyes. 'Up close, it was strange to see Thomas looking this way. Smarter. Clean. Like a completely different person from the homeless man who'd tricked us... I demanded to know where

Landon was or I'd shout from the rooftops. He'd no choice but to let me in.'

'Did you not realise how dangerous that could be?' O'Brien asked.

'*Bien sûr...* but I was beyond reason. Besides, I'd brought a knife.'

'Sorry?'

'A knife... from Yorkshire Trading... four pounds. *Et alors...* I pulled out the knife and threatened him.' Mathis's hands trembled as he demonstrated the motion.

Rice nodded, maintaining his neutral expression.

'Why?' O'Brien asked.

'Just for protection... I never meant to kill him.'

Good luck on convincing the jury of that one, Rice thought.

Mathis looked down, shaking his head, murmuring under his breath. '*Je voulais seulement des réponses...*'

'What does that mean?' Rice asked.

Mathis looked up. 'I just wanted answers. I thought if I threatened him, he'd tell me the truth. I cornered him in his lounge. He backed away, hands up. I demanded to know where Landon was. He promised to tell me if I put down the knife. *Mais non!* Of course, I refused.' His eyes suddenly grew distant. 'That's when I saw it – *un passeport bleu...* on the coffee table. I grabbed it and he told me to put it down, but I opened it...' He pressed his palms against his temples. '*Mon Dieu, c'était impossible!* I saw Landon's name with Thomas's photo... Landon was surely gone. He had to be gone for Thomas to have his passport.'

Rice glanced at O'Brien, raising his eyebrows slightly. '*La tête me tournait...* My head spinning, you know?' His French was becoming increasingly prominent as the memory overwhelmed him. 'I shouted at him to explain this madness! He told me to calm down, to put down the passport like everything was normal. The bastard never broke sweat.'

He sighed. 'I saw the pictures on the mantelpiece. Thomas with a beautiful woman. They looked so happy, like a normal couple. When I asked who she was, he told me – so calmly – about Imogen.' He shook his head. 'She'd died. A heart attack. Then, he told me his real name was Alistair Ashworth. Claimed he was a journalist doing undercover research. Nonsense!'

'Yes,' Rice said, nodding. 'Apart from the name, and the fact that Imogen did die.'

'So I didn't back down. *Non!* I needed to know about Landon's passport, why Thomas's photo was on it.' Mathis's voice grew harder. 'He claimed Landon had sold it to him. I told him it was a lie, that he'd stolen it and somehow put his picture on it.

'Then, the man goes even crazier! He tells me to sit down, to have a drink while he explained everything. For *un moment*, I almost agreed. Then the anger was too much and I punched him.' Mathis clenched a fist. 'He fell back over his table onto the sofa. Pathetic. He looked at me with tears in his eyes and told me Landon had overdosed weeks ago at the canal. Liar! *Je le savais!* But then he said he'd sunk Landon in the canal... and that was different... something in his eyes told me this part was true. I was in shock. Everything was spinning. He stood and walked to the kitchen, saying so casually we should have that drink, that I should calm down. *Comme si de rien n'était!*'

'Sorry?'

'As if everything was normal!' Mathis's voice shook with rage. 'I followed him, screaming for the truth. His back was to me, and I could hear him moving around. Then he turned with another knife. *Et alors...* I lunged without thinking. He tried to defend himself, but too late. I struck at his hands, his arms. When he dropped the knife, I looked into his eyes and saw...' He shook his hands. 'Nothing. Emptiness. *Rien!*'

Mathis's voice dropped to a whisper. 'The rest is... how to say it... a blur... fuzzy. I stabbed him.' He touched his own neck. 'From...' He paused. 'Instinct. Then he was on the floor, blood... everywhere.' He looked up at Rice and O'Brien, tears in his eyes. 'Landon was gone! *Mon meilleur ami...* The only person who truly understood me, was at the bottom of that filthy canal. This man was a monster!'

I don't disagree, Rice thought, but Mathis would have to face the consequences of his actions.

'*Tout seul dans le noir...*'

'Sorry?'

'Landon is alone in the dark.'

'What did you do then?' Rice asked, wanting to return to the confession.

'I thought about calling the police right there,' Mathis said, his voice hollow. 'I thought they'd understand. But seeing him there, face down, blood everywhere, I realised what I had done was *sauvage*. *Alors...* I took his passport, the knives, his laptop. The plan was simple, find a café, use his laptop to leave *une note... une note de suicide*. But of course, I couldn't get past the password screen! I went back to the canal, ready to join Landon, but...' He dropped his head. '*Je suis un lâche.*' He sighed. 'I am a coward... The same coward I've been *toute ma vie...*' He rubbed his eyes. 'So, I threw everything in – the passport, the laptop. Then I just... went back to Bright Day.' Mathis slumped back in his chair. 'I killed a man. I know I can't change that. But that man wasn't Thomas Baker. He wasn't who we thought. He killed my best friend! What do I have left? What? Please... promise me you'll find Landon. He doesn't deserve to stay down there. *Tout seul dans le noir.*'

Alone in the dark. If anything, Rice felt he was getting a French lesson, albeit a very melancholic, tragic one.

O'Brien spoke softly. 'We'll find him, Mathis. I promise you that.'

'If only I'd said something sooner, if I'd confronted him that day at Bright Day instead of being a coward... maybe Landon would still be alive. *Je devrai vivre avec ça.*' He looked up at them both. 'I'll have to live with that guilt forever.'

Rice was sympathetic. 'Mathis, you can't blame yourself for Landon's death. They were the actions of a disturbed individual. The wrong move was taking matters into your own hands.'

He nodded, shrugged, and Rice called time on the interview.

68

After parking outside his home, Barnett took a call from Rice.

Mathis Roux had given a full confession to Rowan Sinclair's murder.

Rice sounded disheartened on the phone, and Barnett could understand why.

Mathis was a man who'd acted desperately out of loss. He probably never intended to kill Rowan, but taking the knife to his home had been a stupid act, and the CPS would be relentless.

They also shared a sense of disappointment over the fact that Rowan would never face the justice system. Death seemed a rather simple escape for a man like that. It would have been so much more rewarding if he'd been able to learn of his failure, and then to face the consequences of his actions.

Barnett winced as he climbed out of his car.

It'd only been a few months since he'd rescued Jess Beaumont from a house fire and burned his legs badly. He was still stiff and subject to sudden twinges of pain. The cold weather wasn't helping matters.

As he walked to his front door, he realised, with some disappointment, that his role in the Rowan Sinclair investigation was now complete. The canal would be dredged for Landon Thambley's body, while Marsh herself was updating Roy regarding the truth of what had befallen his daughter. That she'd fallen into the clutches of a charming serial killer would be traumatic news. The fact that he'd never get to look the murdering bastard in the eye would also be a bitter pill to swallow for a man like Roy.

It would be the responsibility of the other countries to recover the missing bodies of those whose identities Rowan had stolen. No doubt the UK would apply serious pressure on the Brazilian embassy to recover Alistair.

Not wanting to disturb his father, Richard, who was really struggling with his hips at the moment, Barnett didn't knock; instead, he fumbled in his pocket for a key.

When he opened the door, he saw that all the lights were off inside, and that it was far colder than it should've been... The thermostat had been automatically set to twenty-one at this time of day.

'Dad,' he called out.

No answer.

There'd have been a time when he would have panicked, but he'd been through this process many times and, more than likely, Richard was asleep on the sofa, so hadn't risen to switch on the lights.

Barnett closed the door, hung his jacket up and kicked off his shoes.

He flicked on the hall light and started down the chilly hallway.

'Dad?'

Nothing.

The other option, of course, was that his father had gone out. It wasn't completely unheard of these days. Clarissa Trent, the half-sister he'd only discovered the existence of just before Christmas, met Richard once every couple of weeks so that he could tell her stories about her birth mother, whom she'd never known. It would be easier if his father embraced modern technology and sent texts warning Barnett of his absences, like everyone else did! Still, old dogs, new tricks, and all that.

The cold suddenly intensified as Barnett neared the downstairs bathroom.

He groaned and shook his head. His bloody father! Always leaving the window open!

He went in and shut the bathroom window properly.

'It has to stop, Dad,' he muttered to himself. 'Maybe if you had to pay the sodding gas prices, you'd take better care...'

In the kitchen, a note on the table caught his eye. He nodded as he read his father's shaky handwriting. A poker game with a friend.

Grabbing a beer from the fridge, Barnett approached the lounge. He cracked it mid-way and took a long swig. The can felt very light afterwards.

Go easy, fella, you still have some work to do!

He put his hand on the door handle, thinking it strange that his father had shut the door for once, but was rather glad of it, because it might have kept the bloody heat in!

When he opened the door and stepped in, a warm blast of air hit him.

He stepped into the dark room, and closed the door quickly behind him, enjoying the heat. He switched on the light.

He jumped out of his skin when he caught his reflection in the window.

Been a long day...

The mantelpiece caught his eye, adorned with photos of his late mother, Amina. It had been a turbulent time for Barnett just before Christmas, when the full truth about her history came to light. He was still coming to terms with it all.

After closing the curtains, he put the half-empty can on the coffee table and settled into the sofa with his laptop.

Aegis Dynamics.

Neville Fairweather.

Another bloody secretive defence company—

A sudden noise jolted him from the start of his research.

He lifted his eyes from the screen, heart beating, wondering what it was.

He heard it again, took a deep breath, and listened.

The third time, he realised it was just old pipes struggling to heat the house after his father's open-window escapade.

He sighed and then delved into his research, the glow of the screen illuminating his furrowed brow. Aegis Dynamics had been a major player in the early 2000s, with contracts spanning cybersecurity, drone development and several classified operations. Their connection to Gregory Pendleton, the recently murdered ex-employee, was clear, but the specifics of his role remained shrouded in secrecy.

He finished his beer and dug deeper.

Barnett was savvy with the internet. He was quick to uncover a web of government contracts, redacted documents and accusations of clandestine operations. The company's sudden closure over a decade ago raised more questions than answers.

His eyes widened when he hit some really engaging dirt. A series of news articles from the time of Aegis Dynamics's closure... and vague references to a major security breach. Still, rather predictably, the details were sparse, and frustration kicked in.

All was not lost, though. Gardner had asked him because she

knew he was the best at this – and he was not going to let her down.

He'd built an extensive network of contacts across various departments – fraud, cybersecurity, you name it. He picked up his phone and started calling in favours.

Soon enough, an old colleague he'd remained close with granted him access to old employee files from Aegis.

He sensed a long night ahead, but he'd be kidding if he said he didn't enjoy this.

He smiled. Bring it on.

This was, most certainly, his forte.

While the house clanged away around him, he lost himself in a web of mysteries, secrets and lies.

69

O'Brien sat at a worn oak table in Blind Jacks. The low-ceilinged room hummed with conversation and the rich scent of beer. She was checking her phone yet again. Still no word from Gardner. She hoped her boss was holding up okay at the hospital with Riddick.

Three pints landed on the table with a thud.

O'Brien raised her eyebrow. 'Who else are we expecting?'

'Two for me. No chance I'm going home on just one,' he said. 'I nearly drowned today for a start... but more importantly, I solved a case without the boss holding my hand.'

O'Brien coughed obviously.

'Sorry, we.' Rice winked and took a mouthful of beer. 'That tastes bloody good.'

O'Brien took a mouthful of her own beer and gave a refreshed sigh, then wiped her mouth with the back of her hand.

Rice gave an appreciative nod. 'Where have you been all my life, Lucy?'

'Err... in gay bars?'

Rice laughed. 'Oh yes... it's like they always say. The best ones are always gay.'

'I think you'll find that's usually regarding men.'

'Still... same applies...' Rice said. 'I like the fact that you're not always pissed off with me.'

'That's because my father is ten times worse than you, sir.'

He waved his hand. 'No father chat... I implore you.'

'The boss thinks a lot of you,' O'Brien said.

Rice nodded. 'I'll drink to that...' He did. 'Maybe I have it all wrong. Maybe I'm popular after all?'

O'Brien laughed. 'Now then, let's not push it. There's quite a few on the unhappy list.'

'Yep... and we're going to need a fair number of pints to get through it. Could get expensive.'

'Don't be so hard on yourself,' O'Brien said, grinning. 'I reckon we could do it in two pints.'

He scrunched up his face. 'Thanks...' He stuck out his tongue. 'Anyway.' He held up his glass. 'Here's to the truth.' They clinked glasses. 'Just a shame the bastard, Rowan, didn't live long enough to know we caught up with him.'

O'Brien nodded. 'His childhood sounded bleak. I guess all that emptiness made him crave something he couldn't have.'

'Lots of things I crave; I don't start killing when I don't get what I want.'

'What Mathis overheard beneath that bridge... Rowan's confession if you will... Do you think we can take it at face value? Was it really the fact that Imogen couldn't have children that pushed him into killing her?'

Rice shrugged. 'I guess the psychologists will have their say.' He took another gulp. 'We've done our bit.'

O'Brien sighed. She couldn't shake the cold feeling. She

pointed at her head. 'We all have a picture of what we want in here. Most of us learn to live with disappointment...'

'Much healthier that way. Imagine if we started killing over failed dreams. But still, sometimes we look too hard for reasons.' Rice finished his first pint. 'Does he deserve them? Many have a messed-up childhood.' He thumbed his chest. 'I did. I chose to use my bitterness to do some good.' He switched pints.

Since Rice had already waved off the father chat and now he'd mentioned his childhood, O'Brien would be lying if she said she wasn't curious. She took a mouthful of beer for Dutch courage. 'What happened when you were younger, sir... if you don't mind me asking?'

'My old man was a right bastard, Lucy. You may have heard of him. The great DCI Derek Rice. Well, he may have left behind a positive legacy in the job, but that didn't extend to me, I'm afraid. A dickhead, vicious with me.' He swiped the air. 'I don't think he ever said a nice word to me. Seriously, I can't remember a single time. And you know what's really messed up? Part of me still wanted to make him proud. Can you believe that? Even after all the shit he put me through, I still wanted him to look at me the way he looked at his precious reputation.'

'I'm sorry to hear that,' O'Brien said.

'He taught me how to be alone, you know. How to push people away before they could get close enough to hurt me. It became second nature. Easier to be the asshole everyone expected than to risk letting someone in.' He sighed. 'And now look at me!'

He lowered his head.

O'Brien half-wished she hadn't asked. The rapid consumption of one and a half pints had made it easy for him to lay his soul bare. She suddenly felt guilty. 'You've turned out well, sir.'

He fixed her with a stare. 'Have I? No wife, no kids. Just me and my smart mouth, keeping the world at arm's length. All because dear old Daddy couldn't handle a kid who didn't live up to his impossible standards.'

O'Brien reached out, her hand hovering uncertainly before settling on Rice's arm. 'I've seen another side to you recently, Phil. You're not the person you think you are.'

'Don't talk nonsense. I'm an aggressive bastard, and unapproachable as they come!'

'And I'm saying you've been less like that... lately.'

He shrugged. 'Maybe.'

She nodded and took her hand back.

Rice sat deep in thought as he finished his next pint. 'Yeah, well, Lucy, you can thank the boss for that. She's the only one who ever bothered to look past the prickly exterior. Her and Marsh, I suppose. They must have seen something worth salvaging in this old wreck. You know, Emma is something special, isn't she?'

O'Brien smiled, nodded and then, out of the blue, her eyes filled up.

Rice noticed. 'Shit... sorry, Lucy. That was thoughtless.'

She waved him off, wiping at her eyes. 'Behave. It's not you... It's... It doesn't matter.'

'It does. Come on. Hearts on the table. You've had mine beating in front of you for a good while now.'

O'Brien nodded. 'It's just... Emma... and Paul...' She took a shaky breath and shrugged. 'I just feel like I'm drowning sometimes.'

Rice shifted his stool around the side of the table so they were closer.

She met his gaze, her eyes filled with a mixture of guilt and pain. 'God, sir, I feel like such a bitch for even thinking it, but—' She broke off.

Rice smiled. 'Take your time.'

O'Brien finished her pint, took a deep breath, wiped her eyes again and said, 'I've caught myself wondering whether it would be better if Paul didn't make it. Then, maybe, we could be together. Me and Emma?' She glanced at him after she said it, but then quickly looked away. 'Bad, huh?'

'Maybe... or maybe, completely bloody normal. Look, we're all human. With hopes and dreams, like Rowan Sinclair, remember. Self-preservation always kicks in at some point, even when we don't want it to. It is natural to be selfish. You love Emma, and there's this massive obstacle in your way. I'd say it'd be unusual if you didn't have thoughts like that creep in. Not like you'd ever do anything. That's the difference between us, and people like Rowan, I guess. Fleeting thoughts that never become anything.'

O'Brien shook her head. She was crying more freely now. 'Obviously, I get that, sir. Totally. But this goes deeper than that. Emma adores him. She's shattered by his condition. If he dies, she'll be devastated. Inconsolable. I can't help wondering... would she be this devastated if it were me in that hospital bed... if I died?'

'Categorically, yes! Of course she would,' Rice said firmly. 'Emma cares deeply for you, Lucy. You'd have to be blind as a bat not to see that!' He looked around the pub. 'No offence, Mr Blind Jack.'

O'Brien laughed and put her hand on his arm again. She nodded. 'Thanks, Phil.'

'I'm merely a truth sayer.'

'And a good listener. I'm going to treat you to another pint.'

'It's okay, I'm driving.'

'You shouldn't be driving after two anyway, so that's made my mind up. I'll drop you off and... collect you first thing, and bring you to your car? Deal?'

'Bloody hell, you've twisted my arm. What about you?'

'I wouldn't have had another anyway.' She stood to head to the bar.

'Grab me a chaser with that, Lucy.' He took a deep breath. 'A Bell's. Put it on my tab.'

'What would your babysitter say when she comes back to work?'

'She'd tell me I was a dickhead – in a nice way of course.'

70

O'Brien's taillights faded into the darkness.

Swaying, Rice lingered at the end of his driveway for a moment and looked up at the full moon. Despite the crisp cold, he felt content.

Probably because of the three pints and three whiskies in his system.

He noticed next-door's cat perched on his garden wall. He sat down alongside it, and mimed doffing his cap. 'How do, Peaches?'

Princess Peach let out a gentle meow, before jumping down from the wall and rubbing itself against Rice's legs. He smiled.

'Just so you know, lassie...' he said, reaching down to stroke her. 'I'd never have named you this.' He thought of the ten-year-old girl next door. 'Although, she meant well. Still... one thing she did get right,' he said as the cat sauntered away. 'You're a princess if ever I met one... and if you ever need a place to stay... well, I'm all alone in this big old house.'

After Princess Peach had disappeared from view, he fumbled in his pocket for his keys. Standing, he walked down his drive.

The porch light flickered, and Rice made a mental note, not for the first time this month, to change the bulb in the morning.

'Bloody hell... Bells...' he muttered, struggling to fit the key into the lock. 'Hells Bells!' He laughed. After a few attempts, he struck home, and the door swung open with a soft creak. Rice stepped inside, enveloped by the darkness of his home.

He flicked on the hallway light, blinking as his eyes adjusted.

He kicked off his shoes and made his way to the kitchen, imagining Princess Peach marching alongside him.

The cat would fit in here just fine!

So would a dog, truth be told.

Rice had been an animal lover as a child, but it was something else his father had knocked out of him. For fifteen years, he'd begged his parents for a dog. His father had been dismissive, referring to them as flea-ridden and selfish. Since then, Rice had never had the energy to go out and get one.

Thank you, Father, he thought, considering how hard the bastard's icy hand still gripped him, even from the grave.

In the kitchen, the digital clock on the microwave cast a faint green glow. After hitting the light switch, he went straight for the drawer near the sink—

Even when drunk. Typical, he thought to himself, opening it. *Why don't you give yourself a break?*

He knew it was the whisky talking, but he didn't close the drawer. Instead, he reached in for a framed photograph, instinctively handling it gently, despite despising what it showed.

The photo showed a younger Rice in his police uniform, flanked by his father and his auntie. His auntie, who'd been there for him so often following his mother's death when he was ten, smiled broadly, her eyes crinkling at the corners. DCI Derek Rice, however, stood ramrod straight. He'd only looked at the camera at the photographer's request, with a grim, irritated expression that suggested he wanted to be anywhere but there.

Rice regarded his father. 'I led a team today... Dad. Yes. Led. A team that identified a serial killer. Then I went and put another killer away. What was it you once said, Dad? This apple did fall far from the tree? Would you were here to eat your words!'

He brought the picture closer, kissed his auntie's image, then put the picture back into the drawer and closed it.

He stood there for a short time, looking at the drawer, tapping it with his hand, thinking... wishing... that he didn't miss the old bastard.

He hated him with every inch of his being, yet barely a day passed when he didn't think about him.

He grabbed a whisky glass from the top shelf.

71

Barnett's head throbbed.

He closed his eyes, but the image on the screen remained.

Several hours of research had set fire to his retinas.

There was a soft ping and he opened his eyes.

An email from Sarah, an old flame now working in the Defence and Security Organisation, a branch of the Department for International Trade, had arrived.

Attached was the promised list of off-the-books employees for Aegis rather than the registered ones. Fifty-two names in total.

Not expecting much, Barnett skimmed the list with tired eyes, recognising a few names from his earlier research. He rubbed his sore head and yawned—

Then his breath caught in his throat when he read the name at the bottom of the list.

The second to last name.

Number fifty-one.

What?

He leaned forward. It couldn't be... it wasn't bloody possible...

Shit.

This wasn't good at all.

Barnett grabbed his phone and made a call.

Nothing.

The call went to voicemail. He requested a call back, and put down his phone.

He rubbed his temples.

Seeing that name now was wrong. All wrong. It was too unsettling to go to sleep on, and he didn't want to share it with Gardner at this moment – not with what she was going through.

But could he just leave it until morning?

A sound from outside the room jolted Barnett from his thoughts.

A second sound brought him to his feet.

That wasn't the pipes.

72

Determined to fill the empty whisky glass in hand, Rice headed out of the kitchen and towards the lounge, where the Glenfiddich awaited him.

After the day he'd had, another two or three wouldn't go amiss. He looked down and saw that he was still wearing the grey joggers from Leeds District HQ from earlier. It reminded him of the case and he thought of Gardner, feeling rather disappointed that she didn't know its outcome and that he and the team had done her proud.

Would a quick text hurt?

He patted the joggers for his phone. It wasn't there.

His brow creased and he turned and looked around the kitchen. Shit. It wasn't there either.

Bollocks!

Realising he would probably have to call in at the pub tomorrow to retrieve it, he turned and headed back towards the lounge. Deciding he needed a piss, he stopped outside the toilet, deposited his glass on the radiator and opened the door. He winced when a blast of cold air hit him.

Bloody idiot!

He'd left the window open. He reached up, closed the window and then relieved himself.

After flushing, he noticed the smell of bleach.

He looked behind the toilet and saw that the bleach cap wasn't screwed on fully. He rectified that.

After washing his hands, Rice retrieved his glass and continued to the lounge. He opened the lounge door, immediately heading for the shelf where he kept his prized bottle of Glenfiddich. As he reached for it, a soft sound behind him made him freeze.

The door closing.

He gripped the Glenfiddich.

The door clicked shut and Rice turned, holding the bottle by its neck.

73

On edge, Barnett stepped from his lounge and saw his father at the front door, groaning as he desperately tried to hang his coat up.

Sighing with relief, he headed down the hallway. 'Let me, Dad!'

Barnett took his jacket, hung it up and sighed again. It'd been one hell of a day and seeing the late DCI Derek Rice as number fifty-one on that secretive Aegis employee list had sent him into a spin. 'Bit late to be out gallivanting, Dad.'

'Since when was cards gallivanting?'

'How much did you lose?'

'Rather not say...'

'Go on.'

His father shrugged. 'About a hundred.'

'Bloody hell! How's that not gallivanting?'

Using his walking stick, Richard shuffled painfully down the hallway. 'You're sounding more and more like your mother every day, son.' He laughed.

'Responsible?' Barnett said, going to help him.

'Aye... get off, son. I'm fine.'

'Until you're not, and then muggins here is driving you to hospital.'

Once Richard was seated in the lounge, Barnett grabbed him a beer.

'Drink to forget about that hundred pounds, Dad.'

'Behave,' Richard said. 'I'll win it back next week, and another hundred.'

Barnett thought to himself, *Good, then you can use it for the gas bill after leaving the bloody window open!*

'Get *Match of the Day* on from the weekend, please, son.'

Once it was on, Barnett kissed his dad on the forehead.

'What was that for?'

'Can't a man kiss his own father? This is 2025 not 1930.'

'Aye. Kiss away, son, but you've never done it before. Not since you grew to twice my size.'

I did it because you're a good man, Barnett thought. Not the type of man to end up on a bloody list like the one I just read.

Barnett considered sitting down, but thought about Rice again. It probably could wait till morning, but still, after what had happened to Gregory Pendleton, why take any chances?

Barnett laughed. 'Look, I'm going out. I need to check on something.'

'Everything all right?'

Probably. I hope, he thought. 'Yeah... sure...' He had to talk loudly over *Match of the Day*'s music, blaring due to his father's hearing.

Richard winked. 'You finally got a lass lined up? Something special?'

Barnett smiled. 'I'd never abandon you and the footy for a date, Dad!'

'Good boy,' Richard said. 'I brought you up well. If I'd the energy, I'd kiss you back.'

74

From behind the sofa, alongside the door, Jack watched Rice approach the liquor cabinet and reach up.

Taking a deep breath, he stood slowly. Then, keeping his eyes on his target, he sidled to his right, easing the door closed as he went.

Rice was hoisting down a bottle of Glenfiddich.

When the door clicked shut, Rice turned, bottle in one hand, glass in the other.

Jack had already removed his balaclava, so he saw the recognition flash across Rice's face.

'Why are you here?'

Jack didn't respond, instead waiting for Rice's gaze to drop to the silenced gun he held at his side. The colour drained from the police detective's face. 'Jack... what're you doing?'

Jack stayed silent, observing, recognising the slight change in Rice's stance, the subtle tensing of muscles, the readying of the bottle.

Jack raised the gun, his voice steady. 'Put the bottle and the glass down.'

Rice swallowed hard. His knuckles whitened around the neck of the Glenfiddich. 'Jack... what is this?' His voice was barely above a whisper. 'I don't understand.'

'Put them down.'

'Is this about Emma? Has something happened with your sister? Talk to me, I can help.'

'This isn't about Emma.' *Good try, but there's no common ground. Not really*, Jack thought. 'Put them down behind you, on the shelf.' He waved the silenced gun. 'Now.'

Rice's eyes never left the gun as he placed the bottle and glass behind himself on a table.

'There has to be a mistake,' Rice said. 'Why else would you be here?'

Jack waved the pistol again. 'Hands forward and open.'

Rice thrust out his palms as if fending off a wild animal.

I don't feel like a wild animal, Jack thought. *Never really have, to be honest. I can see why others might see me that way, though.*

'Shall we phone your sister?' Rice asked.

Jack simply shook his head. 'I intended nothing like this.'

'Sorry... intended what?'

Jack took a deep breath and watched him. Rice's face was twitching. The fear was really setting in now. He knew he wasn't walking away from this.

'You aren't going to shoot me, are you?'

Jack remained silent.

'Why? What the hell have I done to you?'

The fear didn't bother Jack, but neither did he enjoy it. 'Nothing.'

'Tell me what this is about, exactly. Let me help you. What trouble are you in?'

'I'm not in any trouble,' Jack said. 'At least I won't be... after...'

'After?'

Jack nodded.

Rice shook his head. 'No... that doesn't make sense... none whatsoever! What'll Emma think of you?'

'She won't ever know.'

Rice's eyes narrowed. The denial had given way to anger. 'You do this, you won't get away with it. Your life will be over, too. You think you can kill a cop? And for no reason? They'll put you in a padded cell and keep you sedated for the rest of your days. There *is* no bloody reason for this!'

'Your ignorance can't change anything. There *is* a reason... I'm sorry, Phil, but your fate was sealed a long time ago. Ironically, if not for me, it would have happened much, much sooner.'

'What the hell are you talking about? People depend on me. Unlike you, I'm not a bad person. I help people. What do you do? Suck the happiness from the world. Whatever you think I've done... you should get your facts straight. Ask your sister. I'm a good person. You'll find that out if you do this.'

'You're not listening. This isn't about what you've done or who you are.'

'Then what's it about?'

'It's about what you represent. What you could become.'

'You're not making sense.'

The conversation was dragging on too long. He needed to be out of the door and out of the country. Rose needed to be forever unaware that he'd caused the pain about to come into his sister's life. He steadied his aim.

'Okay... okay...' Rice's voice cracked, raw fear seeping through. 'Tell me why... I deserve that much, don't I?'

Jack's finger tightened on the trigger.

'You'd tell me if there was anything of worth in you... anything at all.'

'I'm worth something,' Jack said. 'My sister probably told you I've no feelings. It isn't true.'

'Then talk to me. If you feel bad about what you're about to do... talk to me.'

Jack shook his head. 'I don't feel bad, but I understand, I recognise... the unfairness of dying for the sins of your father.'

'What?' He looked stunned. 'My father? He's dead!'

'I know. But it isn't enough.'

Rice gritted his teeth and clenched his fists. 'This is an excuse! You're lying – you have to be.'

Jack took a deep breath. His arm was aching with the weight of the gun. 'I once worked in the south for an organisation. Its name isn't important. Among other things, they were stealing sensitive information from major defence corporations that acted on behalf of the government. A terrible move really if you want to stay in business. They should've stuck with drugs. But there was good money in intelligence. Still is. I was approached by a man. You may have heard of him: Neville Fairweather.'

'Christ,' Rice said, shaking his head.

'So, you do know him. He's a major shareholder in a defence corporation called Aegis. It was being hit by the criminal organisation I worked for. Neville approached me and recruited me to inform on the organisation I was supposedly working for, and to protect his interests, and the interests of national security. I'd let my family down for so long with my erratic behaviour. I wanted to prove I cared. So, you see, when you question my worth, you need to understand this was my attempt to show worth. To help my country. For a time, I think I did...'

Rice grimaced. 'Until you realised you were just working for another pack of bastards?'

Jack nodded. 'Yes.' He noticed Rice's hands creeping behind him again.

'Hands!' he said.

Rice brought them forward. 'Empty... look...'

'Problem was, the lines, as they always do, became blurred. The things I was doing for Neville didn't differ from what I was doing before. Then, I went to jail for manslaughter. It wasn't really manslaughter. You want to know the reason? I was ordered by Neville to kill this stupid fool, Charles Keane. He was selling information to the Russians.'

Rice's face was a mask of confusion and fear. He was shaking his head. 'But this makes no sense. Don't you realise? I'm not doing any of these things... not selling anything...' His voice was shaking. 'I have nothing to do with national security...'

'Sins of your father, remember? DCI Derek Rice. He was the one who betrayed the country.'

Rice shook his head vehemently, denial written across his features. 'My father? Nonsense. He wouldn't do that! He was a bastard, but he wasn't a traitor.'

Jack's eyes hardened. 'He invested in the company. Connected himself to Aegis while working as a DCI. He earned good money, using his influence and insider knowledge to support national defence. Unfortunately, your father too, decided to sell information to the Russians. His wanted more. He got greedy.'

'No,' Rice continued, shaking his head.

'Come on, think about it. Yes... there it is... I see it in your eyes.'

'No.'

'Tell me your father didn't have that in him. Tell me that and I'll lose the respect I have for you.'

'Even if he did, I had nothing to do with it. He's dead! It's over.'

'Not while you live,' Jack replied. 'This is how they see it.

Anyone connected has to go. Especially the same bloodline. Betrayal is seen by those above, not just Neville, but those who stretch even further and further back into the shadows, as a disease. They see it as something that spreads in the blood, between generations, across generations... whatever...'

Rice's face contorted with a mixture of anger and disbelief. 'But these people who make the rules – they're no different, you said yourself. Corrupt... greedy. If you know that, if you have this worth you claim, then why do it?'

'Ultimately, I pick a side.'

'Not the good one?'

Jack shrugged. 'On the contrary, I pick the side of my daughter... my sister. If I don't do this—'

'Jack, listen to me. I'd never betray my country,' Rice said, his voice firm despite his obvious fear. 'I'm a good copper. I've dedicated my life to serving and protecting people. Tell Neville and the others that. How can you stand there and tell me I'm guilty of something my father might have done?'

'It won't work, Phil. I know this, but I really have known about you for a long time. Because my sister worked with you, I kept the information hidden. I tried. And it really is nothing personal, and if there was another way, I'd choose it. But, like everything, once the truth bubbles up, things end, and if I don't do this... now... then, those that experience these endings will be Rose... Emma... In a way, you can know that your sacrifice keeps them safe.'

Rice's eyes darted around the room, desperation clear in every movement. 'There must be some other way. Let me talk to Neville myself... The people in charge.'

Jack resisted snorting at the absurdity of the request – it would be crass.

Rice's eyes darted to the gun, then back to Jack's face. 'Please,' he said, his voice breaking. 'I don't want to die like this. Not for something I didn't even do. Think about what this is going to do to Emma!'

For a moment, Jack's resolve wavered. The mention of Emma, of the pain this would cause her, made him hesitate. But then he thought of Rose, of the future he was securing for her, and he knew he'd come too far. He wasn't the person he used to be, he'd changed, but the world hadn't compensated for that.

He needed to see this through to the bitter end.

The silenced pistol made a muffled thwap. Rice's head snapped back, his eyes rolling up as the bullet tore through his skull. His body jerked, knocking into the shelf behind him. The bottle of Glenfiddich shattered on the parquet floor. Rice's body crumpled forward.

75

O'Brien was close to home.

The streetlights alongside the road caused a strobe-light effect inside the vehicle.

She couldn't shake Gardner's face from her mind – the sadness in her eyes when they'd sat together in the hospital car park yesterday.

Her senses were keen enough to spot what went unspoken.

It was over between them whether Riddick lived or died.

O'Brien knew why, and in time, Gardner would know, too.

She'd been a distraction, an escape from the truth – that Gardner was in love with Paul Riddick, and that was an unthinkable prospect. The man was chaotic. Gardner longed for him, but feared what he would bring to her life.

For the first time, with tears in her eyes, O'Brien genuinely hoped that Riddick would pull through.

Gardner deserved to find out if the man she loved was capable of change.

A sudden ringtone pierced her reverie. She frowned. It wasn't her phone. She glanced at the passenger seat. There was no sign there, despite the sound coming from that direction.

O'Brien turned back to the road, but then glanced around again, trying to locate the persistent ringing. It was slightly muffled, suggesting it was coming from the floor.

With a frustrated sigh, she pulled over to the kerb, putting on her hazard lights. The phone continued its electronic plea for attention as O'Brien leaned over, fumbling in the darkness.

Her hand brushed against something solid wedged between the seat and the centre console. She grasped it just as the ringing stopped.

She lifted up the phone.

It was Rice's. It must have fallen from the joggers they'd given him at Leeds District HQ.

The screen was still lit, displaying a missed call from RB.

RB.

She ran through a list of people they both knew in her head.

Ray Barnett?

Makes sense, she thought.

O'Brien considered phoning back, but the screen was locked. She thought about calling from her mobile, but decided she should return the phone to its owner.

She glanced at her dashboard clock. It was late, but not unreasonably so.

She put the car in gear, checked the road was empty and executed a careful U-turn.

She sighed. The night was getting later.

Still, Rice had been good to her today. The least she could do was get his phone back to him before he spent the night worrying.

O'Brien pressed down on the accelerator and the strobe-light effect of the streetlights kicked in again.

76

Emma.

He could no longer deny he had feelings for her.

Back at his daughter's bedroom door, he yearned to see her again – to sit beside her on Lucy's bed as before. But she was gone.

And then he remembered his daughters. His wife. The scent of cinnamon and apples. An origami creation. He looked down at the stuffed toy in his hands. Mr Snuggles.

But halfway down the stairs, there was only silence.

Nothing from above, where Emma had been, and nothing from below, where his family had been.

Had everything been torn away from him... again?

Heart racing, he thundered down the steps and burst into the kitchen.

Across the room, a tall man stood with his back to him, holding himself upright with a cane.

As the man turned, Paul remembered that this cane had once taken a life, and this man was not what he appeared.

The name came to him, suddenly, and Paul said it out loud. 'Anders.'

Anders eased himself down into a chair at the kitchen table. He laid the cane before him and then rested both hands on it.

Anders smiled, but it was a sad, aching smile. 'Hello, Paul. Would you sit with me?'

'No... I don't trust you.'

'That's wise. But this isn't about trust or our history. This is about you and the choices before you now.'

'Where's Rachel? Molly and Lucy?' he demanded, his voice hoarse. 'What've you done with them?'

Anders shook his head slowly. 'I haven't done anything, Paul. You know that. After all, I'm not really here, am I?'

Paul's eyes darted around the kitchen, searching desperately for any sign of his family. But deep down, he knew. They weren't here. They hadn't been here for a long time. Those moments with them earlier hadn't been real.

'Sit down, son,' Anders said gently.

'Don't call me that. You're not my father.'

'No, I'm not.' Anders touched his chest. 'But here, you are, and will always be, a son to me. Now sit and listen.'

Paul sat opposite him. 'Why? There was a time when I wanted to be so much like you. You betrayed me.'

'You were never meant to be like me, Paul. In fact, what you became was so much more. By avoiding my path—'

'I'm a wreck! An emotional alcoholic with blood on my hands.'

'Is that truly what you see? Open your eyes. Those children you saved? The truth you uncovered behind Graham Lock's murder? Your fight to save Nathan Cummings from his father's shadow? I see many things in you, Paul, but not blood-stained hands. I see passion, drive, a willingness to do what others can't. I see the man who sat with me in my final moments when no one else would. Even then, you had the heart to understand my tragedy... to keep me from dying alone.' He lifted his cane horizontally with both hands, bringing it down on the table like a judge's gavel. 'And yet, no one – no one I've ever known – faced tragedy like you did. But does it stop you? Does it steal your fight? You need to see yourself clearly.'

Paul thought of his time at the reservoir, of his father's attempts to help him understand he didn't need to face everything alone. That his drive, his fight, could be channelled with others' support. But that didn't stop the one thing that truly held him back... the pain that tore through his soul with every waking breath... 'I want my family back in this room with me,' he demanded.

Anders looked down at his cane, gave a swift nod and then looked up with a raised eyebrow. 'Why?'

'Why? Are you really asking that?'

'I am.'

'Well, why do you think?'

Anders didn't respond. He continued to wait.

'Because they're everything. They've always been everything. Without them, I'm nothing.'

Anders sighed. 'There was a time when you listened to me, a time—'

'When you lied to me and betrayed me. Yes, I know. I remember.'

'Think further back. To the cave. Mother Shipton's. Remember?'

Paul closed his eyes. The memories flooded back – a damp cave, the glint of a badge, his younger self looking up at Anders with awe and admiration. Their first meeting. The beginning.

He opened his eyes and looked at his old mentor.

'I want you to trust me again,' Anders said. 'I didn't lie when I first saw something special in you, and I'm not lying now. In fact, I can't. I'm dead. Maybe I'm just an extension of you? A symbol?'

Tears welled in Paul's eyes. 'Just tell me, Anders... tell me where they are. Rachel, Molly and—'

Anders cut Paul off by slamming the cane down harder this time.

'They're gone, Paul. They're gone and have been gone for a long time now.'

'No—'

'Fleeting memories.' Anders raised his voice, lifting the cane. 'Like this cane. Like me... Like your father, Colin.'

'No—'

'Fleeting.'

'But what's the point of that?'

'You tell me! It is your point. Not mine. Say it. Speak it. *You* tell me the point.'

'I don't know what you want me to say.'

Anders slammed his cane repeatedly on the table. 'You do, dammit, son. You do!'

And suddenly he did. 'I can't have what isn't there.'

Anders nodded.

'And if I choose what isn't there, then I still can't have it.'

Anders continued to nod.

'So... what do I do then, Anders? What do I do?'

Anders stood and smiled. 'Stop chasing, son.'

'Chasing what?'

Anders turned away, leaning on his cane. 'Ghosts.' He shuffled away.

Paul stood quickly, knocking over the chair. 'Stop!'

Anders did.

'But I don't know what's real.'

Anders raised his cane to point upwards. He turned his head, showing his profile. 'I think you do, son. I think you do.'

Paul looked up at the ceiling, confused.

When he looked down to right his toppled chair, Rachel appeared, pulling a steaming apple pie from the oven. Molly bounded in, brushing past him, waving her colourful paper creation. Lucy snatched Mr Snuggles from his hand.

He looked back up at the ceiling, but when his family began to talk, he dropped his eyes again.

The scene was warm, inviting, and he wanted so much to sit back in that chair.

Lucy was chattering excitedly about Christmas – what presents she wanted, and what Mr Snuggles wanted.

He yearned to embrace this warmth – a warmth more intense than anyone outside this room could ever understand.

Rachel was bringing over the apple pie, her stern look demanding they admire her creation. Everyone burst into laughter.

Home.

Family.

Everything he'd ever wanted.

He looked back up at the ceiling, remembering Emma, sitting alone, waiting on the end of the bed.

He looked down again. His family eating pie. Lucy moving Mr Snuggles's spoon, pretending he was eating too.

Paul started to sit, ready to lose himself in this dream.

Rachel, Molly and Lucy turned to him, their faces radiant with love. They accepted him completely, flaws and all. And he loved them with every fibre of his being.

Ghosts.

'I love you,' Paul said, his voice thick with emotion. 'Always.'

Then, summoning every ounce of courage he possessed, he turned, left the room and headed back up the steps to what was real.

77

Gardner was having the most wonderful dream. She felt Riddick's fingers moving through her hair. 'I've missed you,' she said, leaning into the touch, yearning for their connection to deepen. His touch felt like coming home after a long, treacherous journey.

'Emma.' How long since she'd heard his voice? It moved with his fingers, settling over her like a tangible force. 'Is this real?' she asked.

'Yes.'

She held her breath, afraid to ask more questions, fearing reality would strike and everything would fade away.

Desperate to touch him before he vanished, she reached for the hand in her hair. She felt his fingers... their tips brushed against one another. Moving to the back of his hand, she felt—

The tubes protruding from it.

Her eyes flew open as she tried to comprehend what was happening.

She'd fallen asleep in the hospital chair, hunched over with her head on the bed. Now she hovered between the lingering warmth of her dream and the stark reality of the ICU. Her fingers still touched the tubes in his hand, and Riddick was...

Still stroking her hair!

She rose, and his hand fell away. His eyes were open, locked onto hers with an intensity that made her heart lurch. Behind the hissing oxygen mask, his lips moved.

Adrenaline surged through her body. 'Paul?' He nodded weakly, his gaze never leaving hers. 'You're awake... you're really awake?'

He was still trying to speak, but his voice was too weak to hear above the oxygen's hiss.

She glanced around the room, searching for anything out of place, needing confirmation this was real and not just another dream. But the sterile, mechanical room remained unchanged.

'Paul...' She couldn't believe it. What should she do? He was still attempting to speak, and suddenly she worried he was wasting precious energy. 'Don't... rest...'

He lifted a weak hand and tapped at the oxygen mask. Stubborn as always – he wouldn't let this go.

'I shouldn't,' she said.

He tapped more insistently. The determination in his eyes was unshakeable.

Carefully, she lifted the mask from his face. Riddick took a shallow breath, his chest rising and falling with visible effort.

He spoke, but his voice was barely a whisper.

'You're tired,' Gardner said. 'But... you're looking better.' And he truly was.

Riddick shook his head slightly, frustration evident in his jaw. He would get these words out. 'Emma...' She heard that through the rasping.

His struggle unnerved her – she didn't want him hurting himself.

He pointed at his mouth and repeated. 'Emma...'

She leaned in. A shiver ran down her spine as she felt the warmth of his breath on her ear. He was alive.

'I'm listening, Paul.'

His voice remained barely above a whisper, but each word came clear and deliberate. 'I... don't... want...' He paused for air.

'It's okay, I understand.' But of course she didn't – she just desperately wanted him to rest.

'To...'

Gardner pulled back slightly, searching Riddick's face. His eyes held that familiar determination – the same force that drove him to help others while pushing himself into chaos time and time again. She didn't want that fight wasted on appeasing her, not at such cost.

'Chase...' He drew in another breath. 'Ghosts...'

She put her hand to his face.

'...Any more.'

78

Jack grabbed his balaclava from behind the sofa where he'd hidden it. Checking the safety on his pistol, he slipped it back beneath his belt.

He looked down at Rice's body one last time. The growing puddle of blood mingled with whisky and glass.

Unwilling to risk the bathroom window again, and not wanting to be seen exiting the front, Jack decided his best option was to locate a key for the kitchen door.

He went to the kitchen, tossed the balaclava on the work surface and searched the drawers with his gloved hands.

Nothing.

In one of the drawers, he saw a picture of a younger Rice standing with his auntie and that traitorous father. He sighed. Phil Rice's fate had been sealed back then. He was not responsible for this mess, Jack thought.

But he hoped he would never need to explain any of this to Emma, or worse, Rose.

Still keyless, he headed back to the lounge to check Rice's jogging suit pockets. Better than risking another climb through that window that had already cut open his arm. He found a bunch of keys. Unfortunately, none of the keys fitted the kitchen door.

He stood in the hallway, looking through the bathroom door at the window again. He was running out of options—

An electronic doorbell echoed throughout the house.

Not now, he thought.

He took a deep breath and approached the front door. Through the peephole, his eyes widened.

Lucy O'Brien.

Of all people.

What're you doing here?

He backed away from the door as the doorbell rang a second time.

He turned around, mind racing. *She'll leave soon enough*, he reassured himself.

He sidestepped back into the lounge. The curtains were drawn – she wouldn't be able to see in.

She'd given up on the doorbell and was now knocking.

Not long, now... she'll get the message...

He heard the front door open.

Damn.

He looked at Rice. *Why did you leave your door unlocked, you fool?*

'Phil... are you in here?' O'Brien asked.

Jack reached into his pocket for his balaclava—

It wasn't there.

Then he remembered: he'd left it on the kitchen worktop.

No. This isn't good.

'Phil? I'm coming in...'

Don't, just don't.

'I've your phone,' O'Brien said. 'You dropped it in the car...'

Jack shook his head and looked at Rice again. *Stupid bloody fool.*

And then she screamed.

Jack slipped the gun free from his belt as she came into the room.

She walked right up to Rice, clutching her mouth, not seeing Jack. 'Phil? Phil... God... no—'

'Lucy...'

She turned to look at him wide-eyed. 'Jack?'

'He's dead.'

She took a step back.

'Don't.' He raised the gun. 'Don't move... please.'

Jack remembered knocking O'Brien unconscious over a year earlier, when he'd tried to retrieve his daughter. The irony of their positions now wasn't lost on him. He took a step closer, the gun ready in his hand. No silencer this time. But he didn't want to drop his guard to attach it.

'What did you do?' She was crying, shock evident in her voice. 'What happened?' She looked down. 'What've you done?'

Jack took a deep breath.

This situation was volatile.

He needed it to end.

'Why... why?' O'Brien pressed. 'Why?'

Why indeed? 'Why did you come?'

'To give him his phone.' She looked at the open door beside her. Tears streamed down her face.

'No, Lucy... Don't run...' *I need to think.*

She shook her head.

'I know what you think,' Jack reasoned. 'But I take no pleasure in any of this. Rice's father made mistakes and—' He broke off.

What's the point? he thought. *I can't explain this away.*

O'Brien continued crying, her eyes darting between Rice's body and Jack. 'Please.'

A rare moment of frustration surged through him. 'Why did you have to come?'

She turned to look at Rice again, covering her mouth with her hand. She made a horrible, animalistic sound. Then, she closed her eyes and sucked in a breath. 'Please. Jack.' She looked back at him, pleading in her eyes. 'I know you wouldn't hurt me. I won't say anything.'

Jack nodded. 'I know.' He smiled.

'I have to leave. Let me leave.'

'In a moment,' Jack said, still searching for solutions.

Unfortunately, there really wasn't one.

'You know I love your sister... that I'm with your sister.' She sensed his doubt.

'Yes,' he said. He swallowed. He looked down, chewed his lip for a moment, feeling things he wasn't used to feeling, then he smiled, nodded and looked up again. 'I know.'

O'Brien shook her head. 'Why, Jack? Why? All this... it will break her...'

'Because I don't want to be him any more. I don't want to be that man who hurts his sister... who hurts others... who'll one day be nothing more than a monster in the eyes of his daughter.'

'Then stop,' O'Brien said, clasping her hands together and shaking them at him. 'Stop now *before* it's too late—'

'But it's already too late. What I want... what I need... the change. It comes at a great cost.'

She shook her head and looked at Rice again. 'Phil... Phil... I'm sorry...'

There was no way out. Jack took a deep breath. 'Okay, Lucy. I need you to leave now.'

'Okay...'

She looked at him, her eyebrows rising. He saw the hope in her eyes.

He smiled. 'Head down the hallway to the kitchen. It's unlocked. I left it unlocked.'

'Why not the front door?'

'The kitchen, Lucy... The kitchen.'

'Okay.' She nodded, but didn't move. 'I love your sister.'

'I know. I love her too. So, we're good.'

'Okay...' She turned, glanced at Jack one last time, not completely certain and then burst out the door.

'Bye, Lucy.'

Jack followed her out at pace and watched her run down the hallway towards the kitchen.

He raised the gun, took aim and fired.

79

Gardner and Riddick locked eyes through the ICU room's glass window. The transformation stunned her. The puffiness had receded from his face, and his expression held new purpose and clarity.

While nurses moved efficiently around his bed, checking monitors and adjusting IVs, their movements blurred into a dreamlike haze as his words echoed in her mind: I don't want to chase ghosts any more.

Dr Euan Gresham stood among them, conferring with each nurse before studying his patient. He nodded repeatedly, clearly pleased with what he observed.

He emerged to speak with Gardner. 'His blood pressure and temperature have dropped significantly.'

'The antifungal medication is working then?'

'Among other things...' He joined her at the window. 'I remember you telling me what a fighter this man was,' he said. 'You weren't wrong. I expect that determination has everything to do with this recovery.' He turned to her. 'Coming back from the brink like this – I've seen it before, but it's incredibly rare. I had to prepare you for the worst because I was almost certain that's what we faced. Should've listened when you told me he had nine lives.'

Gardner nodded, her voice thick with emotion. 'To be honest, I thought he'd run out.'

'We're getting more antifungals into him while we've this momentum.'

'Thank you, Doctor,' Gardner whispered, tears welling in her eyes.

Euan smiled warmly. 'Don't thank me – thank him. He clearly wanted to come back.' He rested his hand briefly on her shoulder and gave her a knowing nod. 'For obvious reasons.' Then he returned to the room.

Riddick removed his oxygen mask himself and smiled at Gardner.

She smiled back.

I don't want to chase ghosts any more.

His first words upon waking held such hope, such promise.

Was he referring to his past demons? Choosing life over the shadows that had haunted him for so long?

Gardner pressed her hand against the glass, knowing that was exactly what he meant.

In that moment, as Riddick's gaze held hers and he smiled, she allowed herself to hope for a future she'd barely dared to imagine.

80

As Gardner drove home, the world outside seemed different. The streetlights cast an otherworldly glow, their usual yellow warmth replaced by an eerie blue-tinged radiance.

Were the tears of joy in her eyes colouring this shift in perception, or was something more significant at play? It felt as if she'd woken in another world entirely.

Riddick's smile, the doctor's positivity and, of course, those words: *I don't want to chase ghosts any more.*

Earlier, in the hospital car park, Gardner had tried reaching her colleagues. She wanted to share the good news about Riddick and check on the Alistair Ashworth case. She'd hit a voicemail roadblock. Now, before leaving her car, she tried again.

Still nothing. A small knot of worry formed in her stomach, but she pushed it aside. She wouldn't give in to those feelings, not when the evening had offered such hope and relief.

Taking a deep breath, she stepped onto her driveway. Again, everything seemed altered. Were the bricks of her home a shade darker? Were her windows reflecting an unfamiliar light? She rubbed her eyes, considering the tears, but it made no difference.

Rather than knock for Monika, she let herself in. Inside, she found Rose and Anabelle in the lounge, engrossed in a board game with their au pair. Their faces lit up as she entered, and for a moment, the world seemed to steady.

'Mummy!' Ana exclaimed, rushing to hug her. Rose followed and she embraced them both.

She inhaled their familiar scents. The warmth of their bodies against hers felt real, grounding her. That strange new version of the world was now distant, as if she'd left it at the door. 'Uncle Paul is much better,' she said.

'Yay!' Ana said.

'That's wonderful news,' Monika said from beside the board game.

'Can we visit him soon?' Rose asked, still seeming subdued. Her father's sudden exit this morning surely weighed on her mind.

'Yeah, can we?' Ana chimed in, bouncing on her toes.

Gardner couldn't help but laugh, the sound surprising her with its normality. 'He still needs lots of rest. But I promise, as soon as he's up for visitors, you'll be the first to know.'

'Can we make him a card?' Anabelle asked, already moving towards the craft supplies drawer. 'Good idea,' Gardner said, her heart swelling.

As the girls worked on their cards, chattering excitedly about colours and messages, Gardner felt her earlier disorientation dissipate. The beauty of the moment soothed her senses. She should revel in it. Enjoy it.

'Mummy, look!' Rose held up her card, adorned with a some-what lopsided but lovingly drawn heart. 'Do you think Uncle Paul will like it?'

'Like?' Gardner pulled Rose in for another hug. 'He'll love it. How lucky I am to have such thoughtful girls.'

After tucking the girls into bed and Monika had retreated upstairs to spend the evening online with her boyfriend, Gardner sat alone in the lounge, determined not to drink.

The world had been good to her today – she would reward herself by abstaining. She'd been drinking far too much lately.

She closed her eyes and took deep breaths. She should phone her colleagues, especially O'Brien, but for now, she wanted peace. Peace, and a brief time to savour this pleasant sensation of relief.

A knock jolted her from her reverie. When she opened her eyes, the world felt off again. Sinister shadows seemed to crawl at the corners of the room.

She went to the front door and, through the peephole, she saw a visitor who made her disorientation intensify. Marsh? Rather than feeling off-kilter, the world now seemed to tilt completely.

She'd never been to her home before. It made no sense.

She opened the door. 'Ma'am.' Barnett stepped up behind Marsh. 'Ray?'

'Emma... can we come in, please?' Marsh said.

She stepped back. There was darkness... sadness, perhaps... in both of their expressions. She wondered if this was another symptom of her earlier disorientation – sensing things that weren't there.

But after they entered and she closed the door, she saw the heaviness they carried and knew something significant had happened.

'Why are you here?' Gardner asked. She was certain she heard Barnett swallow.

'Can we sit, Emma?' Marsh asked.

'Of course... but please, tell me why you're here.'

'We'll get to that, I promise.'

As her visitors sat, her heart raced. She couldn't join them on the sofa. The shadows clawing at the corners seemed to have elongated.

'Emma, sit down, please... with us.' The way Marsh said 'with us' was too telling – too reassuring, too comforting, utterly out of character.

'I can't,' Gardner said.

'You can,' Marsh said. 'And you must.'

Barnett smiled up at her from the sofa – the first smile since they'd arrived. 'Please, boss.'

Gardner tried laughing. 'This is strange.' Her laugh and voice sounded brittle and forced. 'I've just been with Paul. He's doing better. The antifungals are working.'

'That's such good news,' Marsh said, offering her first smile, too.

'Fantastic,' Barnett said.

Marsh patted the sofa and Gardner sat.

'Euan is optimistic.' Gardner paused, brow furrowing. 'I need to sort out who's going to stay with him when he's discharged. Obviously, with the kids and—'

'Emma,' Barnett said. She looked at him and nodded.

'There's been a shooting.' He broke off and looked away, tears in his eyes.

'Two of ours, Emma,' Marsh finished.

'No,' Gardner said, shaking her head. 'A shooting? No... how?'

'We don't know all the details. Phil was at home and—'

'Phil?' Gardner stood. 'Phil has been shot?'

'At his home and—'

'How is he?'

Marsh reached up and took Gardner's arm. 'He's dead, Emma.'

Gardner felt the air leave her body. Barnett rose, moving

towards her. She turned away, pulling out of Marsh's grasp. 'His house? How? That's not right... something's not right.'

She thought about the colours, the blurring and shifting shadows... was this a nightmare? Was she still asleep? Did she still have her head on Riddick's lap as he stroked her hair?

'Lucy...' she said, turning and looking at Barnett. 'I need Lucy. I need to talk to her.'

Barnett put his hands on the top of her arms. 'Emma... listen...'

'Lucy... I need to call...'

'Emma...'

'I don't want to hear it, Ray!'

'Lucy's gone too, Emma. She was there.'

And then, it was certain. This was a nightmare, and it couldn't be real. The colours, the shadows... yes, there'd been subtle hints, and she'd been right to acknowledge them, because they weren't just products of tear-stained eyes.

Gardner felt herself slipping downward but she didn't fall. Barnett had her upright still.

'I'm so sorry, Emma,' Marsh said.

Take me out of this nightmare.

'I've got you,' Barnett said, holding her tight.

And then Gardner cried out – a sound she didn't know she could make. A sound that belonged to this nightmarish new world she'd just entered. She held onto Barnett with everything she had as the colours and shadows of this new, terrible world swirled and shifted around her.

Tanya sat at her kitchen table, hunched over her laptop, pausing occasionally to sip her coffee. The podcast was ready. She checked the time. 8.55. Five minutes until launch on her website. She took another mouthful of coffee, reflecting on the years of work leading to this moment.

Her laptop beeped – low battery warning. As she stood to plug it in, there was a knock at the front door. She tightened her dressing gown belt and went to answer.

A delivery man stood there in a cap and hi-vis jacket, pointing to a box at his feet. 'Mrs Reid?'

'Yes.'

'Sign here.' He turned his handset around and she scribbled with her finger.

'Where do you want it?' he asked.

'Sorry... what is it?' He looked down, then up, shrugging. 'I didn't pack it. Heavy though.'

She stepped back. 'Just bring it in the hall.'

The man bent, looping his arms around the box. He kept his

knees bent as he lifted, grunting as he followed her inside. He set it down on the floor.

'Thank you,' Tanya said.

'You're welcome,' the delivery man said, straightening and cracking his back. He reached out and closed the front door.

Her blood turned to ice.

'You look tired,' he said, raising his silenced gun. He touched his own eyelids. 'Bags, here... you been hard at work?'

'It's too late,' Tanya said, stepping back. 'It's been sent already.'

'What has?'

Fighting down nausea, Tanya steeled herself and narrowed her eyes. 'The truth. Neville is finished. As are those closest to him.'

He shrugged. 'Perhaps... maybe... you think there won't be others?'

'Then they'll be exposed, too.'

'By you?'

Her stomach lurched. 'Clearly not. Is killing your answer to everything?'

'These aren't my answers.'

Tanya shook her head. 'Are you Brandon?'

'Wow, you really have done your homework. Impressive. Is my name out there, too?'

'Yes... if you don't... you know... hurt me... I can pull it back.'

He raised an eyebrow. 'Our secret? Show me.'

She turned and led him to the laptop, feeling the gun pressed against her spine. This bluff wouldn't work. Very little could work now. Though nausea threatened to overwhelm her, she still had one chance. Get close to the laptop. Hit the button. Launch the podcast.

A metre from the laptop, he said, 'Stop.'

'I can show you... on the laptop.'

'Show me what?'

'The files I have on you. Take them, then they'll never be sent.'

'And how do I know you won't have a backup.'

'I don't.'

'Go on... show me...'

She reached for the keyboard. The podcast was ready. She moved the cursor over the confirmation. She might be about to die, but at least she had this. A final 'screw you' to the corporations. They'd burn when this hit the internet.

She went to press the button, but the screen went blank, the laptop humming to a stop. The battery. Shit. She looked up at the kitchen clock. Nine on the dot.

'No time,' Brandon said. 'I've got other deliveries to make.'

She heard the thwap of the gun, but that was all.

EPILOGUE
THREE MONTHS LATER

Roy Linders sat across from Gerald and Margaret Ashworth in their lounge. The gentle tapping of rain against the windows provided a sombre backdrop. They knew why he was here. This meeting was about details, closure and the support he could offer.

'They found Alistair in Chapada dos Guimarães,' Roy said, his hands clasped in his lap. 'It's a national park in Brazil, popular with hikers. We have a witness who saw Alistair and Rowan, then acting as Mark Almeida, setting off together. Park rangers discovered him in an area off the main trails. DNA confirmed it was Alistair.'

Margaret gave a small gasp, her teacup rattling in her fingers. Gerald placed his hand over hers, steadying it.

Roy paused, gathering his strength – he'd needed to do that often since Imogen's passing. 'Look... I may be retired now, but I wanted to be the one to tell you. Though our children were never, you know, technically together, I felt I owed you this. Imogen would want me to tell you.'

'Thank you.' Margaret set down her cup with trembling hands. 'And it was before those dreadful emails?'

'Aye. Without question. They never came from him.'

Gerald drew a sharp breath. 'And this man who... who married your daughter... who killed our son...'

'Rowan Sinclair?'

Gerald nodded. Roy knew he was aware of the name, he just couldn't bring himself to say it.

'Does his family know... what he did... what he was...?'

'His mother knows,' Roy said.

'Good,' Gerald said. 'It's the only justice we have. Someone has to feel the guilt.'

Roy thought to himself that Rowan would never have felt guilt anyway – the man was a sociopath. But such thoughts weren't helpful now. 'Aye, and she will. Her son was a troubled soul who stole identities, created new lives, only to destroy them. If only my Imogen had actually married your son, instead of a ghost wearing his face.'

Silence settled over the room, broken only by the persistent rain. Roy forced back his own tears. 'We were all deceived. All of us – you, me, Imogen and Alistair – we were all pawns. I hope you don't mind my being here. It felt right that we should come together, find some peace in knowing the truth. Together.'

Gerald nodded. 'I agree. Thank you.'

Margaret wiped her eyes with a tissue. 'And thank you for confirming those emails... those horrible emails... the accusations... weren't from him...'

Roy nodded. 'Absolutely. They were never from him.'

'Which means the son we thought we'd lost,' Margaret said softly, 'the one who seemed to hate us so much... he never existed.' She looked up at Roy, her eyes bright with tears. 'Is it wrong that I feel relief? Even now, knowing Alistair is...' She couldn't finish.

'No,' Roy said. 'It's not wrong at all.'

Gerald squeezed his wife's hand. 'We got our son back,' he said, his voice rough with emotion. 'Not in the way we hoped, but we got him back.'

'The Alistair we raised – the kind, curious boy who loved adventure and making people smile – that was the real one. That was our son,' Margaret said.

Roy reached across and took her other hand. Three parents, united in loss, sharing the bitter comfort of truth. Outside, the rain continued its gentle rhythm, washing away old pain, old doubts, making space for grief that was, at last, honest and clean.

* * *

Wind whispered through the cemetery as Mathis Roux stood before the freshly dug grave, his wrists cuffed, with a guard on either side.

Though small, as expected, the gathering of mourners was larger than Mathis had anticipated.

It was certainly larger than his own funeral would ever be.

Before his breakdown, Landon Thambley had built a life for himself. These mourners remembered and grieved for that version of him.

Mathis had known a different Landon, one he'd fallen in love with. In a way, he was glad their relationship remained sacred, private.

After the funeral, Landon's former wife approached him, her face red from crying. At her side stood Landon's son, around eight years old. One look at the boy's face confirmed his parentage – he was unmistakably Landon's child.

The guards maintained their distance but stayed alert.

'Did you know Dad?' the boy asked.

'I did. What's your name?'

'Jamie.'

'Well, Jamie, we were very good friends, and you look just like him.'

Jamie's lower lip trembled, and in that moment, Mathis saw Landon in every line of the boy's face – the same stubborn set of the jaw, the same spark of curiosity in his eyes.

'He was a good man,' Mathis said. He looked at Landon's ex-wife, who flinched and looked away. 'It's a shame you didn't get the chance to get to know him.'

Jamie's mother began ushering him away.

But Jamie suddenly turned. 'Thank you for being his friend.'

'Of course.'

'Goodbye.'

'*Au revoir.*'

As the guards led Mathis away, he kept smiling, his mind drifting to memories of nights spent beneath bridges with Landon, sharing dreams and sorrows. He remembered the warmth of Landon's laugh, the steadfast grip of his hand during the darkest moments of withdrawal.

These memories now felt like fragments of a different life, but they were fragments he would cherish forever.

Patty Sinclair's throat was raw from the stomach pumping, and her arms throbbed where the IV lines entered her skin. The doctor had informed her that her liver was failing. She would go into rehabilitation again, but it would only delay the inevitable. Her next relapse would be her last.

She closed her eyes, seeing herself on Rowan's bed, lying alongside him, his small body curled against hers. The memory brought back the scent of his freshly washed hair and the warmth of his skin.

You're the star at the centre of my constellation.

Everything revolves around you.

Patty opened her eyes as a young nurse named Jennifer entered the room to check her vitals. The nurse's face was kind.

'How are you feeling, Mrs Sinclair?'

'My mother used to tell me I was her star.'

Jennifer smiled while making notes on a chart. 'That's nice...'

'She never trapped me... never anchored me down...'

Jennifer looked up with a raised eyebrow and nodded.

'Stars aren't meant to be treated that way,' Patty said.

'I guess they're supposed to shine,' Jennifer said, replacing the chart.

'Yes... exactly... I made a terrible mistake,' Patty whispered.

'We all make mistakes,' Jennifer replied, adjusting the IV drip. 'That's why we're here to help, and the rehabilitation will—'

'No,' Patty interrupted, shaking her head. 'It's not about the drinking.' She drew a shaky breath. 'I told my son he was a star, but I never let him shine. Do you know how long stars can live for?'

Jennifer paused. 'A very long time, I think.'

'Millions of years,' Patty said, nodding. 'Billions, even. But only if they're allowed to burn as they should. I tried to contain his light, control it, make it burn for me alone.' Her voice cracked. 'And when stars can't burn naturally... when they're compressed too tight... they collapse. They destroy everything around them.' She closed her eyes once more, remembering Rowan's face the last time she saw him – the emptiness there, the void where his light should've been. 'I thought I was making him special,' she whispered. 'But I was just teaching him how to burn out.'

The nurse's hand settled gently on her arm. Patty opened her eyes, meeting Jennifer's compassionate gaze, but turned away. She didn't want to talk any more.

Outside her window, the sun was setting. Somewhere in the darkness beyond, she thought, her son's light had finally been extinguished, consuming others in its final, devastating explosion.

Sitting in a wheelchair at the front of a small, hushed crowd, Riddick gazed at the two plaques, gleaming despite the weak daylight.

In Memory of DI Philip Rice – Colleague, Friend, Protector.

In Memory of DC Lucy O'Brien – Compassionate Soul,
Devoted colleague.

The grounds of Knaresborough Castle stood silent, a gentle breeze rustling through the leaves of the two newly planted oak saplings.

Riddick, despite a difficult week of nausea and fatigue, held himself erect. His face was determined. Though he might not have looked the part, thin and weak in a wheelchair, he was determined to project strength and respect.

He'd never been close to Rice and O'Brien. In fact, there had been some rather fractious times between him and the DI. But they'd been his colleagues. Part of *their* family.

Most importantly, they'd been close to Emma.

He looked around, hoping she was here – behind a tree perhaps, or standing in the shadows of the keep where they'd first met. But of course, she wasn't.

Gardner was gone.

She'd chosen to leave Knaresborough and him behind – and who could blame her? After all he'd put her through. And after everything that had happened with O'Brien and Rice? How could someone be expected to just carry on as normal?

He'd let her go.

He'd vowed not to chase ghosts when he came back.

And now, even though the thought broke him in two, Gardner had become a ghost to him.

Ray Barnett turned to the crowd. He too was taking the loss hard. He'd lost weight, and his usually imposing frame had diminished, both under the burden of loss and his neglect of a robust fitness regime.

Barnett thanked everyone for coming – to pay their respects; to not say goodbye, but rather, honour their lives. Then he moved into the usual anecdotes – used to both lighten the atmosphere while, oddly, really driving home the sense of loss.

'Phil Rice was... well, he was a right pain in the arse, if we're being honest.'

A ripple of subdued laughter.

'Opinions on everything, wasn't afraid to ruffle a few feathers.' He nodded at Marsh. 'Hey, ma'am?'

She smiled in return. 'He never dared!'

More forced mirth.

'God help us all if we got between him and the last biscuit in the tin,' Barnett said.

Riddick wondered if this was true. He'd spent very little time socialising with Rice in the staff room. In fairness, he'd spent very little time socialising with anyone. Today, sitting here after narrowly escaping death, he realised that he was quite alone. But with that came a sense of hope, a sense of promise. Rather like these saplings here – they'd grow. He, too, had chosen to do the same.

Barnett's expression softened. 'Would you like to add anything, ma'am?'

'Yes,' Marsh said. She coughed and lowered her head. For a moment, Riddick thought she might actually cry. She didn't. 'Beneath that gruff exterior was a heart of gold. Phil cared deeply about his work, about making a difference. He may not have always shown it in the most conventional ways, but his dedication to justice was unwavering.'

Everyone clapped, and then Barnett spoke about O'Brien.

'Every team needs a heartbeat, and Lucy was that beat. Kind words, a listening ear, or a shoulder to cry on. Chances are, if you ever found a cereal bar mysteriously appearing on your desk when you were having a rough day, Lucy was behind it.'

After the laughter had passed, Barnett's voice caught. He turned away. 'Sorry.'

Everyone waited patiently.

When he turned back, he stood up straight, took a deep breath and said, 'Lucy had a way of bringing out the best in people, of reminding us why we do this job. Her compassion and her unwavering belief in the goodness of others made us all strive to be better.'

After the ceremony drew to a close, people began to disperse, many stopping to lay flowers or share quiet words of remembrance. Riddick watched Barnett kneel beside his wheelchair.

'You think she's okay?' Barnett asked.

Riddick nodded. 'She's strong. Stronger than me.'

'Stronger than all of us put together,' Barnett said.

'Aye. She'll be fine. There are people down there for her, in Salisbury. Up here, she didn't have enough. I understand that.'

'She had you.'

'Don't,' Riddick said.

'Sorry.'

Riddick smiled. 'It's okay.'

Barnett said, 'She may just need time.'

Riddick didn't answer. He didn't know what Gardner needed, but he was certain that it wasn't him – at least, not any longer.

He stayed for a while, watching the sun's rays dance across the newly planted saplings, feeling the weight of everyone he'd lost.

Then, he gave a swift nod to Rice and O'Brien, vowing he would be back on the job within twelve months, before wheeling himself back into the real world.

* * *

One Year Later
Salisbury

Gardner hung her coat up at the door and sighed.

Today had been an intense one.

They were investigating the death of a young woman, Harriet Spring. Gardner was convinced it was the ex-boyfriend, but new evidence had thrown all of that into doubt. She felt like she was back at square one.

Still, she shook it off, as she always did, before greeting Monika and her two children.

After a quick catch-up on the sofa and several cups of coffee to perk her up for the long night ahead, she got them ready for bed and tucked them in.

Monika, who no longer had a boyfriend, but still disappeared in the evenings to talk with friends and family back home, said goodnight.

Gardner made herself a strong coffee and went to her office. She unlocked the door with the key that she kept on herself at all times.

There was no copy.

If she did ever lose it... she would have to break the door down.

She checked behind her and opened the door, stepped inside and locked it behind her.

By ten o'clock, she was, as she always was, exhausted.

She wanted, as she always wanted at this time, to go back downstairs for another coffee.

But she knew that would be bad news.

It would result in an all-nighter, and she didn't fancy being on the receiving end of one of those again – not with Harriet's killer still an unknown quantity.

But she couldn't ignore the feeling that she was closer than she'd been in a while...

She stood and turned, surveying the wall, which was covered top to bottom in photographs, newspaper clippings, scribbles and lines in permanent marker, Post-it notes and pinned documents.

These past couple of months had seen an escalation.

The lines that wove out from that central image of Neville Fairweather had multiplied at an alarming rate.

She felt closer than ever before, but how close she actually was still remained a mystery.

She thought about Tanya Reid, and how close the podcaster had come.

Was Gardner there yet?

There was no way of knowing.

Tanya Reid, and her work, had been turned to ash in a housefire.

She tapped a photo of Brandon West. The cleaner. Then, moved her attention to an image of her brother, Jack. Where had he gone? Had he had any involvement with what had happened? Or had, he too, been erased by Neville and Brandon?

Either of the two possibilities made her feel physically sick.

She focused her attention on a patch of corporate logos, linked with spidery squiggles to the faces of the great and the good. She read a few news clippings detailing seemingly unrelated events, but the devil was most certainly in the details.

Eleven was her cut-off point. It had to be.

She had a family... she had a job... she would never put them last. No matter how much it sometimes hurt.

So, at eleven, she sat down in her chair and rubbed her temples.

She took a deep breath and then opened the top drawer.

She deliberately kept these photos hidden, so they didn't distract her while she was researching, and so they didn't dampen her mood while she fought for the truth.

She looked down at the pictures of Rice and O'Brien.

Then, her eyes welling up, she put them back in the drawer and closed it again.

She looked at her reflection in the computer screen. Her hair was shorter now, her face thinner... she was eating far less, what with being so busy... and effectively working two jobs now.

She tapped the drawer, and thought of her lost colleagues.

When I get there, it will be worth it.

She opened her email to Riddick that she'd written ten months ago. It was an email she'd still never sent. That she may never send. She read it, as she did every day. It all still rang true. Every word.

And it could happen. One day it really could. She could hit send. Tell him everything. About how she felt, how she longed for him and how their connection was one that shouldn't be ignored...

But...

She turned and looked at her wall again.

She had her own ghosts now.

And she wasn't ready to give up on them just yet.

* * *

MORE FROM WES MARKIN

In case you missed it, the previous instalment in Wes Markin's gritty Yorkshire Murders series, *The Winter Killings*, is available to order now here:

www.mybook.to/WinterKillingBackAd

ACKNOWLEDGEMENTS

Maintaining Gardner and Riddick's intricate and tempestuous relationship over six novels would never have been possible without the unwavering support of my editorial team: Emily Ruston, Candida Bradford and Susan Sugden.

Deepest gratitude to advance readers and wonderful bloggers – Kath, Donna, Sharon, Phyl, Melanie and countless others.

My children continue to light my path with joy, while my family – Jo included – provides endless patience for this corner-dwelling storyteller.

Although *The Black Rock Killings* brings a sense of closure, at least in terms of the relationship between Paul and Emma, those characters continue to thrive in my dreams. Will they be back?

I can't give you certainty, but I can give you this:

Never say never.

ABOUT THE AUTHOR

Wes Markin is the bestselling author of the DCI Yorke crime novels, set in Salisbury. His series 'The Yorkshire Murders' stars the pragmatic detective DCI Emma Gardner who tackles the criminals of North Yorkshire. Wes lives in Harrogate.

Sign up to Wes Markin's mailing list for news, competitions and updates on future books.

Visit Wes Markin's website: www.wesmarkinauthor.com

Follow Wes on social media:

facebook.com/WesMarkinAuthor

x.com/MarkinWes

ALSO BY WES MARKIN

The Yorkshire Murders

The Viaduct Killings

The Lonely Lake Killings

The Crying Cave Killings

The Graveyard Killings

The Winter Killings

The Black Rock Killings

DCI Michael Yorke thrillers

One Last Prayer

The Repenting Serpent

The Silence of Severance

Rise of the Rays

Dance with the Reaper

Christmas with the Conduit

Better the Devil

Jake Pettman Thrillers

The Killing Pit

Fire in Bone

Blue Falls

The Rotten Core

Rock and a Hard Place

THE

Murder

LIST

THE MURDER LIST IS A NEWSLETTER DEDICATED TO SPINE-CHILLING FICTION AND GRIPPING PAGE-TURNERS!

SIGN UP TO MAKE SURE YOU'RE ON OUR HIT LIST FOR EXCLUSIVE DEALS, AUTHOR CONTENT, AND COMPETITIONS.

SIGN UP TO OUR
NEWSLETTER

BIT.LY/THEMURDERLISTNEWS

Boldwood

Boldwood Books is an award-winning fiction publishing company seeking out the best stories from around the world.

Find out more at www.boldwoodbooks.com

Join our reader community for brilliant books, competitions and offers!

Follow us
@BoldwoodBooks
@TheBoldBookClub

Sign up to our weekly deals newsletter

https://bit.ly/BoldwoodBNewsletter

Printed in Great Britain
by Amazon